B o

B

Group Therapy

GROUP
THERAPY

Shelby Hearon

Atheneum 1984 New York

*I wish to thank the National Endowment
for the Arts for its support.*

*Lyrics from "Open All Night" copyright © 1982 by Bruce Springsteen.
Used by permission.*

Library of Congress Cataloging in Publication Data

Hearon, Shelby, ——
    Group therapy.

    I. Title.
PS3558.E256G7 1984   813'.54   83–45500
ISBN 0–689–11444–3

Copyright © 1984 by Shelby Hearon
All rights reserved
Published simultaneously in Canada by McClelland and Stewart Ltd.
Composed by Maryland Linotype Composition Company,
Baltimore, Maryland
Manufactured by Fairfield Graphics, Fairfield, Pennsylvania
Designed by Mary Cregan
First printing January 1984
Second printing April 1984

In memory of
HAZEL HYDE SMITH
1903–1983

*In all forms of group family it is uncertain who is the
father of a child; but it is certain who its mother is.*

FRIEDRICH ENGELS

One

I

Journal: Houses with Names

WHEN I was little, we had River Bend.

River Bend was Gran's tidy white frame house, thirty minutes from Austin, Texas, on the Guadalupe River. A Swedish family had built it and had later added an upstairs for the wife's parents, which we, my cousin Nan and I, used after Gran bought it. My mother's sister, Aunt Caroline, also had two sons, but I don't remember ever seeing the boys there in the summer. It seems to me that from the start there was only Gran and the four of us: Mother and Aunt Caroline, and Nan and I.

Delia, a black maid, would come to Gran's on Fridays and leave a china platter of bacon-deviled eggs in the Kenmore and, on the yellow Formica kitchen counter, a cut-glass tray of fried chicken, very spicy (Delia used a special recipe she'd read in the paper which used ten different secret spices). And a pitcher of lemonade for Nan and me, and a cooler of iced, minted tea for Mother and Aunt Caroline. Plus there would be a fresh cake, usually carrot, sometimes spice with sea foam, sometimes white

3

with a caramel filling, in a round aluminum cake box. The cake box and tea cooler wore ironed, starched white cotton covers, cut and stitched to look like little Dutch girls. The upstairs beds always had fresh, pressed sheets with tiny flowered borders and matching sets of pink towels, smelling slightly scorched from the dryer.

From River Bend we could walk down a slight back-slope to the shallow, clear stretch of river which belonged to the subdivision. It was like a private beach along the Gulf, this part of the cool, glassy, meandering river bend which was ours. There was a promontory on our side, a bit of land which jutted out, with a plank dock and an old tire swing and a nice flat spot of ground on which to picnic and from which to swim. From the dock, on the bank, you could see the rocks on the bottom of the water, varicolored pebbles worn smooth and harmless; there were no weeds, no snakes, no sudden muddy eddies. The sisters wore big straw hats, adorned with artificial grapes or cherries: tea-party hats, sunbathing hats, summer hats, River Bend hats.

It was a weekend house for Mother and me, a vacation house for Aunt Caroline and Nan. For the four of us it was our real home, our only remaining house with a name.

The story about houses begins with the fact that our family came over on the next boat after the *Mayflower*, a grevious delay that vexed the sisters always. "We had relatives on the *Mayflower*, but they died," Aunt Caroline used to explain, and we would nod, although neither Nan nor I ever understood how that could be possible. The Sayres, which was the family's name then, lived for three hundred years on what was always called the Cape. (Nan, when small, used to forget and call it the Shawl. "My grandma lived three hundred years on the Shawl, Delia," she would boast wanting to try the story out on someone to be sure it impressed. "Cape, baby." Delia would correct her, adding, "That's nothing; my grandma lived considerably longer than that on her own Cape. Times change. These days the ladies are glad to settle for the Outskirts, and don't you forget it.")

The house on the Cape, Sayre House, fell into the hands of in-laws and then strangers, who changed the name. Mother and Aunt Caroline would tell this as part of the family story. And how after that, when Gran was young and married and named Marjorie Sayre Miller, the family had owned a big house in Austin, which should have been called the Sayre House, but wasn't.

The old part of Austin was laid out on a square, with the north-south streets named, in order, for the rivers of Texas (so that by the time you learned that Guadalupe Street was one block over from Lavaca, you'd learned it was that order on the map as well). The numbered streets ran east-west, with First on the south at the Colorado River and Twenty-fourth on the north at the University of Texas, with the Capitol halfway between, at Twelfth. Its domed Capitol, wide streets, and winding river reminiscent of Washington, D.C., the original Austin was as orderly: hemmed neat as a handkerchief by Waller Creek on the east and Shoal Creek on the west.

Gran's house, a Victorian showplace, had been built in 1852 in the town's residential heart, on the corner of Fourteenth and San Jacinto. When it was a hundred years old, it had received a Historical Preservation plaque in a formal ceremony and been christened, not the Sayre House, but the *McAllister* House, for the prominent mayor (father of the present female mayor) who had saved it from the path of a new freeway.

Gran was by then widowed and living at River Bend and didn't care. The house had been in disrepair, falling down she said, when she'd moved out, and she'd been glad to have the conservationists take it. But Mother, raising a daughter alone in an apartment, and Aunt Caroline, the wife of a struggling Presbyterian minister in the Deep South, were crushed. Once again the family's house was owned and named by strangers.

Mother, when she got her divorce from Mr. Pinter, my father, had taken the fine, old name of Sayre, to salvage it somewhat; Aunt Caroline, who couldn't do that with a husband alive, always used it as a middle name, Caroline Sayre McCall, on her engraved notepaper.

When Nan and I were born, Mother and Aunt Caroline had searched the entire genealogy for just the right names for us—Lutie and Nannie—and had drawn small branching trees of just who the first Nannie and Lutie, for whom we were named, were and how far back we went. We didn't like our names, embarrassed by them in the days of classmates called Judy and Pam. Besides, I felt in some way responsible, as Nan wouldn't have been there if it hadn't been for me.

Aunt Caroline, the elder sister, had had Bubba and then Langley G. and, proud of having two sons, had rested on her laurels. Two was enough for a church family, and at that time Uncle Elbert had not yet got Grace Church in Savannah. But then Mother, in her late twenties, already leaving Mr. Pinter, had got pregnant with me. And having made a daughter, as is her way to make what happens look as if she intended it, she began to make Aunt Caroline feel inadequate for not having made one, too. "Who are Elbert Junior and Langley going to marry?" she would ask. "What control do you have over that? Families dissipate that way when they don't have girls. Daughters keep a family going," she said, until, four years after I was born, Aunt Caroline had Nan.

6

And then we were the cousins, and each sister had her girl.

In those days Nan and I felt inferior in every way to the splendor of our mothers. They were beautiful, with champagne-colored hair, gray-green eyes, high foreheads, and smooth skin that they said went back to the grandmother on the Cape. They were tall, regal women, both of them, larger even today than Nan or I. They seemed, when we were little, extraordinarily *real*: Their cheeks had color, and their lips; their voices carried; their shoulders had breadth; and their hands, strength. Their bearing conveyed presence. We, small girls, seemed insignificant and inessential. Paper children, with outdated names, cut from a pattern book.

My fourth summer at camp, I remember, Nan came down to go to camp and spend the summer with me. After the session was over, we stayed on at River Bend, paddling around in inner tubes, sunbathing on the dock, having those lovely Delia-made picnics, wondering if we would be like the sisters when we grew up.

Then Gran had her stroke.

At first Mother and Aunt Caroline tried to get Delia to come stay at the house, but she did daywork—making more money hiring out to five households than she could working for any one woman. She did come, for a week, in the evenings after her other jobs were done, to clean up Gran and bathe her and leave us a meal on the yellow counter top. But that wore her down, and she told Mother that was no good for her, that she would come the way she always had, on Fridays.

Next, they tried a licensed vocational nurse; but the cost was too high, and she would do only nursing, not being hired help, as she explained. Finally, Mother located a high school girl who was taking Distributive Education and needed the money and who came from a big family and so would know how to cope with and be sweet to Gran. That was the way Mother presented her.

But it turned out that she, Jimmie Wallace, was barely fourteen, not much older than I, and didn't know the first thing about cooking or cleaning or nursing old ladies. All she really knew was how to get around my mother.

I was so jealous; I was sure that she was not what she pretended to be, that she had made up Distributive Education, and that she'd probably run away from a foster home which didn't want her back.

Mother would reach out and touch Jimmie's frizzy hair and pat her sallow cheek and tell her she was a marvel. "I've never seen Mama look better. You're amazing. Doing Delia's work and the nurse's, too. You're an angel. Isn't she, Sister? Imagine, keeping everything spick-and-span and teaching Mama to use the walker and going to summer school besides. What would we do without you, Jimmie, honey?"

After she came, there were no more deviled eggs with bits of bacon or spicy fried chicken, no more cake with caramel filling. The starched Dutch girl covers had vanished from the cake box and cooler; the kitchen floor was grimy with dirt overlaid with wax. Mother seemed blind to all of it when any other time I was sure she would have fired on the spot anyone that sloppy and incompetent.

Jimmie would sit on the dock, passing out Kentucky Fried Chicken, paid for with Mother's money, to the sisters and us and talk as if she were one of the adults.

"Marjorie's a tough cookie," she'd say brazenly, calling Gran by the first name that no one used. Talking about her with a familiarity that even her daughters didn't dare. "She's a tough old bird, your mom," Jimmie would say to

Aunt Caroline. "She's a pistol, isn't she, Flo?" she would ask my mother.

I couldn't bear it. Watching my mother respond with a laugh, her creamy skin dimpling around her mouth, her eyes growing bright—she was so beautiful then.

It wasn't until that fall, when Gran moved with us into the new place that Mother had bought west of town—a farmhouse that faced a line of brittle scrub oak and a dry creek bed—that I understood about Jimmie Wallace. That she had kept the house on the Guadalupe for us, for one last summer. That letting the nurse go, firing Delia after seven years on one week's notice, putting in her place a white girl who could be had for next to nothing—all was a way to postpone the inevitable. I realized that Mother and Aunt Caroline had been as aware as I was that Jimmie wasn't what she said, had never worked before, had no credentials. They'd made themselves believe what they wanted, to have one last summer in their tea-party hats, their sunbathing hats, their River Bend hats.

Mother bought the house in the cedar brake west of Austin when it wasn't even in a subdivision and not connected with either city water or gas, gambling that it would be worth a hundred thousand in five years' time, naming it Redoaks for a stand of eight young trees on the back of the acreage that turned, amid the evergreen live oaks, a brilliant crimson in the fall.

Redoaks is west of the ninety-eighth meridian and, therefore, over that invisible line across which, in a matter of a few yards, the rainfall level changes and the county goes from wet to dry; indigenous plants, such as the scent-drenched purple mountain laurel, will not grow, grass browns to the ground in the blistering summer sun, dust whirls in the air when you jog, and dogs chasing wild turkeys in the amethyst evenings look like foxes on a desert landscape.

By the time I started high school at St. Stephens, Gran was a yo-yo. She would expand into the house, yard, countryside, busying herself with tending me and the gardens despite the loss of function that persisted to some extent on the right side of her body.

When she was expansive, she'd get her hair done at Marcie's in Oak Hill, our nearest community; she'd take me to the Big Wheel for fried chicken and biscuits when she was nostalgic about Delia. She had me drive her to St. Luke's Church on the lake, where she could look through the wall of glass down on the water and worship with her own kind; she had me accompany her on Saturday afternoon expeditions to Scarbrough's Better Dresses, to get herself a dark silk (which was usually no longer really silk but seemed so, from the feel and price, to her): a nice dress, with self-trim and covered buttons, and deep hand-turned hems, and generous armholes. She would enjoy a drive around to see what had been done lately with the McAllister House or the cemetery where her husband was buried or take in a garden tour if it was that time of year— the Azalea Homes, the Bluebonnet Trail, the Rose Shows.

Then she would begin to recede. Regular as a tide.

First she would not leave the house, never mind that her hair was dry as straw, hadn't been washed or tinted for weeks, was shut up in a tangled gray spider web of a net, with a handful of pins. Never mind worrying about the grocery store; she wasn't all that hungry anyway. We could make do with the okra and squash. She would sit on the wide porch of our reproduction farmhouse in one of the granny rockers and watch the day come up, letting the morning get started and cast its bright shadows around her, shine through her tea glass, move across the lettuce garden and the dog pens next door, warm her slippered feet and sagging cheeks; she would stay there, watching, until the sun sank behind the house, vexed it did so behind her back.

"Go on about your business," she'd say when I was home. "Don't worry about me." She would forget I was Lutie, or who Lutie was, and call me Florence, for my mother, or Caroline. "Did your mother ever have children?" she once asked, watching the noon sun go by overhead.

Then she wouldn't be able to leave her bedroom anymore. I would have to feed her from a tray when I got home from school. It would be an effort to coax her to move out into the hall and across into the bathroom that was hers and company's.

Finally, for an awful spell that lasted three days, she would not leave her bed, not to eat or tend herself, not for anything. She fretted and wept and talked about a daddy and mother I had never heard mentioned, and I had to soak her sheets in Massengill's and spoon-feed her milky oatmeal.

The end of my senior year in high school she died. Mother was attending a conference of arts and sciences alumnae, as a representative of the vice-president, and I couldn't reach her. I tried the Joe C. Thompson Center, the LBJ Library, and even Lakeway, which The University sometimes used, but no one had a conference scheduled. I called our doctor—the general practitioner who signed my forms for camp and school and treated Mother's sore throats—and he confirmed that Gran was getting old. But he wouldn't come out. "It's not my domain, honey. It's mental. That's not my bailiwick. I can send out a tranquilizer, but that's about it."

"She can't breathe," I told him.

"Hysteria," he said. "Nobody dies of it. It's the way

kids hold their breath until they turn blue; when they pass out, they're breathing again just fine. Sounds like you're the one could use a bit of tranquilizing."

But she did die of it. I called Marcie's Beauty Shop, and they called an ambulance from the county service, as there was no public ambulance then, and it came right out. But she was gone. The attendant who picked up what remained of my grandmother said her lungs had filled up.

It was then that Redoaks became a weekend place. For the years that Gran was bad, Mother had come out only on weekends from her apartment in town, to check on us and be glad we were looking after each other.

With Gran gone, she renewed her options. The house was already worth more than she had estimated; people flocked to the county's all-white schools, glad to brag that they were on the road to the Johnson Ranch, that they were in the hill country, that they were buying old-settler land.

The red oaks themselves had grown towering and thick in the years we'd owned it. Because the cistern water was our own, the only charge being the electricity to pump it, I had watered everything. The trees got a steady slow hose at night in the hot months from May to October; the kitchen gardens, squashes and pumpkins and pole beans, and the lettuce patch, double-fenced against rabbit and deer, were soaked each evening at twilight.

Mother offered me the chance to stay on, rent-free, while I went to The University. "I wouldn't charge my own daughter, the idea; besides, having you there instead of some unreliable tenant will be an advantage for both of us. I'll sleep better knowing you'll be in a safe place—these days even the dorms aren't safe—and we'll have a weekend place. What do you say, Lutie? Let's keep it."

So we did, and I became custodian of Mother's house with a name.

Which history of houses explains why she is so angry I am leaving.

2

THE last thing before she left Texas, Lutie had breakfast with her mother. Her mother had heard the news of the job offer a month ago, when she'd told her that her friend Mavis Conroe had called to say there would be an opening to replace someone on leave of absence from Vassar College. Mavis had been on Lutie's dissertation committee at Texas, and when she said, "You'd be perfect for the job," she was also offering Lutie a chance to teach somewhere else for a change and thus return as more than an adjunct, for Texas never hired its own. "It's short notice," Mavis had said, "but there's no way to have an interview before August, when enough of the committee is back."

Lutie had told her mother all that, but Mother never heard what she wasn't ready to. So now, in the baking August heat—already at not yet 8:00 A.M. it had hit ninety-two degrees—Lutie told her again.

"It's actually in the soc department," she explained, "even though it will be women's studies."

"You don't know what you're getting into."

"Oh, Mother, don't be angry."

Florence Sayre was. She bit her lip and pushed back the plate of biscuits and eggs at Sid's. "I was so homesick,

Lutie, when I was up there. You have no idea. I wrote my mother every single day." She was back in a past it was painful to visit. "Do you have any idea what the world was like then? Cheaper, for one thing. Did you know I could take fifteen dollars to the commissary and buy food for the week for the three of us? I'd take three five-dollar bills and keep track of the amounts in my head. Chuck roast was thirty-four cents a pound; you could get a week's milk and eggs for two dollars and fifty-five cents. Nowadays fifteen dollars doesn't buy you dinner anymore."

Lutie had heard this before. It was part of the story which began when she was a baby, Mother was still married to Mr. Pinter, and the war was over.

"The military is very hierarchical. I tell the vice-president that when he complains about The University. That he has no idea. When the wartime commissions were revoked and I was a sergeant's wife, it was night and day different."

Mother's job brought her in contact with a lot of important people; she was something of a semiofficial hostess for University functions and, since it was a state school, for state functions as well.

Her reputation as a woman who had raised a child alone and made a name for herself was her highest accomplishment, and Lutie admired her mother for it.

Her mother had just been selected for one of the five Outstanding Austin Women Recognition Awards to be presented in December. These were given annually by the local chapter of Women in the Public Eye and the *Austin Express* (the service group administering the secret ballot selection and the newspaper doing the publicizing) and were much coveted.

Mother's area of achievement was public health. She was responsible for getting four hundred new beds for the community hospital. Not the beds themselves, actually, but for creating a volunteer effort that raised the money and aroused a sense of need in the city. It had been an uphill fight due to the fact that a lot of citizens thought that extra beds meant freeloading vagrants from around the county; but Mother had persevered, and the new wing was to be named for her: the Florence Sayre Wing. Which was a dream come true.

"You have this nice teaching job down here and lots of friends and a nice place to live. There's no earthly reason to dash off—"

"Mavis has already set it up for me."

"I don't know how someone like that seems to have such a hold on you, I really don't."

"You met Mavis, Mother; she was on my committee."

"I'm not interested in the history of the woman, which has nothing to do with the matter." Florence Sayre looked reproachful. "You don't know what you're getting into. I was so homesick when I was away up there and you were a baby—it's so hard for anyone to understand now what army life meant in those days. But you were strictly on your own. Everyone was transient. Not that most of them knew better. You have no idea, Lutie, but there are whole groups of people who don't have any sense of family, at least not as we know it."

Had it not been for her cousin Nan, Lutie would never have been able to pick up and go. She'd reasoned that Nan, who created and marketed needlepoint designs, might like to try her talents outside Savannah; also that Nan, never married, might like to try her wings. Lutie had called and asked her if she wanted to house-sit, and Nan had jumped at the chance.

Nan's older brother Bubba had recently got married, and that was an irritant to Nan. Aunt Caroline had encouraged the wedding, soon after Uncle Elbert died, so that Bubba could be married from The Manse, a lovely historical old house where some U.S. president had married, while the family was still in it. The church, embroiled in its search for a new pastor, let them remain, and the wedding gave Aunt Caroline a chance to entertain from The Manse one last time and put under social obligation those friends she now sorely needed.

Bubba had obliged, and all the family had attended. There had been only one fly in the ointment: the bride's name.

"It's *Mickey*," Nan had told Lutie over the phone. "You can imagine Mother. Mickey Denny. That's the sum of it. Mother said, 'What sort of people would give a daughter a name like that, I ask you? Even for a boy it's a nickname.'"

What Aunt Caroline had done, and Nan had mailed Lutie a copy of it, was to send out announcements of her son's engagement to Miss Mary Michael Denny. "She says she's doing her a favor, that she has to live here and she might as well be presented right," Nan reported, amused and cross at the same time.

Nan, like Lutie, was short and nondescript in her coloring and features; they were just as they had been as little girls. But Nan somehow ended up looking quite glamorous, because she had a lot of animation to her features and gestures, and used a lot of make-up—layered eyelashes and colored shadow and a glossy mouth—and wore vivid, original clothes. Lutie admired her cousin and always saw her with fresh eyes; at the same time getting together with her was also like being back twenty years in those early River Bend summers.

Nan arrived to house-sit, and she and Lutie had two nights, slumber-party nights, at Redoaks, while Lutie tried to let her in on all the secrets of the overwhelming dwelling.

17

It had been hard to know where to begin.

The first problem of course was the limy, sediment-filled water. If there was a norther, you had to let the pipes drip so there was no chance of their bursting as company arrived (that had happened); but if you let them drip, then the calcareous water made a film that hardened into rock, an instant stalagmite where it hit. So you had to keep special salts in the Culligan water system tank, so that the drinking water was pure and company was never aware of this ongoing war with the limestone soil. Living west of the ninety-eighth was like living in a roofless Carlsbad Cavern.

Lutie put an extra can of Drāno down the kitchen sink, to be sure that the calcified water didn't stop it up (that had happened too, just once; she'd been standing there, a plumber's helper in her hand, the food not ready, when the first car of Mother's friends pulled into the drive). Next, she'd scrubbed the bathroom tubs and bowls (the big bath upstairs, the small guest bath that had also been Gran's downstairs) and gone over them with tile wax, to take off the gritty white film the water left. And she'd bailed the cold, tan backed-up water out of the dishwasher—which wasn't really usable, but needed to look as if it were, so that you could load it while the last of the helpful University guests looked on.

Then, because it was August and baking hot, the next item had been the ticks; the only things besides the cedar and scrub oak that flourished on the drought-prone, flash-flood land.

Ticks around Redoaks came in seven varieties of the common dog tick, the worst, called the starback, nesting, in the hot months, in every inch of ground, bush, and animal. Lutie kept on hand a strong solution from the county vet harmless to humans, intended for dipping hunting dogs, which she mixed in a washtub, two tablespoons to the tub, and used to hose down the front porches and spray the small sumac bushes near the back and along the flagstone walk from the gravel drive.

Besides the water and ticks common to the area, there were also vexing malfunctions particular to Redoaks which Lutie despaired of ever covering in detail for Nan. She'd left notes all over the place: "Be sure the burners are turned all the way off. The knobs tend to slip and if you leave them partly on sparks will fly out, and by the end of the day the burner will be shorted out."

She would think she'd surely covered everything, and then something else would come to her. For example, the upstairs floor was the downstairs ceiling. Literally. That is, the copy of an old 1840s stone farmhouse was quite authentic—and economical for the builder—in that the wide-plank pine boards which formed the floor also constituted the ceiling. There was no insulation, Sheetrock, duct space, nothing, in between. A cough in the upstairs bedroom could be heard in the living room below. That had not mattered; privacy was not part of the house anyway. The problem was not noise, but the fact that if you forgot when you took a shower and left the curtain on the outside of the tub, then by the time you were in the kitchen making breakfast coffee, water would be dripping on the dining table. (That had happened, too; water had dripped into the corn pudding cooling for a company brunch.)

Then Cecelie the cat had to be chased off the living room carpet, a prize expanse of wool twenty feet by twenty (the four main rooms, in frontier tradition, being each a square). It was deep purple-brown which Mother called aubergine, which had cost $15 a yard installed when that was a fortune. It was stunning and set the color scheme for the room. The walls were café au lait, the woodwork cream, the love seat sofa and two wing-backed chairs upholstered in a chintz of brown, cream, aubergine, and deep red. When company came, Lutie filled the four large cream-colored clay pots, which sat in each corner, with waxy green branches—holly in winter, ligustrum in summer—and sat the antique deep ruby crystal wineglasses on a silver tray on the large, refinished oak buffet.

(She never went into the living room except to fill the vases, lay an oak fire in the six-foot stone fireplace, or remove all traces of the cat. Even when Dabney had lived there with her, the room had remained for company only.)

Mother would tell her University people, "You can't miss our place." She would say to the vice-president's friends, "When you see the brilliant foliage and the porches which look like Tara, that's ours."

"Ours" was how Mother spoke of it, although Redoaks was hers. She paid the low monthly payments on the mortgage. Gran, when she was alive, had paid the Pedernales Electric Co-op bill and Lutie's tuition at St. Stephens. Lutie and Dabney, both in graduate school (he in classics, she in sociology), had paid the utilities and furnished the food for the weekend gatherings.

"Do look after Cecelie," she said to Nan.

"Who's that?"

Nan had moved her things, three large summer-tour suitcases, into the upstairs bedroom.

"You know, my tabby."

"I tried to think. Hired girl?"

"No such luck."

"Roommate?"

"Then I wouldn't have had to draft you."

"One of your hill country shrubs, the flowering Cecelie?"

Lutie showed her the cat food, the flea collars, the Kitty Litter, the vitamins.

Nan pointed to the stove. "Who's supposed to make sense

of these instructions stuck all over the place? For God's sake, Lute, I mean, do you leave them here all the time?"

"They're for you."

"I think our mothers have warped your brain. I mean it. My mother would love to do that. Post stuff like 'Turn off faucets tightly to the right when leaving bath,' I mean it. You should see her ensconced in that new duplex, the renovated slave quarters the church ladies found for her. I have to take my shoes off when I enter."

"You've saved my life by coming."

"They love it, our mothers. 'We're trading daughters.' Mother said it, and then yesterday Aunt Florence said it. I wonder who is in charge of deciding how they'll respond."

Lutie drove her to the Big Wheel, so she could see where you went out to eat, and by the HEB supermarket that stayed open until midnight. They had an iced tea on the porch as the sun went by overhead and talked about the old days when Gran was alive.

She left Nan asleep upstairs in the big bed, with Cecelie curled on the kitchen table waiting for breakfast, to meet her mother and say good-bye.

They walked across The University campus as the tower chimed quarter to eight. Even Mother, in an executive role, had to be at her desk on the stroke of eight, and could not leave before the stroke of five. Lutie had taken advantage of the fact in picking her time to say good-bye.

Mother was in a pink linen two-piece suit with a white pleated blouse. The suit had once been a dress but looked new with the top open like a jacket, the blouse under it. Mother worked all the time to keep her clothes in fashion.

She walked her mother to the Tower building which housed the vice-president's office. It was an old ritual, their having breakfast out, which she had done while she was in graduate school before she married, and again, after. The campus was crowded already in the glaring morning light, alive with tanned students in pastel shorts.

"I'll call you when I get there," Lutie promised as the clock began to strike the hour.

Her mother forced a smile. "You don't know what you're getting into."

3

A T first it looked as if her mother had been right.

Lutie did not get the job.

"You what?" Mavis Conroe had asked her. "You brought *furniture?* For an interview?"

Lutie had been slow to understand. It seemed that nothing had been definite. Nothing had been offered after all, except plane fare.

"I never meant to imply . . . I thought you'd get a free trip up; we could have a visit, get caught up. I never got the whole straight of what happened with you and Dabney, did I? Besides, I thought you'd be perfect for the job, and there was a chance, I told you. With your work on matrilineal descent. It seemed a natural. But *furniture?*"

Lutie sat with her friend, her former adviser, over a cup of bitter New York coffee, her trailer parked in Vassar's visitors' lot.

Mavis stirred in two spoons of sugar.

"What happened?" Lutie ventured.

"They didn't like you. Oh, I don't mean you, naturally, you personally. They just couldn't see you for it; you didn't look the part. They couldn't see you teaching women's studies. Up here, with your accent and those

23

clothes. And then, when you said, 'Yes, ma'am,' to the chair. Well, that creamed it, for sure."

"But you said someone was going on leave—"

"They did, but she had a friend. Up here there's no scarcity. I'm sorry, really. I should have foreseen, you're so—"

Lutie tried not to show the degree to which it hurt, that she didn't have the job and that she had disappointed or maybe even embarrassed her friend. Mavis had been on her committee; she had expected that would be all it took.

They sat in a steak place in Poughkeepsie while Mavis had a drink and let the full predicament settle in on her.

"What must I do?" Lutie asked.

"Let me think about it."

The next day Mavis, as Professor Conroe, called every soc department in the state university system. There was one spot, part time, one semester, not advertised: to replace a Professor Cleveland Birdsong, who'd been named acting chair of her department while a search was on, at State University of New York at Purchase.

"Birdsong." Mavis sniffed. "I hate it when women make up those names. But you're in luck. It's down in Westchester and ready-made for you."

Dr. Birdsong conveyed she was delighted to look no further and to let Lutie take over her two sections of Intro Soc ("The concept of 'I' as a product of social organization"). Earlier Lutie would have been disappointed; she'd come thinking she could teach some version of her dissertation (the atavistic survival of matrilineal descent as evidenced in the American South), but coming as it did to the rescue, the job seemed a miracle.

So she turned her old Chevy plus trailer around and headed down to Westchester, where, after two days, she located an efficiency apartment in a three-family house, eight minutes from SUNY Purchase, for only $275 a month. (Which amount was more than Mother paid on Redoaks, principal, interest, taxes and insurance, but was apparently quite cheap for up here.)

It seemed to her the height of luxury that everything worked: the drains, the oven, the refrigerator, even the bathtub. Mrs. Vaccaro, the landlady, was glad to have her, since her own daughter was off in Florida and didn't write. The place had its own outside stairs, a little porch, a sugar maple in the front yard, a pear tree next door. She was two blocks from a service station, a luncheonette, a diner, and a grocery store. At the end of the street was a small baseball park, and beyond that, a bigger park, and then a mammoth turn-of-the-century dam.

As Lutie sat in the immaculate kitchen, signing a six-month lease, Mrs. Vaccaro had asked her, "What's your nationality?"

It wasn't a Texas question, and Lutie hadn't known what to say. As she looked blank, Mrs. Vaccaro pursued. "Where do your people come from?"

Lutie, finally understanding, had said, "England."

"You just visiting then?"

"No, ma'am. They came hundreds of years ago." Lutie had laughed.

Mrs. Vaccaro got defensive. Her mother, she said, had come from Italy as a young girl and had never learned the language.

Lutie touched her arm and explained that the reason her own family had left England so many years before was that England was an awful country, and the reason that Mrs. Vaccaro's had only come a few years before was that Italy was too marvelous a place to leave unless you had to. And that had made things all right.

She had wanted to put out a bird feeder right away and a bowl of water for the neighborhood cats, as Cecelie was the one thing she really missed—it felt strange to go to sleep without her curled on the covers—but Mrs. Vaccaro had remarked that she always put mothballs out to keep the cats off her flower beds and that she hoped the racket of the birds wouldn't bother Lutie, that they were always a pest on their way south in the winter.

Lutie furnished her living room–bedroom to her liking. She had the wicker couch and two wicker chairs, which had once been Gran's, a small rug (department store Oriental, nothing special, in nice shades of deep blue). She had one hanging bookshelf and, under it, set her daybed directly on the floor to sleep and study on. Over the couch, facing the three high windows which looked out on leafy oaks across the street, she'd mounted her blowup of the Arch of Septimius Severus from the Roman Forum—the one good thing she'd salvaged from her time with Dabney. To match the walls which were a dim rental green, she'd bought four green cushions for the daybed, and two potted ferns. With Rome as a backdrop, it all fit nicely into her quarters in the tiny village below the massive dam.

Mother had said she would call on Wednesdays and Sundays. She had MCI and so would call after eleven midweek and before five on the weekend. She promised that she hadn't forgotten that New York was an hour later and that Lutie must say if she was too sleepy to talk.

Mother also wrote from work on Monday mornings, to keep her daughter up on all the details not important enough for a long-distance call. She liked to write from her office as administrative assistant to the vice-president in charge of academic affairs at The University of Texas at Austin. She liked to type on office paper, to give her comments on the scene a stamp of authority.

This week her mother's letter recounted the to-do they'd had when, at the premiere of the movie *The Best Little Whorehouse in Texas*, someone had mistaken their aging blond mayor, Ginny McAllister, for the real madam of the defunct Chicken Ranch, because she was talking curl to curl with Dolly Parton, and had asked them to pose together for a picture.

... We were all proud of McAllister. She never lost her composure. "Now why would you want a photograph of a lady mayor?" she asked, and averted an embarrassing situation. Can you imagine such a mistake? But it got a lot of press and even ended up being rather funny, and they both got roundly bussed by Burt Reynolds. It was quite an occasion. I'll enclose a clipping for you.

I've invited the V-P and his wife out to dinner for a platter of scrimp. Wish you were here to go along. I won't descend on Nannie at Redoaks until she gets settled in. She tells me that The Jabeau has taken a number of her needlepoint designs on consignment already. Caroline and I are proud of our girls.

Love,
M.

(The *scrimp* for *shrimp* was the sort of mistake her mother often made when she was anxious. Lutie was used to it; it reminded her of Gran.)

She put the clipping of the mayor, along with the weekly letter, in the file box at the back of the linen closet where she was going to keep correspondence.

On the front of the white frost-free refrigerator she'd posted a list:

Exercise
Grocery
Dressmaker
City
Group

For *exercise*, which she had decided would be a daily walk, she'd bought Symonds's *Tree Identification Book*,

27

Peterson's *Field Guide to the Birds East of the Rockies*, and a history of the county which said that the Kensico Dam Pavilion had once been a famous place for Sunday outings at the turn of the century.

Grocery she had already found in her neighborhood, and *Dressmaker* should be easy; you could look them up in the *Yellow Pages*.

City she planned to get to know gradually, riding the local train from nearby White Plains into Manhattan; walking, map in hand, from Grand Central to Central Park (she'd figured that anything called Central had to be within a certain distance); and then riding the train home.

Group would be harder; she was less secure about how to pursue that. Yet after what Mavis had said about the wrong impression she had made on the committee at Vassar, it was foremost in Lutie's mind. It was threatening to know that you were seen differently from the way you intended. That's what a group would do: show you who you were, reflected in their eyes.

Lutie put a cut-up fryer in the easy-to-light white rental oven, with a lemon to flavor the drippings, set the temperature at 350 degrees and the timer for an hour.

She set out her gray cotton place-mat and her white cotton napkin and put a tall glass of iced tea with lemon in the frost-free refrigerator to wait for her. This was a device she had adopted in the absence of Cecelie: deciding that any such object—the oven timer set to go off, an alarm clock, a phone message to be answered—implied your return, expected it.

When you lived alone, you wanted to feel welcomed home.

Beside her place-mat she set her journal, a stitched wide-ruled college notebook, and her gold-tipped Mont Blanc fountain pen, which she had bought with the proceeds of her divorce, wanting one special possession that she could keep. She'd had the pen, and four wells of Mont Blanc black fountain pen ink, for four years, and had never used it. The problem was that she'd been afraid the pen might leak. Pens did that: leaked and stained your index finger, smudged your palm, dripped on your papers. She knew that from schoolday ventures with Esterbrooks. The truth was that the dysfunction of inanimate objects at Redoaks had been so threatening, so constant in her life, that the idea of a leaky pen had seemed the last straw.

At home she'd taken her walks in the mornings, had got up early, at dawn, and gone out as the school kids were lining up across the cattle guard at the end of the gravel road to wait for the school bus. Something about that had pleased her: starting out in her Adidas in the mornings like a youngster going to school.

But here she found it pleasant to walk in the early evening, to leave when it was light and return when it was dusk. Knowing that the families on the short shady block were out in their backyards cooking on grills, wearing short sleeves in the steamy air of August; that the men and their friends were gathering at the ball park at the far end of the street for a game of baseball; and, on the smaller diamond, that little kids were playing without a coach.

She had timed her walk at exactly an hour, second-floor back door to second-floor back door, screen latch to screen latch.

She walked down the sloping asphalt drive, newly tarred in preparation for winter, and down the two blocks of Clove Street to the baseball park, where a dozen people, sitting in folding chairs on a rise above the diamond, cheered the left fielder's catch, and the sides changed places.

She edged around the children's swings and slides to one side of the field, past the empty smaller diamond, and started on the tiny dirt path which took her from the small

29

neighborhood park under an old stone bridge into the vast expanse of public space which was the dam pavilion. To the right of the open plaza she began to climb an old brick road, once used for carriages, now abandoned. The bricks were set length down, the way she had seen them in Rome, so that only a tiny rectangle, the end of the brick, formed the face of the road, making a mosaic of thousands of tiny rust-colored cubes, the depth of the brick: a roadway which would not turn or wobble under wheels. She loved the road, which was always empty, its edges overgrown with vines (poison ivy, Virginia creeper, something that looked like the Deep South's kudzu, and, here and there, ropes of grapevine sprawling over brush and sapling).

Towering hardwoods met at the top over the road and her head, letting in only shafts of early-evening light, which struck branches, vines, and shrubs on the way down. The bricks stopped at a set of stone stairs, sprouting weeds in the cracks, which led onto the dam. Lutie stopped, too, to look over at the sloping dam face, its great black-marbled gray blocks mitered together with no visible mortar, as if fit tightly and neatly enough to keep the wall of water behind them sealed by their juncture. High across the front a row of stone shields alternated with bundles of stone fasces, the whole design hewn and faceted like giant gems. Its size and proportion were Roman, and with good reason: New York water commissioners had brought stonemasons from Italy at the turn of the century, craftsmen who had camped at the base of the dam while it was being raised, whose village had been drowned by its filling. You could stand here and imagine them hauling the granite from the nearby quarry, homesick for the Baths of Caracalla, for the arches of antiquity two stories high, for the sight of the beauty they were used to; re-creating, as best they could, the palatine proportions of Rome.

At each end of the dam were stone hemispheres, cut by

a two-lane road, facing each other. The arches to the north looking into the deep cold water; the arches to the south facing down to the dry fountains and reflecting pools of the plaza below. Piazza del Kensico it should have been called.

In the open space below, people were spreading blankets on the grass and setting up folding chairs carried from their cars. Instruments tuned up for the midweek band concert. By the time she reached the far end of the dam "The Star-Spangled Banner" broke out, and everyone rose, to celebrate a late-summer evening in a once-glorious park.

As she started down the series of steps which descended through a grove of white ash, she looked at her watch. It had been thirty minutes, and she was still thirty minutes from her home on Clove Street. The circular stroll filled her with well-being. She would do this every day: walk around the plaza, rising to its right, descending to its left, closing in the listening crowd with the drawstring of her feet. The hour encircling the distance.

That was Lutie's way, to take on what was strange bit by bit until each aspect of it became familiar.

(Voices from home echoed in her ear. "Oh, Lutie, you think too much," said her mother. "You'll domesticate Hell itself," said Dabney.)

4

_____

Journal: Victimless Crimes

HERE is Mother's latest letter and my answer to it. Both of which show, I think, that we are finding it harder and harder to keep in touch, now that almost six weeks have gone by.

Dear Lutie,

The big news down here, dear, is our private spaceship launch. I understand it made your New York Times. *They call it Conestoga, and the booster was an old Minuteman rocket. Anyway, you can imagine the excitement here. The company simply bought a lot of spare equipment from NASA and sent it up, just like that. They hope to offer flights in two or three years. Imagine, making it look so easy, showing that private enterprise can move faster than NASA and not have all that paper work and accountability.*

We got to go, the V-P and some others of us. And there was a party afterward. The sad part was that Toddie Lee Wynne died of a heart attack minutes before the launch went up; we were all most distressed about it. He was not

the only money behind it, but you know the Wynnes: He
was the heart of the venture.

Well, the other news is a letter Caroline sent me the other
day. I can't believe she still had it, but she was going
through everything she'd stored after Elbert's funeral. It
was a letter I wrote her when I was pregnant with you, in
Washington, D.C., saying, "I feel so lonesome up here, a
pregnant girl with a pregnant cat. Just think how it will be
Christmas when I come home to see you and Mama. I'll be
something to behold." You can see where my mind was
then, and I can imagine you are getting just as homesick
up there now.

I don't sleep the way I should with you such a long way
off. Sometimes it gives me quite a scare just thinking of
you up there. But I look forward to our phone talks, and
I'm counting the days until you're home. The fact that it
will coincide with the awards occasion will make December
a special treat.

Nan and I stay so busy with our separate lives I've hardly
seen my favorite niece.

Love,
M.

I answered her on my blue Crane's paper, with my
initials, that she got me for my birthday last March, so she
could see that I liked to use it.

Dear Mother,
I wrote you that I had a dressmaker. Well, she has made
a gray dress for me, fitted in the waist, and a petticoat skirt
in red and yellow and black paisley that I can wear either
under it or as a gored skirt itself. It looks—at least I hope
it does—rather like the Ralph Lauren ads. I'll wear it down
to Aunt Caroline's for Thanksgiving, which I am looking
forward to a lot. Do you and Nan have plans?
I'm looking forward to being able to take advantage of

being on the East Coast to make the trip, on an excursion flight, as everything is so close together up here, compared to Texas. It takes not much more than an hour, imagine.

I took the dressmaker a buttermilk pie when I picked up the dress because she did such a nice job. We sat and ate a piece together and watched her favorite serial on TV—did you know there is a soap called "Texas"?

I also have another exciting trip planned for the weekend after Halloween. Mavis Conroe, you remember, who set up the Vassar interview for me, has invited me to the Hamptons. That is the place to go up here, or, rather, places, as there is a Westhampton and an Easthampton and a Southampton and maybe more than that for all I know. I'm not sure which one is where her friend's house is, but they are all a long way out on Long Island, which is hundreds of miles in length, stretching almost all the way under Connecticut—just imagine an island reaching from Austin to Houston! So I guess not everything up here is close together after all.

There is a harvest moon, and so it is rising early, and I can see it at the top of the pear tree in the yard next door. The almanac says it is the moon nearest the autumnal equinox and rises soon after sunset for several days. I guess in the old days that meant more light to work the crops. The almanac also says that Venus is the morning star. That's one thing that is certain: The sky here is very little different from the sky at home. I can see Orion's belt and both dippers when the night is clear. Wouldn't it be fun sometime to see the southern sky?

Love,
L.

It bothers me that Mother and I don't seem to be writing about what is really happening, and that gets harder to do on this end, as perhaps it does on her end, too.

For example, her letters are full of news about her University adventures, but they contain nothing at all about how Nan is doing out at Redoaks or whether Cecelie is all right. If I ask her on the phone, straight out, she'll say something like "Your cousin is busy as a bee getting her Christmas needlepoint designs ready. I hardly see her." Once I asked specifically about Cecelie, whom I'm really missing, not having her around to curl up on the bed at night, and Mother moved right on, the way she and Aunt Caroline do when they want to change the subject: "We've had summer weather for the first two home games; too hot even for dark cottons, can you believe that?"

I wrote Nan once, to remind her to be careful about the shower dripping through into the kitchen, and about the trouble with the washer, and about being sure to add salts to the Culligan system, but all I've got is one postcard, with a kitty on the front and a balloon drawn in with the kitty saying "hi," which is the kind of card we used to send each other in camp days.

For my part, I have never admitted to Mother, or to Aunt Caroline, that I didn't get the job at Vassar. At first it was my pride, and now it is too late. So I can only write about my teaching very generally and not in a way that really shares the wildly costumed performing artists who are my soc students at SUNY.

The other reason it's hard for me to write about much is that it is a different world up here, and different rules apply. And it is going to take me awhile to figure them out.

For example, last night I had to call the police from the washateria for something which would never have happened at home.

I had looked up from making lesson plans to take my walk at the regular time, seven, not noticing that daylight was getting shorter, so that by the time I started down my outside stairs to take the brick road to the reservoir, it was already dusk. And I could see that by the time I got through the baseball park and under the bridge to the big pavilion that it would be night. That might have been all right—but it seemed foolish to go through a grove of trees in the dark when I wasn't sure. I've been working on not making any assumptions up here until I have more information.

The main reason for the delay was that my hair was wet, and I didn't want anyone to see me like that. I can't get used to how slowly everything dries up here. I'll wash out my panties, the way I did at home, and a few hours later they are still wet; I'll wash my hair, the way I would at home, and then put my face on, and my clothes, and expect to be able to brush my hair out and leave—and it's still wet.

Distressed at the thought of missing my hour's exercise, feeling out of control to be off schedule and with drippy hair, I decided to try the washateria that I pass every time I go to the grocery. It is in the same neighborhood, by a nursery which I like to pass anyway to see the blooming plants. I knew that the center would be safe, that no one would care about my hair, and that behind it was a nice hilly residential area which would be a good place for an evening walk, and no one would be alarmed at my strolling by. So I could do that while the clothes were in the wash and dry cycles, thirty minutes each, and get my hour in after all.

Part of it was that after Redoaks and the backed-up plumbing, one of my ideas of luxury was to put everything in a big commercial machine that worked—and wouldn't overflow or back up with water as chalky as white shoe polish. I had been waiting because I didn't have a lot of things with me: three sets of sheets, and three of towels, the jeans that I wore to walk and study in, a few old shirts. The rest, underwear and good skirts and blouses, I'd been washing by hand. But now I gathered everything together, including dishtowels and pajamas, and it looked like two good loads. I had already bought, to have on hand, a box of Arm & Hammer detergent, the kind that doesn't put a lot of phosphates in the sewage, and I had collected a peanut butter jar full of quarters just to be prepared.

At the beginning everything went fine. There were four other women in there, and they seemed light-hearted and relieved to be there, out of the house and getting things clean in machines that worked, the same as I was. Everyone was taking her time folding and sorting, making tiny piles of children's socks or men's undershorts or washcloths.

The washing machines were much bigger than I was used to, and I could put everything I had into one; in fact, they were the size that you could have put three normal loads in. They took nine quarters, but that was fine, because I had brought forty with me just to be on the safe side. I set the control on hot, as I always do for everything when I wash commercially, not being fooled by the management's wanting to save money on its costs and convincing you that you should be using only warm or cold water.

The machine could not be opened until the spin cycle was completed, and that made me relax about my walk. Not that I thought any of the women would want my old beige towels and sheets since what they had were mostly flowered and bright-colored; still, knowing the machines had a time lock was reassuring.

Then, just as I was about to go out the back door of the washateria and walk around the residential neighborhood and stop for a look at the potted chrysanthemums across the fence at Handelman's Nursery by moonlight, three scrubbed young people came through the front door and stopped me. The boys were wearing pastel jackets and starched shirts and light blue polyester trousers, and the sweet-faced girl had on a smocked dress whose gathers fell discreetly across her huge breasts. I could tell at a glance that they were Christians, by which I mean the way people use the term nowadays and not meaning the same as Uncle Elbert's church in Savannah.

While I was deciding this, the trio walked up to me, and the most scrubbed-looking boy said, "We're doing a survey. Do you mind if we ask you a few questions?"

Now I could tell that they weren't doing a survey, or they would have had questionnaires or some other materials, and they would have identified right off the organization they were with (or pretending to be with, if the real experiment was to see how people reacted to being approached in a public place). Also, they would have taken a sample of all of us who were there, but they only wanted to talk to me. So that was a giveaway right off, because I was the only white woman in there, and blacks are invisible to their kind of Christian.

I could see by the wall clock that we didn't have time to skirt around if I was going to get my walk. "I'm a Presbyterian," I told him directly, this not being the unrelated answer it seemed.

"If you were called to Jesus tonight," the other, blonder boy asked, responding to my statement, "would you be at peace with your soul?"

"I think so," I answered, reasoning that you were probably never ready but always had a feeling of unfinished business (the clothes in the machine) when your time came.

I could feel the four other women behind me, over at the folding shelves, listening, confident that they wouldn't be bothered with all this, but curious anyway to see what I did.

"If you were called before your Lord tonight, could you justify your life to Him?" This was from the leader again.

"I wouldn't presume to make excuses to God," I told

him, and I looked right at him, so that he could see that I was not an amateur at this business.

Then the large-chested girl asked, "May I tell you how I found the Savior in my life?"

Ordinarily I would have said yes, the way I always let Mormons come in and say their say because I know they have to report that they have talked to a certain number of people. But this time I didn't feel that I could; there was only twenty minutes left in my wash cycle. So I said, "No," but in a nice way, and sort of waved at them as I went out the back door. They could see I had my Adidas on and so wouldn't have to take offense.

I tried not to be frustrated by the delay. That is one of the main things I have to work on while I'm up here: that things don't stay the way you plan them.

Behind the nursery was a lovely steep hill that went sharply up and around a curve, and I wondered if they had trouble with ice in the winter here. I was thinking of our part of the hill country west of town and how, when it ices over, which it does half a dozen times a year, it is impassable, with everyone planing and skidding all over the highways and roads.

It smelled cool and was very clear. I could see the full moon high in the sky, farther to the south than it had been when I moved here. It looked wondrous, sitting, as it seemed to, in the branches of a big yellow sugar maple.

Coming back, heading down toward the parking lot and the washateria, I felt good, back in control of things, when I saw this car in front of the nursery ramming into a parked car. A burly man was backing up his Datsun and then accelerating and plowing into the driver's side of an empty red Toyota. I stood stock-still, watching for a few minutes, the way you do when something happens that you don't know what to do about, and then walked closer to the edge of the lot near him and wrote down the numbers of the car licenses inside the back of my checkbook. And he looked up and saw me—and went right on with his wrecking. Nobody else was around; so no one else saw him. Then I noticed that the Datsun was also bashed in, all along the passenger's side. It gave me the complete creeps. I saw him look up again, and then I went into the washateria.

To call the police. What else was there to do?

I told the other women, but when they looked out, both cars were parked, and he was nowhere in sight. The women said that the police wouldn't do anything, but they didn't mind that I called, and even showed me where the number was, taped on the side of the phone box.

What happened then was bizarre. I put my clothes in one big dryer, and put in three quarters, which gave me thirty minutes. But my mind was not on the idea of a walk anymore. I looked out toward the nursery again, and I saw the man driving by at top speed in his Datsun. It made me mad, his leaving before the police got there to see what happened.

I was taking my clothes out of the dryer when I heard another car and got out back in time to see him again, this time speeding off in the red Toyota, with a taxi following behind him. At that moment three police cars arrived, and I told them about the trashing of the two cars.

The police milled around, listening, making a huddle in the near-empty lot as their radios talked to each other. Then the first said, "Nothing we can do without a complaint. Somebody has to file a complaint."

And the second said, "Probably mad at his wife."

The third said, "It's the full moon. We get a call a minute this time of month. You wouldn't believe."

I went inside and finished folding my sheets.

The other women were really sweet; they didn't say, "I told you so." They talked until I calmed down, telling me that he was probably ripping off an insurance company, that the police never do anything. But in a supportive way.

When I got home, I was still rattled and sat on my glasses and broke them across the bridge of the nose. Not being able to drive without them and not having even a make-shift pair held together with a paper clip (I'd lost those), I walked this morning to an optician that I'd passed when I was locating the train station. The walk took two hours, so it turned out that I got my exercise after all.

They put my lenses in a lighter frame, a caramel color I'm not used to that was a perfect fit. I paid them $27.50 from my emergency fund and, walking home, had plenty of time to consider what I'd learned from last night: that nobody up here minds what you do if no one complains.

Two

5

THINGS went too fast up here. You didn't have a chance to take your time. Lutie's intention had been to master each part of her new life slowly, to get it firmly in her mind, the way she had her evening walk up the carriage road to the Roman dam—but it had not worked out that way.

At first she was going ahead with the list on her refrigerator.

She'd found her dressmaker, Mrs. Rodino, in a nearby village called Hartsdale, through the *Yellow Pages*. After she'd made her a dress, and that had turned out nicely, Lutie had gone to the Neiman-Marcus in White Plains to see what was new and found that they were showing pants cut just above the ankle, nipped at the bottom. And that all the outfits were black with red, a bright crayon red that made all the deep wines of last year out of style.

She never liked to copy exactly, so she took the main idea—that of a single brilliant color with black—and got two yards of royal blue wool and two of deep green, to have made into the pants, at a store near Neiman's called B. Altman's. She also got some part wool, part synthetic material to have made into a black jacket with the new big shoulders. That look was faddy and would go out of style, so the material was cheaper, but would look nice for this year.

She studied the Vogue and McCall's pattern books to figure out what to do with the old tan cashmere coat Mother had saved from her army days, which was gathered from round shoulders and had no belt or buttons. She decided that it could be cut off and belted so that it had a Russian look. And she got a black muffler and wool cap that fit with it perfectly.

Mrs. Rodino wasn't too enthusiastic about cutting off such a length of cashmere. "You can't buy one like this for love nor money." But she had done it; after all, Lutie was from Texas, so that explained it.

She liked her dressmaker a lot. Mrs. Rodino lived in a settled neighborhood with flower borders and glassed-in front entries. She was thrilled to have Lutie as a customer, because of the soap opera "Texas," and each time asked if what she saw on her set was genuine. If that was right the way Lurleen talked, if they had floods like that down there, and if she, Lutie, had ever known anyone named Billy Joe or T.J. And Lutie could tell her that the floods always came in the spring and that all the girls she'd been to school with named Lurleen had talked that way.

She scheduled Mrs. Rodino's fittings at eleven, so they could get their business done while they watched the set. The dressmaker kept her eyes primarily glued to the screen, her mouth full of tiny straight pins, catching a hem here, taking a tuck there, chalking a line around the hips. During commercials Mrs. Rodino talked about her mother, who had died two years ago at ninety, and how she missed her every day of her life. She liked to hear that Lutie kept up with her own mother, although she thought Texas a long way off, and how could she have left that way? And then, when the show was over, she served coffee and Italian pastries called *sfogliatelles*, to pay Lutie back for the buttermilk pie.

Lutie had got familiar, too, with the supermarket called Finast (which was next to the washateria), and had made the acquaintance of the nice woman, named Mary Sue, who okayed your check and who always remembered her and said, "Here you are, dear, have a good day," when she handed back her card.

Lutie had matched the leaves she gathered on her walk to those in her tree book and had used her bird book for the very first time last week. She had seen on the outside stoop, where she kept a small, discreet pile of breadcrumbs, not anything that would be noticeable to Mrs. Vaccaro driving by, a mottled gray and white bird that was the shape of a robin, but not the color: a robin in a camouflage suit. The Peterson's guide showed a bird that looked much like it: a juvenal bluebird. And Lutie could see that the bluebird looked nothing like the blue jay back home but was a robin sort of bird.

And her mother still called on Wednesdays, after eleven, and Sundays, before five, on her MCI, and she still wrote her weekly letters, giving the exciting details of her rather public life. This time, about her adventures with the Arabs:

... *We were all taken to Lady Bird's ranch, with a lot of formality. It was a delegation of visitors from the University of Isfahan, making a tour of our fine Middle Eastern Studies Center. My dinner partner, if you can use such terms, was no other than a Mr. Farmayan, one of seven children of the richest family in Iran (or Persia, as they are saying more and more these days). I was nervous, but he put me at my ease; you have no idea how alike Texas and Iran are, what with the desert parts and fertile valleys and horses and*

47

*whatnot. He had a lot of questions, which I tried to be
knowledgeable on. The V-P caught my eye across the
sparsely potatoes—so I guess I acquitted myself properly.*

*The most amazing tidbit to pass on is the young couple
who raise Arabian horses and do a lot of entertaining of
Arabs, who had Brown and Root come build them a lake
at their country place outside Houston—so they could have
a spot to have barbeques around. Can you imagine?*

Love,
M.

So everything had been going the way it should, slowly,
with her learning new things the way she wanted.

And then Mavis called to say that she'd found a group
for Lutie.

She had mentioned Lutie's name to the former husband
of a friend of hers, a woman who was going to law school
at forty, whose former husband was a jerk as a husband
but ran a good group, and that it would be the very thing
that Lutie was looking for. Mavis had called him on the spot
and turned in Lutie's name. "There, I've made amends for
dragging you up here. Now let me hear how it turns out.
And I'm going to drive down to Westchester after I get
my classes settled. And I'm counting on our weekend in
November. We'll have a long visit. The infighting up here
you wouldn't believe, but who am I kidding? Anyone from
Texas would believe anything. It's the same everywhere.
How is Birdsong these days? Now you have to go, promise,
as I stuck my neck out. Therapists don't like to take anybody they don't know—that is preaching to be saved, but
they are like that. So it's all set. He's the best; even she
admits that. Picky to live with, one of those constipated
boy wonders grown gray, but the best. I'll give you the
address."

Lutie tried to take it all in. "That's really nice of you, Mavis." She had wanted to say no, but how could she? "I was going to wait, maybe until after midterm, to start looking for a group. I'm just now getting settled. But of course, that's grand. Certainly I will." She took a deep breath. "When does it start?"

"Tomorrow night."

Lutie had been into the city only once, and it had slowed down her resolve to go in every week. She had tried to write about it in her journal but had sat an hour with her Mont Blanc in her hand and couldn't get it organized into any sort of form.

The city was like that.

She'd taken a local train from nearby White Plains, parking in a small mall nearby, so as not to have to worry about if there was a space, since the station lot seemed totally full of commuter cars.

She had picked a local so that she could take her time and get used to the scenery and the names of the stops from here to Manhattan. It was the same way that she didn't like to take airplanes but preferred to drive places (even if it wasn't a matter of money) because you could see where you were going and what you were passing through and how it changed—so you didn't suddenly arrive in a wholly strange place.

When the train made its second stop at Hartsdale (which she knew because of Mrs. Rodino, so she was feeling good about that), there were only three of them in her car, a black woman two rows in front of her and a really old white woman dressed in a tan coat older than Mother's, not as nice but the same cut, and black bedroom slipper type shoes, very worn down, and a new pink wool scarf wrapped around her head. All of which looked strange, for Westchester in September. And the woman had a paper shopping bag and a big black purse of some kind of cheap plastic material. But the thing about her that caught Lutie's attention was that she couldn't sit still. It reminded her in some way of Gran, in her yo-yo phase, not wanting to leave the room but being dragged out into the bathroom.

The woman kept asking the conductor, "Does this stop at Mount Vernon?"

And he would say, "It's the local. Makes all stops." Then she would ask him again when he walked through, and he would say, "It's the local. Makes all stops."

Finally, the other woman leaned over and told her, "It's three stops away."

And when they got to Scarsdale, the old woman asked again, "Is this Mount Vernon? Is this Mount Vernon? My daughter's meeting me."

And she fooled with her new pink scarf and wrapped her overcoat around her and craned her head all around, and the other woman reassured her, "It's two more stops. I'll tell you."

Then, at Bronxville, it was the same thing. "My daughter's meeeting me. Is this Mount Vernon?" Too frantic to hear what they told her.

Lutie in time could feel herself get nervous, because anxiety was always contagious, wondering if the train really would stop at Mount Vernon and if anyone would be there. A few minutes later the conductor, acting in a routine way, walked through the almost empty car, shouting, "MOUnt VerNON, MouNT VERnon." And he waited at the door while the old lady gathered up her shopping bag and purse and clutched at her baggy old coat and stepped out on the platform.

It was high up, and she had to go down some steps, and Lutie and the other woman craned their necks to watch her descend. To try to glimpse if anyone was really meeting her. Finally, they looked at each other and smiled. Thinking they could be that daughter, waiting.

Lutie had meant to make a lot of trips, getting to know the procedure of leaving, arriving, and coming back. She had calculated the $6 (off peak hours) round trip as part of her entertainment. It would be foolish to have the semester in New York and not grow accustomed to the city, and she intended to break some small part of it down, a few blocks at a time, and make them her own—the way you took new words in grade school and used them until they were yours.

But that first time things had got out of hand almost at once. She had come up out of Grand Central on Forty-sixth and turned left and, looking at the map, thought she would hit the street that turned into Central Park West and so make a square, going up to the park on one side and coming down from it on the other. But somehow she got on a diagonal street and ended up north of the edge of the park, in some other area of town. Realizing it, she turned around and retraced her steps, finding herself at Lincoln Center. Once there, it had seemed the reasonable thing to do to take advantage of her mistake, and see a performance at the center, and count that as one of her special events. She was in luck; there were a few seats available for that night to *La Forza del Destino*, by Verdi.

But the ticket she could get cost $30.50, and that was almost all the money she had left. She'd left home with $40, which seemed a vast amount of money when you weren't going to do anything but walk around, and the train ticket was only $6; but suddenly she had spent $36.50 of her forty, and that left her a little nervous. She had left her Neiman's card and her Mastercard at home, because she didn't want them to get stolen and she certainly thought there would be no use for them. But now what had seemed a prudent emergency amount to carry had vanished. She had $3.50 left—and the rest of the afternoon and early evening until time for the performance.

Which meant that she couldn't eat supper, but surely in the city you must be able to get an iced tea and walk around for $3.50. But even that didn't work out all right. For one thing, it took money to go to the bathroom. She had used a quarter at Grand Central, which she forgot to subtract, and then she used another, an extra in her pocket, to put in the little glass dish in the rest room in the lobby of the Waldorf-Astoria (which she happened upon in her walk). While she was in the hotel—which seemed very much like home, and she realized it was because the carpet was the same pattern as a hotel in San Antonio where she'd had lunch with Mother and Aunt Caroline—she decided to have her tea. She found a coffee shop, on a lower level, called Oscars. The check, without tip, came to $3. So she had the choice of not leaving a gratuity or not going to the bathroom again before she left. She felt as nervous as the lady in the sweltering overcoat on the train: she had never not left a tip in her life.

She was at the door of Lincoln Center a half hour before curtain time and in her seat as the production began. The opera was the most beautiful thing she had ever seen. The crowd scenes looked like paintings by Breughel whenever the curtain opened, and when the monks, all dressed in white with candles in their hands, came out of their doorway, chanting, it made you want to cry. She liked the basses best, and never got tired of hearing them. There were two intermissions, and it went on and on, and people left before it was over, but she didn't; it was so beautiful. Although the opera was supposed to be taking place in Spain, you could tell that Verdi was Italian even if you hadn't known, because the sets, when it was "outdoors," looked exactly like the Forum in Rome and quite took her breath away. When the orchestra played the theme, as it did whenever the curtain opened, and the broken pillars were in the background and the arches and columns in the foreground, and a soft light in the "sky," it made her want to stop it right there, forever.

And then the hero and the brother began to duel, and people rushed about, and it was over. The only opera that she had seen before, when Mother took her to *La Bohème* by Puccini in San Antonio, had also ended with the heroine dying, half lying down, singing a tragic, heartbreaking duet with the hero. This one did, too, and the soprano had a wound in her side and was bleeding to death but sang with him to the last note, the farewell kiss. That must be the way operas always ended, and she imprinted the sight and sound on her mind.

Back out on the street, it was pouring down rain. Quickly she checked the M Central Harlem Line Metropolitan Region schedule in her pocket and panicked. She had barely enough time to make it to the last train. The opera had been hours long, but it had never occurred to her that trains stopped running. It was a quarter to one, and the train left at one-thirty; she would have to run. Because people were standing out in the middle of Broadway, shouting and waving their arms in the rain and almost getting hit, and yellow cabs with their lights on were zooming right past, not even slowing down, Lutie knew that even if she'd had the money, she would never have been able to catch a cab.

She ran steadily all the way, being careful not to slip, cutting over at Forty-sixth, only to find the door locked. Frantic, she ran around the side of Grand Central until finally she found an entrance. She had five minutes, in which she used her last quarter in the bathroom, located her gate, and sank in relief onto the train.

The station had seemed odd in the middle of the night, but not scary. There weren't many people there, and most

53

of them looked as if they'd been drinking a lot and were tired. She was, too. Her legs were shaking, that she had made it, that it was the right train, that she was headed home. There were two boys in her car, one of them with a beer can and one of them with a cigarette, because it was a smoking car. And the boys were talking fast and a lot, the way boys did, saying "fuck" a lot, and showing off for each other, and so she relaxed because that was something you knew about if you were around colleges.

The conductor was a woman who said that there was no additional charge for returning after peak hours. This made Lutie lean her head back and let out a deep breath; she had not even thought of that possibility. She would have to make better arrangements next time: take more money, allow more time. Maybe bring a sandwich. And a pocketful of washateria quarters.

When the train started out of the tunnel, the lights overhead blinked out and stayed out a minute, and you could see all the lights of the city because it was dark in the car, and that was spectacular. Her skirt and blouse were soaking wet, and she began to think about getting into the tub in her new rooms, where the water was clear and you had all the hot water you wanted.

Then the lights went off again, and this time they stayed off. After a few minutes she felt fear in her chest and tried to calm herself down. The boys raised their voices, saying "fuck" a lot louder, but it was not them she was scared of; it was just a general thing of being in the dark and not knowing what was happening.

Finally, the woman conductor came through on the loud-speaker and said that they were going to stop at 125th Street and that everyone on the two dark cars was to get off and move forward to the front cars, which had lights. So Lutie and the boys walked down until they got to a lighted doorway, and there were other people with them, from the other dark car. For a few minutes it seemed that the train was moving, and Lutie started to run, but it wasn't; it was only an illusion. There were a lot of blacks standing around on the high platform, and Lutie smiled at them, feeling better, more at home.

When the train stopped at Mount Vernon on the ride back, she peered out into the dim early morning for some sign of the woman in the pink scarf and old coat and half expected her to get on, clutching her shopping bag and plastic purse, but there was no one in sight.

Riding home, Lutie recalled the other time she had been as scared and out of control, although in a different situation. It had been out at Redoaks, right after Dabney had moved out, and she was starting to see other people. A divorced man who lived out in the same area had seen her jog by in the mornings, as the schoolchildren went to wait for the bus, and got acquainted with her. He'd stopped by her place for coffee and then invited her to come around to his house for dinner. Lutie knew what that meant: that he wanted her to spend the night. She was grown and single, and she thought she was going with her eyes wide open. She'd worn the satin underwear left from her honeymoon, the kind trimmed in real Brussels lace, which you couldn't get anymore. She had never been to bed with anyone but Dabney, whom she'd met at St. Stephens, gone through undergraduate days with, and married in graduate school. So she was nervous but resolved to do well at the matter of dating.

When she got there, he'd put two T-bones on the counter and had poured wine for both of them and put fresh asparagus to soak in a marinade. He explained that he was a developer and interested in seeing housing be on the fore-front of making a change in living patterns for women. Lutie had two glasses of wine, which went straight to her head because she never drank anything, and then she began to notice that he kept going off into the back of the house and coming out more and more hyper.

"Well, what are *you* staring at?" he asked. "You think I'm going to take my clothes off the minute you arrive? Is that it?" His eyes looked tiny, and he was jumping all over the place. It was then that the fear moved in and sobered her. "I'm not in a hurry," she said, trying to sound convincing.

A few minutes later he came out with only a towel on, wrapped around his waist, nothing else. He'd had a shower and whatever was in the back room and was swinging his arms and shouting something at her about how she could just wait for it until he got good and ready.

The rest reminded her of taking your driving test: You had to stay in control and act as if you knew it all cold. She'd said, "Let's eat first," and gone to the kitchen and located a skillet and put the steaks on and poured a little of whatever was on the asparagus on top of the steaks so they'd sizzle, and he'd laughed and moved around the brown and gold living room with its brass trays mounted on the wall, goading her with his voice, accusing her of trying to seduce him, and she kept saying, "I'm in no hurry, let's eat first." And then he'd gone off into the back again, and as soon as he went through the doorway, she'd run out the front and started off down the gravel road that she walked in the early morning. It was a two-mile stretch to her house (she knew the distance exactly since his house was halfway around the circular loop from hers), and she calculated later that she'd made it home in eighteen minutes —something of a record.

She'd got inside and latched all the windows—which, on the ground floor, as in all old farmhouses and thus their copies, came down almost to the ground—and pulled down the shades and gone upstairs to the big bedroom saved for

Mother on the weekends. The only room with a lock on the door. She'd taken the phone off the hook and gone to sleep in relief.

When she woke, the cows were already going to pasture. You could lie in either upstairs bed and watch the steady line of black and white milk cows, Jerseys, amble single file between the two property fences behind the lot. In the early dawn they loomed large as elephants and seemed, like elephants, to be holding on to one another, tail to trunk, because they walked so close together.

Later, leaving for school, she'd noticed that the rockers on the porch had been moved, and the gate left open. But she'd counted on the fact that a developer wouldn't damage a house, no matter how high he was or on what.

He'd seen her take her walk a few days later as he was driving to work and had leaned out the window and laughed. "I do believe you went home and went to sleep. You're some cool customer."

It had made her realize she'd been in way over her head and needed to move a lot more slowly.

At two-thirty in the morning, after her maiden trip into the city, her mother called. "Lutie, where have you been? I called at eleven, our time, and then twelve, and then two your time. I was frantic. I would have called the police but I couldn't remember what jurisdiction Cranberry Park was in. Do give it to me, for goodness' sake, so I can write it down, here by my phone. What would I do if anything happened? How would I even know? Where on earth have you been?"

Lutie told her mother about *La Forza del Destino*; she made it sound as if hordes of people like her, in their good summer linen skirts and blouses, had gone into the city and come back out again. She made it sound like the bus trips that Mother took with the V-P and official visitors to the

57

out-of-town Southwest Conference football games because she knew that they often didn't get back until almost dawn, and they were certainly safe and acceptable, and Mother enjoyed it a lot whenever she got invited to go, to see Texas play Baylor at Waco or TCU at Fort Worth, and could wear something burnt orange to show that she was a loyal Longhorn fan.

"I was frantic," her mother repeated, to make sure Lutie understood how awful it was to be far away, and out of touch.

"You mustn't worry. A bunch of us went together to the city."

6

B u t now, before she was really ready, she was going into the city again. This time resolved to take twice $40, to do nothing but go to group and come back—and to remember to take a pocketful of quarters from her peanut butter jar.

Mavis had given her the address of the therapist, on West Eighty-second. It was his, Dr. Donaldson's, apartment as well as his office, Mavis had said, because people didn't like to go out at night to the phobia clinic where he worked, which wasn't in such a good part of the city. Lutie consulted her map and figured she had walked almost that far last time when she got on Broadway by mistake and kept waiting to hit Central Park.

She had thanked Mavis, who was rushing off to a meeting, having checked Lutie off her list for now. (She admired the way Mavis got things done and imagined her keeping notes by the phone which read: "Get L. Sayre a group; get M. Smith a good dye job; get B. Jones a lover. . . .")

She took her spending money out from between the pages of Harry Stack Sullivan's *The Fusion of Psychiatry and Social Science*, in the chapter called "The Illusion of Personal Identity." It was a habit of hers, to make a joke like that, selecting that as the location for funds that you were going to use personally. In the same way she'd put her emergency money—for when something happened, like the old Chevy, which you sometimes had to start by making a connection under the hood with a screwdriver, breaking down or needing a new solenoid or fuel-line hose or fan belt, or herself getting a sore throat or breaking her glasses again—in a book called *Stigma*, in a chapter on "Deviance," which is how you could think of a breakdown of any kind.

This time she put all the money left for the month in her wallet and got a really complete guide to Manhattan at the drugstore with the help of the woman named Denise, who was as friendly as Mary Sue at Finast. (Denise would say whenever Lutie came in to buy a lipstick or shampoo, "And yourself?" and Lutie didn't know yet what the answer to that was supposed to be. It must be the way that if someone at home said *"Gesundheit,"* when you sneezed, you answered *"Danke schön,"* even though you didn't know German. Here one person must say, "And yourself?" and the other gave a set reply. Once she had heard a man say back, "Not to complain," but Lutie was not sure if that was the standard answer.)

This time she took an express train, which was almost full when she got on. When the conductor walked through, shouting, "EXpress, ExPRESS, One Hundred Twenty-fifth and Grand Central," she looked around to see if anyone in a wool scarf was frantically getting off. But people looked uninterested, preoccupied, reading their papers, as if this were old information they didn't need.

When the train stopped at One Hundred Twenty-fifth, Lutie looked out the window and saw the same crowd of blacks who had been there the night she'd had to walk down the platform with the boys who said "fuck" and she had had no money and been scared and tired. She waved out the window to them now—remembering what a comfort the crowd had been to her that night. She felt better, waving out the window, as if she had some familiarity with the territory, and smiled at the surprised faces that stared back at her.

When she came up out of Grand Central, she calculated and saw that she would be late. She could figure it took one minute for each short north-south block, and about three for the long east-west blocks—when it wasn't raining and you weren't running. And so she would need about an hour to get to West Eighty-second, depending on how far west the address was. (She hadn't yet figured how you computed the numbers; in Austin, if a location was 200, that meant it crossed Second, and if it was 600, it crossed Sixth. Here there didn't seem to be a rule, and she didn't have time to work one out.)

It was five o'clock now, and she needed to be there at six. That was calling it too close; it took longer when there were a lot of people on the streets to walk around.

So she thought about all the money she had with her and stepped right out in the middle of the street, missing a cold storage truck by six inches, and caught a cab—a feat which thrilled her. She gave him the address, and he asked right away, "What's that between?," to which she replied, "If I'd known that, I wouldn't have needed a cab."

"Don't get smart, lady," he snapped.

"And yourself?" She fell back on a familiar phrase.

"I got no complaints."

Reassured that she knew her way around, Lutie leaned back against the seat and watched out the window. Seeing that the cabby got on Broadway and sped north, she relaxed, knowing that it took you west of the park, so that he must know what he was doing and wasn't going to ride her all around the city. "What's your nationality?" she asked him, deciding to be friendly.

"Same as yours, lady, American." He snapped again.

She didn't say any more, and after a bit—when they were in a part of town beyond where she'd walked before, blocks past Lincoln Center, and there was a Chinese restaurant on every street corner and sometimes one in the middle of the block, and she was wondering if this was the famous Chinatown—he turned around and said, "Denver."

And Lutie could see that he was younger than she was and trying to act as if he had been here all his life. That would be one way to get to know the city, to drive a cab, and maybe he was doing it for that, to get acquainted with it, before he settled down to be an artist or lawyer or something. "I've been to Denver," she told him, because naturally everyone in Texas had been to Colorado.

"Yeah?" But he sounded as if he had closed the subject, so she didn't add anything more.

"Here you are," he said, wheeling around and setting her down across from a Chinese restaurant. It had cost her $4.75, and she didn't know what to tip him. Deciding that a $5 bill wouldn't be enough, she reached into the pocket of her bright blue trousers and added two of the quarters she was carrying for bathrooms in New York.

She found herself in the foyer of an apartment building, telling a white man in a uniform, who was watching a television set, whom she had come to see.

He didn't answer or look away from the set (which she saw showed the inside of an elevator) but gestured to a black man, also in uniform, who said to her, "That's the tenth floor." She glanced at him and saw that he looked very much like a Cuthbert. In Savannah everyone tried to get a Cuthbert for household help, knowing they were the best. Every really good family, Aunt Caroline had told her, had Cuthberts dating back to the Civil War. You could recognize them on the street because of their elongated heads and short upper lips and how they looked you right in the eye. You could even pass a bunch of children in the old park that was now a public playground and see one of the children playing and know that he was a Cuthbert. And sometimes someone from an old family would call the boy over and say, "Who's your folks, son?" and he would tell her that his folks were the Wilson Cuthberts or the Flournoy Cuthberts, and she would be able to place him immediately.

Lutie didn't embarrass the elevator man by asking such a thing, but she looked at him directly, as if they had mutual connections, and punched the button for the tenth floor.

She was early, as it turned out. The group was meeting in a very large living room, which was the therapist's but which had something of the air of a dentist's waiting room because of all the chairs set out, and the magazines laid around, and the general air of being a widened public hall. She and the other arriving group members were asked to remove all items such as wedding bands or crosses at the door, things which would provide personal clues about them, because this was a group on Image.

The therapist had put out a big pot of coffee on an old dropleaf table in the hall, and while she sat in the living room, sipping a cup that was too strong and bitter for her taste, the man who looked like a Cuthbert came in again; only this time he was in a chauffeur's uniform, helping some tiny woman in a leg brace to her seat. Lutie didn't know why he'd changed clothes or how he went from one job to another that fast, but when she smiled at him in recognition, he only frowned and left the room.

She had worn her new blue trousers, and the new black jacket with its big padded sleeves, and her best white hand-stitched cotton blouse. She felt that she looked citified and fashionable, although anyone who was discerning would know that any woman her age in glasses and homemade

63

clothes was a schoolteacher. As the other people drifted in, however, she began to feel less and less confident about what she had worn. Nine of the twelve of them were female, and all were in what Lutie thought of as home clothes: unironed jeans, baggy cords, loose shirts with rolled-up sleeves, tight T-shirts with no underwear, hair tied back or cut shorter than a man's. It disconcerted her. Maybe they knew something about what you were supposed to do in groups on Image that she didn't, and had come incognito in a sense.

The therapist, Dr. Donaldson, came in last and sat with his back to the hall. He was in a white shirt with the sleeves rolled up, loafers, and no socks and was smoking a cigarette. She felt her face turn red at the horror of finding herself overdressed in the biggest city there was.

The Cuthbert appeared again, this time in a three-piece suit with a navy striped tie, a gold watch chain, a leather valise—looking for all the world like a medical doctor or an insurance salesman. She couldn't help grinning as he took off his jacket and vest and rolled up his sleeves and crossed his right leg over his knee in the same direction as Dr. Donaldson, to whom he then turned and asked, "So what have we here?"

It was clear that he was part of the show.

The other people shifted uncomfortably when he started talking because they had thought at first that he was one of the group members, dressed for success the way blacks did, and now they could see that they had been manipulated to think that.

The therapist introduced himself as Joe and the Cuthbert as Dr. Sammy David, his partner and co-leader. Then Dr. Donaldson explained the idea behind Image and how "this is new for us, and we are learning as we go along, the same as you, about what we, our clothes and our gestures, convey to one another, and we want you to share whatever comes to your mind as we go along."

64

After that he had the group members give their first names, which was all they were allowed to reveal, and then they were to write on a piece of paper what they could guess about the person sitting to the right of them and the same about the person sitting on their left:

        age
        marital status
        occupation
        background

They were to keep it to a few short words like that—he had sketched them in the air, like a list—and to keep it factual. No adjectives.

Ball-points and tablets were passed around.

Lutie looked, covertly, at the woman on her left, and then directly. She couldn't write down what came to her mind, which was *depressed, defensive*. They were not, he said, to use adjectives. After a minute, she wrote:

        divorced
        38
        no children
        creative
        college-educated

That was all she could think of. She thought the woman at least forty-five, so hoped to cheer her up. The creative part was because she couldn't imagine, looking at her, in her tan T-shirt (which said "WATERLOO"), with her sagging breasts and stringy black hair and sad face, what kind of job she could have. She thought about simply putting "white, female," but to put what was obvious seemed cheating.

The woman on her right was younger and tougher, and her hair was cleaner, and she had on running shoes and a sweat shirt (which showed mountains and said "WOMEN

BELONG ON TOP") and looked rather masculine or perhaps only athletic. Lutie struggled with all that, then wrote:

> single
> no children
> 30
> graduate student
> organizational interest

Again she had subtracted a few years, because the woman looked to her to be in her mid-thirties, slightly older than Lutie, and she didn't think she was a student at all; she imagined that she worked at some agency, but she felt she got the idea across with "organizational interest." The girl looked angry, that was the main thing, and you couldn't say that. In some way Lutie had decided to express that by the idea of organization (weren't all organizations angry? Wasn't that their purpose?).

She wanted to add on the first woman's list "feels confused" and, on the second, "feels slighted." But she was not sure if that was too personal or too negative, so in the end she didn't—although she thought if the group was going to do any good, you should learn what sorts of secret signals you were sending. It wasn't going to provide what she had come for if they both just said the obvious about her:

> single
> schoolteacher
> 32

Then they traded lists, the idea being that nobody would be embarrassed in front of the leader by having them read out, yet everyone could get a quick, thumbnail idea of what messages she or he was sending in the first few minutes of the first night, some idea of how they came across on first impression.

Lutie read from the woman on her left (the T-shirt):

> rich
> married
> unemployed
> East 60s

And from the woman on her right (in the running shoes):

> rich
> married
> doesn't work
> East 70s

She felt tears sting her eyes and looked at each of them, only to see that they were equally cut by what they read.

"Jeez, you don't know how to tell age," the track suit said. "Jeez, I'm only twenty-three."

"That's all right," the woman with the sad face told her, "she added eight years to mine. Don't feel bad." She crumpled the sheet of paper and threw it on the floor.

Lutie looked at Dr. Donaldson to see if he realized that he had upset them all. She looked around the room and saw that nobody seemed in any better shape than the three of them in her arc of the circle. The tiny woman with the cane, who reminded Lutie of Gran, had got red in the face. A young man, who moved around in his chair like the developer at home and who was trying to convey how sexy he was, looked as if he were about to leap out of his skin. All of them had got less, or maybe more, than they'd bargained for.

"Well," the therapist said, with a half laugh, "that wasn't the best of ideas, was it? We thought, you see—"

"What's with the sidekick anyway?" a cross gray-headed man named Ira asked. "First he comes in with a briefcase; then he turns out to be a shrink. Maybe all the rest of you are plants. How are we supposed to be able to trust you anyway?"

"When we got the idea," Donaldson said, "it was to show how clothes are what you remember. You'd seen Sammy two times before, but no one knew that because he was in uniform and—"

"Correction, Joe," Dr. David interrupted. "This one caught me right away." He gestured to Lutie.

"That right?" The therapist nodded but went on with his story, trying to take the sharp edge off the atmosphere.

But the man who brought it up wanted to have his say. "So what's the point? We didn't come here to hear that we put down spades in uniforms. The fact is you don't notice anybody you meet that way. You want to try describing to me the last waitress who served you a cup of coffee? What's the point of that, I say?"

Everyone was upset, which must have been part of the point.

Then they were asked to turn to the people on the right and left to find out who they really were and what they did. The woman on Lutie's left, with the depressed air, Danya, was a librarian with three children who wanted to leave her husband but who couldn't afford it because she had a cyst on her ovary that needed to come out. She was thirty, and this was her first marriage.

The woman on Lutie's right in the warm-up pants and sweat shirt with the cropped hair was an assistant editor at a big publishing house who had been passed over for promotion and had a married lover, which is what worked against her, and didn't make half what her writers did and had to write their books for them. She was twenty-three, and they were to call her Fudge.

Lutie told them that she was divorced, an assistant professor of sociology, and from Texas—which was all she had to tell.

"That explains it," they said, and relaxed a little with her.

No one was what she or he looked like. The tiny woman with the bad leg was a pediatrician; the man who looked like a yardman in coveralls was a lawyer; the cross man who had been arguing about Sammy David was a painter; the frantic developer type was unemployed. It gave you something to think about.

Lutie thought that the purpose of the group was to help, not to make you feel worse about yourself, and that the leaders didn't know what they were doing. They had the group members get out their pads again, and this time they were to write down what they *wished* their neighbors had said about them, and this time adjectives were in order.

Lutie wrote:

> independent
> individual
> in control

Danya (the T-shirt) wrote:

> young
> gorgeous
> available

Fudge (the track shoes) wrote:

> married
> happy
> lots of hair

And then nobody was mad anymore, and they all looked at each other, and they could see that things weren't how they should be for anyone else either and that nobody was doing any better job than anyone else of projecting what he or she wanted to be. And it made them want to help each other come true.

There was a good bit more. They talked as a group about

what details they associated with what they would like to be, and what things they first noticed in general about other people, and what that said about them, and they began to get a sense of what they would be working on together. For next time, Dr. Donaldson said, all of them were supposed to come in uniforms, which they could borrow, invent, or even rent, so that for the second session they would be disguised on purpose, like actors, appearing as a definite stereotype. That, he implied, would defuse tonight's meeting in a way and help them get off on a different foot to explore what they were in the group for.

"Should it be someone you'd like to be?" someone asked.

"No restrictions. Any uniform," Donaldson said. And served them some cookies that had a lot of chocolate in them, and tasted homemade but weren't, and told them he'd see them next week.

7

Lutie was standing by the elevator with the last group to go—wondering if the coffee she had spilled on her blue trousers would come out in cold water if she got to it the minute she got to Grand Central, figuring it would be an hour's walk—when Dr. David called her back. "Sayre, I believe you left this?"

She turned to see, and the elevator left without her. "What?" She had her bag, her jacket.

They brought her back in the apartment and settled her on the tweedy couch with a cup of hot tea before she knew how it had happened. (She had no memory of saying the coffee had been too strong to drink.)

". . . So you spotted Sammy right off?" Dr. Donaldson asked.

Lutie nodded. "Wasn't I supposed to?"

"Nobody ever has."

"But you never did this before."

"Variations. We've done variations."

"I don't know what was so difficult about it." Lutie was sitting with her knees pressed together, needing to go to the bathroom and worrying about the coffee stain.

"Go see if it'll come out," Donaldson said, gesturing toward the dark circle above her knee.

"How did you know?"

"One of the fringe benefits of a long marriage." He was smiling at her anxiety, but it ended up looking as if it were his anxiety.

In the bathroom she applied cold water in soaking doses to the stain, holding her pants under the faucet, having to risk that the wool would not shrink, watching until the brown ring slowly diluted and then faded away. She pressed a cold cloth to her eyes and forehead. Maybe they had guessed that she got upset about being overdressed.

"I should go," she said when she was back.

"Sit down, stay. We like to eat when it's over. It's a relief to us when we see that people have pulled themselves back together and we haven't done any harm. Are you all right?"

"I enjoyed it. At first, I thought you didn't know—"

"That's the risk."

She took her shoes off and accepted another cup of tea, although she preferred it iced. Soon the apartment began to smell wonderful.

"What is that?" she asked.

"It's my secret," Donaldson said. "For French cooking I throw a stick of butter in the skillet and add a chopped onion and a splash of wine and then whatever is around; for Italian I put a little olive oil and butter in a pan, add some red pepper flakes and a saucer of heavy cream, and it works wonders on whatever you dump in it. Pasta is what's tonight. How does that sound?"

"Wonderful," she said. "Like Italy."

"You've been there?"

"Oh, yes," she said. "I loved it."

"Linguine I have, about a pound. That seems to be it."

"Do your creamed hard-boiled eggs, Joe. That'll be

72

lavish." Dr. David was sprawled out on a chair, giving instructions. "Where you from?" he asked Lutie while Joe rummaged in the kitchen.

"Texas."

"That's all?"

"I have an aunt in Savannah—"

"That explains."

"And yourself?"

"Columbus. I guess you haven't been around here long enough to know that everyone in New York is from Ohio. Joe and myself both went to Ohio State, although not at the same time. He is an older man, as should be obvious."

"Where do the people who live in Ohio come from?"

"They crawl over from West Virginia."

"I don't know Ohio. Is it the North?"

"After five years here I'd have to say that it was the South."

"You look like a family in Savannah, is how I recognized you so fast." She told him about the Cuthberts.

"You know," he said, "I haven't had this conversation since I came to Manhattan. *Help. Household.* Those words aren't used around here. Not to my face."

"Is Sammy David your real name?"

"No. It was Davidson. But when Joe and I started working together, the Davidson and Donaldson seemed to us a fatherless crowd, and we decided it might make our clients nervous. Besides, I thought I might as well get a little instant name identification."

"Did you think that up, about the different uniforms?"

"I do that all the time. I find that anybody trusts me if I'm in a lackey suit. Sometimes I come in when I have a patient, one who's on edge, in a hospital orderly suit, and then he'll tell me everything, or I come to my office in khaki pants and shirt, like a car attendant, and my patient will level with me about what her husband, the old goat,

73

has really done, where in my three-piece suit she won't open her mouth."

He rooted around for a cigarette. "That's where the Image group originated."

"Is that your major interest?"

"Phobias."

"How did you get into that?"

"That's the fat men on the stairs story." He made a sort of smoke haze around his head, the way you might imagine old men to do when they began a favorite story. "My mother used to do daywork for a set of twins, who were in their mid-fifties when she first went around. They were portly then; but time passed, and they got so fat, she would tell the story, that they claimed they couldn't put their shoes on with their clothes on because they couldn't bend down, so she would describe for us these roly-poly naked sixty-year-old men tying their shoelaces, and then we would ask her how could they put their trousers on after they had their shoes on, and she'd mimic them, putting one hand on her hips and pointing her toe and sliding it into an imaginary pair of pants, arching her foot like a dancer, and we would fall out laughing. I have no idea how much she made up; surely she never saw them that way. But anyhow, one day, inevitably, she went to work, and there they were, dead as doornails, naked as jaybirds, wedged on the staircase, where they used to sit to put their shoes on, side by side, unable to budge up or down. Shoelaces tied."

Lutie watched Dr. David, Sammy, warm himself up with the story, which he obviously saw clear as day in his mind. "So how did that make you go into what you did?"

"Wanting to find out the answer. Though I'm not sure to what. Why they couldn't put one another's shoes on, dressed. Or why they had to sit on the stairs. Or why they didn't have Mother put their shoes on. Or why they didn't wear house slippers that they could slide on. How come they got stuck that day, and how come they didn't the day before? Was one of them refusing to move? I don't know. . . ." He flashed a grin. "Just *how come*, the whole thing. How come my mother thought it funny, all those years?"

She liked the story and told him so. She was beginning to get relaxed.

"How'd you like our session?" he asked.

"I overdressed."

"You dressed up, and they dressed down. That's something you have to get used to. South, you dress up to go out; North, you dress down when you're off duty. You comb Zabar's in your ten-year-old pants and tennis shoes with holes in them."

She considered that. "I would be uncomfortable."

"Where'd you get a name like Lutie?"

"My cousin is named Nannie. That was our mothers' idea, to hunt the family tree for something old-fashioned."

"I have an aunt Nannie." He laughed. "She changed her name to Clydette Wandine."

Lutie laughed, too; she was on familiar ground. Talking to Sammy was easier than to anyone she'd met since she got here. "Why'd she do that?"

"Why'd your cousin stick with Nannie?"

"Because that's what her mother named her."

They both knew what he would say to that: "Because that's what my aunt's mother named her, she had to change it."

When Joe came in, they were comfortable together.

At the table Lutie realized she was deeply hungry, and she ate two plates of the linguine, hot with red pepper and fire and creamy and cheesy just like in Rome. "That is really good," she told Joe, feeling content.

He took the bottle of supper wine for him and Sammy and moved them into the living room, which looked less

75

like a dentist's waiting room with all the people gone and the extra chairs put away.

"How'd you get into sociology?" he asked.

"She's from the South," Sammy told him, as if that was an answer.

She didn't have a proper reply. She knew that Sammy had learned to tell his story about the fat men who couldn't bend over to tie their shoes as an explanation of his interest in phobias, which both did and didn't have anything to do with it. She didn't have a story like that. "I guess it was Gran," she said truthfully. "When she had everybody around, Delia and my mother or even, later, Marcie at the beauty shop and the clerk in Better Dresses, then she was all right, and when she didn't, then she wasn't." And she told them about Gran and how she yo-yoed in and out, but they forgot the point and began to talk about what could be done to help people like that these days—because they saw everything the way psychologists do.

Lutie tried to explain that what had happened to Gran would have happened to anyone who'd lost her house and had to live with kinfolk who didn't want her. And in the back of her mind she knew it was true, that she probably had got interested in her field because of how Gran had been at River Bend and then how she'd been at Redoaks, watching the sun set behind her back.

Joe was continuing by giving his approach to therapy. "Nobody changes, is the first premise. Nobody is going to change. What you have to do is to get them to see what they're already doing and going to do anyhow and then to figure out how to do a better version of it. For them to. Say you have a patient who always has affairs with married men. You don't delve into why. You get her to see that, whyever, she does; for whatever reason, if they got too close, are there too much, really belong to her, then she bolts. So you get her to make a list of men who travel eight months of the year and never see their wives—professional athletes, rock musicians, traveling salesmen—and you tell her to find one of those. Or she comes in complaining that she isn't getting enough attention from this guy, and you ask her how would she feel if she got that much from one of her married lovers, and she says that would be heaven, two nights a week, flowers, a call every other night, and so you tell her to pretend he's married and get off his case."

"Isn't that discouraging if nobody changes?"

"It feels good to show them how they can take the same givens and change their situation."

They enjoyed arguing about it. Joe poured the men another glass of wine, and brought her some more tea, and didn't seem as bossy as he had in group.

At midnight Lutie excused herself because she figured that it would take her at least an hour to get to Grand Central and she would have to thank them, and the Forty-sixth Street side of the station would be closed, and she would have to go around, and it had been too pleasant a time to have to run all the way—the way she had last time, after the opera, in the pouring rain.

"I have to go," she explained.

"We can't let you set out this time of night. Why don't you stay over? I'll put you in a cab first thing in the morning?" Joe consulted his watch.

Lutie hesitated; she wanted desperately not to have to deal with the long walk and the frantic haste and getting home at two-thirty in the morning. But she knew she hadn't learned yet how to be single and stay over. "I can't," she said, looking at both of them.

"Sure you can," Sammy said. "Southern girls can do that, and nobody blinks an eye. They simply lock their doors

77

and prop a chair under the knob, and nobody thinks less of them in the morning."

"If you're sure you all have room?" She weakened.

"Us all?" Joe looked startled.

She had seen only one bedroom and the study.

"Southern girls," Sammy interpreted, "they don't have the least idea about mens."

"Don't you both live here?" she asked, bothered to have got it wrong.

"Does she think we're gay?" Joe asked his partner.

"You ask her. I'll be on my way. Sweet dreams."

Lutie sat very still after Sammy left. She didn't know what to do. She felt it wasn't right for a therapist to sleep with his clients, any more than for a teacher with a student, but she decided she had let herself in for whatever happened by not leaving when she should have.

"Let me go to the bathroom," she said. She was floating away from all the tea. Behind the closed door she sponged her face again, and washed under her arms and between her legs, and put fresh lipstick on, and brushed her hair. The night with the developer in the country came back to her, but at least Joe wasn't someone like that. She shut her eyes and, against her will, remembered how it had been in bed with Dabney, with him calling her cold as a Kelvinator, things like that she was better off not to remember. His doing it by himself in Rome, with her right there . . . She put that out of her mind so as not to freeze up. She wondered if she should take a towel with her into the bedroom, for afterward, to tidy up.

She wasn't on the pill, hadn't been since a year after Dabney left, and she would have to explain that. She didn't know what you were supposed to do when you spent the night. Maybe you always took a little bag with you, just in case? But that seemed awful, to come prepared, everywhere you went.

78

She thought of leaving her glasses off but didn't because she couldn't see without them.

"I'm ready," she said when she came out. She went into the bedroom and pulled the red plaid spread down and sat, waiting, on the side of the bed.

Joe came and sat beside her. "How long have you been divorced?" he asked.

"Four years."

"Got a boyfriend?"

"Not really."

"How was it with your husband?"

"What do you mean?" She didn't want to talk about that.

"I had a dog once, a Husky, named Beulah, and she had come to me from an abusive situation, so she would jump a mile if you lifted your arm, and she wouldn't let me come near her for about two months, and then, one night, when I came home from the clinic, she came into where I was starting to work and threw herself on the floor, on her back, As if to say, 'Cut my throat or whatever you're waiting to do.' You look like Beulah. She had a pretty coat."

"I don't understand."

"I'm saying we got off on the wrong track. You look like a camel laying your neck down to have your throat cut. Did you know they did that? Is there anything else but tea you drink? That was my last tea bag."

"Iced coffee. I'll fix some from what's left in the pot. Can I help you clean up?"

He fixed a glass for each of them, with milk and vanilla and a lot of crushed ice, which he made by wrapping cubes in a towel and bashing them with a hammer on the drainboard. He put brandy in his.

"What made you come up here?" he asked her when they were settled on the daybed in his workroom.

So she told him about the job and the semester away. And how she loved where she was living, and about her walk up the carriage road, and about the dam and her students at the performing arts college where she was teaching.

He listened, and after a bit he took her over and showed her a big framed portrait of two boys who looked like the boys on the train who said "fuck" a lot, the ones with the beer and the cigarettes in the dark rail car. And it made her wonder if all boys that general age looked alike.

"These are my sons," he said.

"How old are they?" she asked. "What are their names?"

"That's the missing piece of the puzzle," Joe said. "That's it."

"What?"

"Lutie, one of my boys is four years older than the other. Which is which?"

She studied the pictures, but they were both so big-boned and had the same heavy features, and neither had a mustache or anything, and she was about to give up, but then she saw that one of them had the big jaw that tomcats get when they are grown. It was the way you knew that they were grown, when they got that big, wide face. So she pointed at that one and said, "Him."

"Did it honestly take you that long?" He took her arm and set her back on the daybed. "Shut your eyes," he said. "Now describe Sammy to me."

She told him about the Cuthbert look, the forehead and the upper lip, and about his shoulders being narrow for his height, and about his hands' having just a few flecks of missing pigmentation, which was unusual for his age, and that he probably came from a big family. . . .

"Now don't open your eyes." He took her hand in his, but in the way a doctor does when he is about to go over the results with you; it wasn't in any way a pass. "Now describe me," he said.

She panicked. She tried to picture Joe, but she couldn't.

Whenever she tried, she got the general image of all the boys on the train and general boys like that, the ones she'd had in her class, whom she couldn't tell apart without a seating chart. "Sammy is taller," she finally said, lamely.

"Shorter than Sammy. You could pick me out of a crowd."

"Brown hair. I don't know—you look a lot like your boys." She was afraid she was going to cry with embarrassment.

"Which of us is older?" he asked.

"Don't tease me," she said. "If you want to talk about it, that's okay, or if you'd rather not. But don't tease me."

"Look at me, Lutie."

She raised her eyes, but she couldn't. He had a big nose. A forehead. Ordinary eyes. A mustache. She looked down. All she could focus on was that he had some hair on the backs of his hands. And looking at that much of him made her have to blink her eyes.

"You must have had a louse for a father," he said.

"I don't remember him," she explained. "I was three when we left."

"What was his name?"

"Mr. Pinter."

"Do you ever hear from him?"

"I used to get birthday cards."

"What else?"

She struggled. "Mother didn't want to be married to him."

"Why not?"

She turned her hands over. "Those were army days." She shrugged.

"Which of us is older?" he asked, but being lighter.

"That isn't fair," she told him, relieved that they could get off the subject. She suddenly felt worn-out tired. It was late.

He sighed. "Why don't you lie down here and I'll go get a blanket? We'll need to get up early to put you on the train."

The last thing she remembered was the weight of the covers on her shoulders as she fell asleep in Joe Donaldson's workroom.

8

Journal: The Night We Met
Was Not the Night We Met (I)

I HAVE a new routine, where I go out on the stoop
under the night sky, the way I did at home in July to
watch the eclipse, wrapped in a blanket because it is in the
forties now, and wait for Le Rouge and Le Noir: two
neighboring cats.

I fill the pockets of my old blue sweater with Seanips,
which was Cecelie's favorite treat, and whistle very softly,
and they always come. Sometimes, lately, they've been
waiting for me, and when I open the door, they'll come
running up the stairs. The red tabby tom caught on right
away, and he eats first, digging in my pockets where he
knows the treats are, and then sits curled in the circle of
my crossed knees and permits the little black male, not yet
really a tom, still with the narrow face and slight body of
a kitten, to have his supper. He, Le Noir, comes to my
elbow and paws at my sleeve until I give him a palmful of
the deep-sea treats.

I don't know how the cats get out; they must scratch at the door to be let out, but surely, when it snows and is much colder, they will stay inside all winter. I've never seen a cat in cold weather, not really; whenever it ices over at home, Cecelie gets on the bed and stays there until it warms up, but that is only about five times a year.

At any rate, by that time I'll be back in Texas; school is out, even counting for turning in final grades, the third week in December. That's nine more weeks, as yesterday was the Ides of October.

Even if I wasn't leaving, Joe and I might not be seeing each other after December anyway because that happens. People get to a stopping place or get stuck with one another and drift apart. That's how I'm thinking of it. It's the same way that I wouldn't become uninterested in group just because it's going to end. We assume a termination to most things: a diet or a degree. I don't understand why we can't do that with the people we know in instances like this. . . .

I fell asleep on Joe's daybed and caught the train back out to Westchester the next morning. Because I didn't have classes on Thursday and could take my time, I walked from his apartment, so I could think over what had happened.

The main thing was I didn't want my having stayed all night and had supper with him and Sammy to mess anything up in group, because I like it a lot. The second week when we were to wear a uniform of some sort, I came as a waitress (using a white blouse and a white summer skirt and making a hat out of a lace doily from the dime store and an apron from a bigger one, pinned on). Danya, the librarian, came as a policeman, and Fudge, the assistant editor, wore a nightgown. Other people had made up uniforms, too, and then we all analyzed what we'd worn, and everyone said they could see that being a waitress was just like being a schoolteacher, that it meant you thought you had to wait on people, and then they could understand, and they liked me better.

I was direct and talked to them about where I was coming from, which was that the one major maxim of Mother's and Aunt Caroline's was: Don't look hungry. (I had grown up with them quoting the part from Louisa May Alcott's *An Old-Fashioned Girl* where Polly "turns her silks" when she falls on hard times and the part from *Gone with the Wind* where Scarlett takes down the emerald velvet draperies to make herself an elegant bustled dress to rescue Tara in. These were part of our family's language, these scenes. When Uncle Elbert died, Mother said at once, not even thinking about it, "Sister will have to turn her silks." And, after we lost River Bend: "It's time to sew up the velvet drapes.")

Then the next time we were to come to class dressed in a way that fit how we really saw ourselves, something closer to the truth than what we'd been pretending the first night or making fun of the second. I came as what I am: an academic in the social sciences who has a temporary job. I wore hose, my hair pinned back with tortoiseshell barrettes, an old tweed skirt, a plain shirt and jacket. And I carried a stack of books—George Herbert Mead and Lewis Henry Morgan—and an old book satchel. And I sat with my feet flat on the floor, the way my seventh-grade teacher had done. And we talked about all that.

Meanwhile, the rest of them were doing the same. Danya, who had come the first night in the T-shirt and black skirt and droopy hair, looking like a dancer who is too heavy and sad to dance, so you got the idea that she'd failed at what she really wanted to do, began to "dress for success." She wore tailored suits, bow-tied blouses, high heels and had her hair waved in the way that made her look like a high school principal or someone who sells cosmetics. And when she got cross, it made you feel that the principal was mad at you or the saleslady thought you were uninformed, and so it worked. And Fudge, who'd worn the sweat pants and running shoes and hostile air of being on her way somewhere and you were in her way, had started to wear gypsy-looking clothes: soft-shouldered gauzy blouses and long, bright skirts. And to admit that what she really wanted was to look very female and not to have to compete all the time to get what she wanted.

It all fit in with Joe's theory that nobody really changes but that we can figure out better ways of being who we are anyway.

Next week we're supposed to come back again in what we wore the very first time (which we had to write down that night, so we couldn't "forget") and then look at each other and see how much we can see of what we saw the first time and how much we can now see about them because we know them, and they know us, better. I am looking forward to that, a lot.

I stayed all night the second week, also, the waitress week, and Joe wanted us to be lovers, but I told him that I hadn't been on the pill since a year after Dabney left and that I had a diaphragm, but that I hadn't used it since I got up here and didn't have it with me. That made him mad, and so we had a fight. He called me some bad names and himself some for getting mixed up with someone like me. Then we phoned Sammy, and he came over and said it looked as if we were a mess together and that we were the last people on earth he could imagine getting together. Naturally, we knew what he was doing, and it got us out of the heat of our fight.

So I stayed, and he used something, and he said I was just like that camel laying my neck down to have my throat cut, and I said that if he was going to do it with me, he couldn't fuss at me for how I was about it. That how I was was a long story, and I wasn't about to tell it to him then.

I did tense up. I knew it. I froze. I could remember all the bad things Dabney used to say, what a cold fish I was, and remember how after Rome he'd made sure to tell me about all the times he used to lie in bed and do it by himself while I was cleaning Mother's house. And I felt such shame about that, and hurt and anger. So all Joe got was the distance; I couldn't help that. It wasn't Joe's business why. I was not interested in what had gone wrong with him and his wife, Carole, as far as sex was concerned, and I told him so. And I told him that if he called me Beulah after his Husky, who had flopped down on the floor for him to hit her, one more time, I would not stay over again.

So I invited him out the next Friday night, to my neighborhood. I didn't worry about his staying over, the way I would have in someplace like Austin, because I knew that people didn't mind what you did if nobody got hurt, such as the man and his two bashing cars; besides, the people were mostly working, married couples who had their own lives and own fights, which you could hear without a lot of trouble. So they weren't interested in anybody else's business.

The streets in Cranberry Park didn't smell like backyard grills anymore, because the chilly evenings were here, and so I didn't get the smell of cooking or hear the crowds at the baseball games. The World Series was on TV, and if you were out in the early evening, you would see flickering lights through the windows and hear the muffled sounds of the announcer coming through the panes.

I thought our first night at my place might be more of what had happened at his apartment, with Joe fussing at me for the way I was with him and deciding that it was all a waste of his time if I was going back to Texas anyway, and my getting farther away from him. So on the whole I wasn't anticipating anything but regret to come from having him out; but I wanted to ask, since I'd stayed with him twice, and it seemed the thing to do. And at least by then I knew it wouldn't be like the bad experience with the developer at Redoaks, when I'd had to run all the way home and lock the windows.

Joe was not that kind of person, a psycho; he was the normal kind, glum.

What happened, though, was that we had a wonderful time and got very close and have been that way ever since, but it was an accident, having to do with my liking cars so much.

At the start we were in my living room, and he'd admired my blowup of Rome, and we were in the wicker chairs, talking casually as if it weren't obvious that we would end up on my daybed and then be wondering what to do with ourselves after that. I had figured out that I'd suggest that we put on jackets and sweaters (because it was cold) and go up to the all-night diner, which was four blocks away, and have bagels and cream cheese, which I was getting to like. I hadn't ever eaten there, but I'd gone into the diner on Thursday, knowing he was coming, and checked it out. I'd wanted someplace that was like the Holiday House at home, where I loved to go—tired of fixing Mother's garden-grown company meals—and get a big Number 4, with chili, cheese, onions, and tomatoes, someplace where you could eat out in public something which you could never fix at home.

My idea was that Joe and I could go up there and be out in public and have things to look at and people to listen to and wouldn't get into a fight. There was no Sammy to bail us out this time.

But for all my planning, it was late before we got to the diner.

When Joe came, before anything happened, he went in the bathroom, and when he came out, he asked, "Is that your car in there?"

He was talking about my other blowup. "That's my enlargement."

"What kind is it?"

"It's a Morgan." I loved the car and didn't mind talking about it. "I found a picture of it in a car book at a news-stand, and I had these students who run a place called Blowup enlarge it for me. And then I framed it. It's my second favorite kind of car."

"What's your favorite?"

I couldn't tell if he was asking because it was more or less required or if he really cared. It is a myth that men are interested in cars, I've learned that. They take for granted that they can go and come places and don't get the same thrill out of revving up an engine and getting away that a woman does. In my experience. "A Cord," I told him. In case he did want to know.

"Never heard of it."

Which is what I mean.

He sat down in the wicker chair and kept on smoking his cigarette. I'd forgotten about an ashtray, which I didn't have, but I'd set out a saucer for him to use. He was in corduroy pants and an old sweater and looked older than he did in his navy suit at group.

"It looks like this." And I drew in the air with my hands the big fenders and rounded hood and flaring front. Not that he could get the idea, of course; but it made me see it in my mind, and that was a pleasure. When he appeared to get the idea, I relaxed a little bit.

"But that isn't what you picked me up in?" he asked.

"That's my ten-year-old Chevy. Couldn't you tell? You rode in it."

"I didn't pay that much attention."

"Cars tell a lot. I bet if the people in group told what kind of car they have and what kind they'd like to have—"

"This isn't Texas, Lutie. Most of them can't even drive."

But I thought he was teasing me. That was all right, because it was on a favorite subject. "Don't you remember," I asked him, "the night we met I wanted to know what kind of car you drove?"

He looked at me, sitting in my jeans on the daybed, with an odd look, and he said, "I don't remember much about that night we met, except that it wasn't 'the night we met,' the night we met. And that you fell asleep in my study and I sat up half the night." He looked slightly cross and then asked, "What did I tell you?"

"You said a Saab."

"True. But that's expedience. That's not a real indicator."

I laughed because that's what pepole always say about anything you try to judge them by: This blouse isn't the real me; this sofa isn't the real me.

He got that and laughed, too, but he went on. "The Saab was hers, Carole's. She was big on *Consumer Reports* and getting what was maximally safe or economical—I think the Saab is both."

"It's ugly." I tried to think of him the age of the boys on the train. "What did you used to drive? Back in Ohio."

"An Austin Healey, used, with a roll bar. And a perforated oil drum."

And I liked him a lot better, just the fact that he could say that.

"What would you drive if you could?" he asked.

"The Cord." I'd made that clear enough.

And then he said what turned us around. "Show me," he said, "Show me the Lutie Sayre who drives a Cord."

I closed my eyes and tried to gather myself into one place, to shape myself, to get inside a Cord owner. And it came to me clear as day. I knew, I *knew*, exactly how it would feel to have parked my car down in the drive and climbed the stairs. The steps went with it fine; perhaps this was my studio or my hideaway. When I opened my eyes, I was deep into being a Cord owner. "I want to shake off the day, Joe. Would you get yourself another beer and open me a diet Dr Pepper while I take a shower?" (You might not think that Cord owners would drink diet Dr Pepper, but on the other hand, they would have the confidence to have what they wanted and not to ask for mineral water just to be in fashion.)

I went into the shower and washed my hair—which suddenly felt dingy from the day on campus and a restless night last night spent thinking about Joe coming. When I came out, I accepted the cold drink and, still being the Cord driver, propped two pillows behind me and began to towel-dry my hair. "Sometimes," I told him, "I have to shed being a schoolteacher."

"It's amazing," he said, pleased. "I wonder if I was that different when I changed the oil pans in the Healey every day?"

"Probably."

When I was ready, I untied my bathrobe and dropped the belt. I didn't have anything on underneath, but I was so wrapped up in my car ownership that I wasn't at all embarrassed. "Let's make love," I told him, "and then go get a bagel." I could say that because Cord owners made love all the time and they didn't worry about it, and it was the same to them as getting a good hot bagel with homemade cream cheese, and at the end of a long day of teaching, you sometimes needed to do both.

"The night we met you looked like an orthodontist's wife. . . ." Joe laid his clothes in a heap by the daybed, and I was glad to see that he was no longer a Saab driver, because he didn't fold them neatly at all but threw them down, and I opened my arms to him.

"The night we met was not 'the night we met,'" I reminded him, and we smiled at one another because we were proving that it was. And I didn't freeze up at all or go away, naturally, being the type of person who drove a Cord automobile.

Then, when I was back to thinking about the diner, he said, "We can't go out; your hair is still wet."

And I'd forgotten again, still expecting that I could wash my hair and relax awhile and then have it dry and ready to brush in place when it was time to go.

"Cord owners," he said, "sometimes sit in the kitchen and watch him stir the pasta with a wooden spoon."

"I don't have one," I said, not pleased because this was what happened at his place, and this was my place.

"I do," he said, and produced not only the spoon but green noodles, still damp and limp, fresh from the place he liked so much called Zabar's.

I had seen the sack when I picked him up, but I hadn't taken in that he meant to cook. In my apartment.

"All I need," he said, "is for you to put the hot water on and direct me to an egg yolk while I get things started."

I sat down, brushing my hair. "Cord owners, while they watch, sometimes discuss scholarly matters."

"Austin Healey owners with leaky pans may not know what you're talking about."

I told him about my teaching and how primarily that

consisted of getting students to look at the same facts in a new way, as Leonardo did when he wrote "The sun does not move," to a world which still believed in sunrise and sunset. And then we ate the green noodles with grated cheese and cream from his deli sack, and it tasted very delicious; but I could see that Austin Healey owners, whatever they pretended, wanted to take control of whatever space they were in. That was fine when he was a group leader, but here it made me feel crowded.

"Don't make yourself at home," I told him.

"Am I?"

"You are."

"Carole said that's why she had to resort to higher authorities: *Consumer Reports*, pediatricians, law school." He looked unhappy with himself.

"How does it feel when you do it?" I asked.

He lit a cigarette at the table and looked glum. "That if I could pick you up and sit you here and beat the egg yolk and cream here, then nothing would get out of hand."

"Stage manager."

"That's what Sammy says. He's right. You're right. I often think of rooms that way. If I'm at a party, and it's a new place, and I'm getting that anxious feeling of not knowing where everything is or what's happening, or if some game is being played that I can't see, that I'm a dummy in a hand that's being dealt that I don't know about, I'll do it. I'll literally do that: think 'This is stage left,' 'That's stage right,' 'That's the fourth wall, e.g., the audience' "—Joe talks that way, saying *eee gee* for e.g. and *eye eee* for i.e., just as if he were dictating into a machine, when he gets nervous—"over there. And then I have a frame of reference for what's going on."

"That's why you like group; you can tell us what to do."

He smiled, conceding. "And what to wear."

93

"You said that was Sammy's idea."

"*Image* was his. Uniforms, all that—mine."

"That's why you told me to be a Cord owner."

"Under my direction you were a star."

"It was fun. It worked." I conceded.

"Carole would call that manipulation."

"Calling it manipulation is manipulation."

"You're the one who manages the group."

"That's not true at all."

"Nonsense. They've been under your control since the first night when you recognized Sammy and let everyone know it. They're afraid of you. They try to write you off as a bossy old academic, but they're afraid of you nonetheless."

"So the only reason you asked me to stay over the first time was that I took the group away from you?"

"Something like that."

I was laughing; I didn't believe any of that, but it made me feel comfortable with him and no longer cross about the pasta. "Let's go to the diner for coffee anyway," I told him.

"Hair's wet still."

"How can it be?" Vexed, I discovered he was right.

"Cord owners go into a rage when they can't control their environment."

"They do." But I wasn't going to be put off again. "I'll tie it back with a scarf."

"So I have no choice this time but to put my shoes on and go out into the cold?"

"So you must want that since you're here."

"I must, mustn't I?" He looked as if he did. "The night we met was a definite loss of face." He got his jacket and pulled it on over his sweater. "I'll let you in on a secret: Once winter's here, the steam heat gets so dry you can wash your hair and it will be dry by the time you put your shoes on. Just wait."

"I'll be back in Texas by then," I reminded him.

The present changes the past, is the point, and what was enough is not enough now. Before we were lovers, I could make do with the landlady, Mrs. Vaccaro, and the dressmaker, Mrs. Rodino, and Mary Sue at Finast, and Denise at the pharmacy, and my butcher, who has a daughter in college, and Dr. Birdsong, and my flamboyant students, and the women in the washateria who always remember me as the one who called the police the night the moon was full. But now I can't anymore. Now I am lonesome without him.

It's the way a room seems bare when you take down the Christmas tree, whereas it didn't seem bare before you put it up.

9

Journal: The Night We Met
Was Not the Night We Met (II)

L A S T night Joe brought out his boys, who are with him on Saturdays, and Sammy came with them, as he does whenever we need helping out. Sammy's part was to take the boys back so that Joe could stay over. Joe says it doesn't make him anxious, to let the boys know that he is sleeping with me, but that we needn't rub their noses in it. His words.

Part of the point about Fritz and Noah's coming to my place is, I know, some sort of test of me. Ever since Joe made me shut my eyes that first night and describe him, and proved that I couldn't, he's been trying to show me that I never do see men, that I'm blind to all the ones who count. He tried to get me to tell what I could remember about Mr. Pinter, but I told him we'd been over that. Then he asked about Aunt Caroline's husband, Uncle Elbert, but

I told him that he was dead and, besides, had always been at the church whenever I visited Savannah. As for my cousins Bubba and Langley, all I could say was that Bubba had been pudgy from the start, and Langley only lately. All of which made him mad. Although it's the truth.

He says he is going to do a book called *Whatever Happened to Men?*, but I'm not sure whether that is directed at me or at Carole, as he still aims a lot of emotion in her direction. I offered to tell him what I could about Dabney (that his head was too large and his shoulders too narrow for his frame, for example), but he is not interested in hearing about my former husband.

His sons' names bothered me before I met them because they didn't match. Naming is so important at home, and I could have figured out about sons named, say, Fritz and Karl or Noah and Adam. Names that went with one another. But *Fritz* and *Noah* didn't fit together, a fact which could mean trouble.

I worked a long time on the food for them, looking back in my journal to see old recipes, noting that I hadn't fed anyone since the big Fourth of July buffet at Redoaks for Mother. I decided on Mexican food and filled three glass cake pans with green enchiladas, which I made with real green tomatoes from Finast and canned green chilies and lots of cumin, and filled them with chicken and grated muenster cheese, and they were spicy but not too hot for novices. I also made two cheese pies, which resemble quiche but have no milk, being three kinds of cheese, including cottage, and eggs and butter and a touch of vermouth. And I put jalapeño slices on top, to be in keeping with Mexican (at home I would add zucchini to the recipe and put onion slices on top, to give it a country effect).

I wanted to do a buttermilk pie, but that looked too much like the cheese pies; besides, I thought that with teen-age boys you should have chocolate, which is in some ways a substitute for sex. I was never able to make decent cakes at Redoaks because of the unpredictable oven; but here I did a double fudge cake from my southern cookbook, and it turned out perfectly, dark and chewy and not even a hint of scorch. In fact, it turned out so well I made a second, a sheet cake, and put it in the freezer, to have on hand for next time. And by then I was almost sorry that there were only the four of them coming.

As it turned out, I didn't have any trouble telling the boys apart or remembering their names. There was ruddy Fritz, with his heavy man's jaw and the thicker thighs that go with it, for the strutting way of walking that a tomcat has, and there was young dark Noah, with his hairless face and sweet, dazed smile and long, skinny legs. It was Le Rouge and Le Noir, in the flesh. (Also about their names, I noted in my head: Fritz for First and Noah for Next.) The way Fritz staked out his territory at once by claiming one of the wicker chairs, so that one of the grown men would have to sit on the daybed or floor, also reminded me of the red tabby. Whereas Noah, who, at twelve, was almost six feet tall but still a child, wandered around, not exactly staying put anywhere but constantly asking me could he help me in the kitchen.

I had nothing for him to do—the food was ready, and in a place this tiny I have to be organized to have it look clean. Finally, I decided he could bartend and said, "Why don't you take everyone a beer, Noah, would you mind? I have German, Mexican, Canadian, and Texan." (I was proud of that.)

"What d'you want, Dad?" He was pleased with his assignment.

"Noah gets to wait on us," Fritz said in a very sarcastic

tone. "She can't even tell who is the nigger around here—"
He shot that out, to gauge its effect.

I waited for Joe to get up and smack his eldest in the face, but neither Joe nor Sammy moved. All I could see on Joe's face was a deep wish that they hadn't come.

I said, "That's my chair, Fritz," and went and stood by it until he moved, grudgingly. Then I said, "It must be *you* who can't tell who's who around here."

Then I waited, still irritated, while Noah brought all the men a beer and had one himself—which I though Joe would object to, since it was clear that Noah, at his age, shouldn't have one. But he didn't.

It was clear to me from the start that Joe Donaldson didn't have any control whatsoever over his sons and that that was his real anxiety about bringing them here and also the reason for his trying to run everyone else's life.

Sammy seemed different, too, although it took me a while to figure out. He'd come in a leather flyer's jacket and had a sort of war hero look pasted on his face. (And he was giving words the wrong endings, the way he did when he was in front of a lot of people in a social way, but I hadn't seen that before: saying "hamburgro" for "hamburger," "figro it out" for "figure it out," "weathro bureau" for "weather bureau." Things like that.) I could see he didn't feel at home with Joe's boys, or maybe even with Joe out here in a strange county, not the way he did with group, where he had a definite function, or with the two of us alone in the city.

"Where's the TV?" Noah asked.

"No TV." Joe answered for me.

"I *told* you," Fritz announced to his brother. "I asked Dad did she have Atari or Intellevision or what, and he said no TV."

"I forgot." Noah looked around vaguely.

I wanted to say that I didn't have anything against a set, that it was an economic matter, not a moral one, but there wasn't any point in saying all that.

The point was that Joe's sons wanted something to *do*, and I couldn't provide it. My first reaction was to get mad at Joe because he hadn't anticipated this and helped me. He should have known how it would have been with them in a small space, should have had some ideas from what he was used to doing with them on Saturdays at his place. But then I realized that if you're used to the city, it's hard to think differently.

I tried to recall what people did at home, but I already knew. What they did at home was eat. That—the meal, the food—was the whole point, whether it was at River Bend or Redoaks or The Manse in Savannah. If you were getting together with someone, you were getting together for a meal. And so there was the time of getting there, and then the time before you ate, and the long eating itself, and then the time after you'd eaten, when you might wait on dessert until you'd moved into another room and visited a moment, or you took a tour of the house (at The Manse), the waterfront (at River Bend), the gardens (at Redoaks), and then you came back and had a dessert, which was always a ceremony, and then, after a decent time, a little conversation about friends, it would be the end of the evening or the afternoon.

If I'd figured out how it would be different with the boys, we would have planned a movie, of which there were a lot nearby (well, fairly close). Or I would have checked ahead around the dam area, the way I'd checked ahead on the diner for Joe and me, to see if there was someplace with a pinball machine or what they called Pac-Man or something like that. I would have researched it, the way I like to do.

But it was too late at that point, since it was getting more and more awkward, and I could see Sammy and Joe were not going to have any ideas because their minds were jammed with the anxiety of what was bound to happen with Fritz and Noah cooped up and beginning to pick at each other. So I made a decision—but I wish I hadn't waited until after Fritz got himself another beer, which he shouldn't have had.

"I always take my walk at this time of day," I said to four male faces, which could not have been less responsive. "It's beautiful at this time of year, with the leaves turning. And we can see the lake at the top of the dam."

There was dead silence from Joe and Sammy, and Noah, not really hearing, asked again, "Can I help with something?"

But finally, when I got my jacket on, so they could see I meant it, Fritz got up from his place by the door, shot a sullen look at his father, and said, "Might as well. Nothing else to do."

If he hadn't got up, we'd be sitting there still; it was clear to anyone on the outside that what they all waited for was how it was going to be for Fritz.

I felt a great relief when we all were going down my outside stairs, on our way—bundled up slightly against the chill. It was a lovely late afternoon, and I was sure it would help the boys to walk off some of their nerves, and the men, too. Some kind of scrub football team was practicing on the baseball field, and some smaller kids were playing on the little diamond. Parents had their toddlers on the swing sets and were talking to each other in little clumps of threes and fours.

It was later than I'd been used to walking—and, because of daylight saving, would be dark when we got back—but that was fine, since I wasn't doing it alone, and it would give me an idea of how safe it was at night.

I'd debated putting the green enchiladas in the oven,

turned on low, and the cheese pies with jalapeño to warm, while we were gone. But decided that I might need the time, that is, need to use up some time, if things didn't get any better when we got back; we could wait while the food heated, and I could put Noah to work with iced tea glasses and putting the napkins in napkin rings and things like that. And maybe Fritz could be bullied into taking the Seanips out on the stoop and calling his lookalike to eat.

We started up the brick road, and I was proud, for some reason, as if it were *mine*, in a way I'd never felt at Redoaks. And proceeded to tell them which were the maples and beech and oaks, as if they didn't know and I was the native. But they didn't know, and I might as well have been, for all the attention they paid to what felt like my home turf.

At the top I read aloud the carved inscriptions over the arches at the brick road end of the dam, first the one we'd walked through, "HE COVERETH THE HEAVENS WITH CLOUDS: HE PREPARETH RAIN FOR THE EARTH," then the one above the arch which framed the dark, deep lake, "HE GIVETH SNOW LIKE WOOL. HE SCATTERETH THE HOARFROST LIKE ASHES."

I was thinking that Uncle Elbert could probably have quoted chapter and verse to locate the lines and that these out-of-breath people with me wouldn't even know they were from the Bible.

We stopped awhile—because they were winded—to look out across the reservoir ringed with fall colors, with no sign of the gulls that circled in the late summer: a lovely expanse of water, which, in the departing afternoon sun, looked amber and gold with the reflection of the trees and sky. Joe rubbed his hand along my shoulders for a moment while we stared down at the lake, and then, as we moved to gaze down at the plaza on the other side, at the dry reflecting pools and leaf-filled fountains, he wandered ahead.

By the time we reached the far end of the dam it was almost dark and getting colder. Again I read the inscriptions over the Roman arches to my silent crew: on the lakeside, "HE CAUSETH HIS WIND TO BLOW AND THE WATERS TO FLOW," and, toward the grove and our descent, "HE MAKETH THE GRASS TO GROW UPON THE MOUNTAINS." I was imagining the Italian stonecutters laboring to carve, in letters as high as Fritz, these Old Testament words, selected by a forgotten committee of New York water commissioners.

As we started down the stone steps, a sharp wind blew the leaves at our feet, which was a thrill, because at home almost nothing is deciduous, and so you don't have the pleasure of scuffling through piles of fallen red and yellow, gusting down the stairs ahead of you.

Halfway down Fritz asked how much longer this was going to take, and Noah whispered to his father that he needed to go to the bathroom. After some discussion the rest of us started on down the steep steps as the younger son wandered off into the underbrush.

It was about sixty seconds, maybe twice that, before Noah hollered out, "Oh, shit," and came running through the brush. But he didn't have to tell us the trouble. The strong smell of skunk preceded him.

My mind got very still. We were as far from my place as you could get, so at least thirty minutes (or more, because they were slow walkers). It was too cold for Noah to take his trousers off. The butcher's shop, where I'd started going for meat, was only half a block from the dam pavilion, on the edge of the little village which abutted Cranberry Park. Five minutes from where we were, at most. They would have to wait; there was nothing else to do. I thought about leaving Sammy with the boys, but I didn't want to get him in trouble, leaving him in a dark and secluded grove of trees with two white boys, so I decided to take him with me. Joe was their father—he could stay.

"It takes tomato juice," I explained, realizing that they didn't know what to do, anything at all to do, or have the least idea why I was suddenly heading off down the steps in the other direction. "Joe, you get him to roll off what he can with leaves, and we'll be right back. Come on, Sammy."

As we jogged along down the stairs and out of the shrubs onto a sidewalk in front of a Catholic day school, he tried to tell me what was happening, suddenly his old self again. "Carole wants Joe back, see, so the more trouble the kids make, the more they can blame it on him for being gone."

I nodded, mostly glad to see the old Sammy that I liked so much. But I didn't perceive it the way he did, that teen-age boys were something you could explain with things like mothers and fathers. But rather that boys like Fritz had their full jaws and all that went with them and were wanting to prowl and weren't old enough yet to ride the train at one in the morning and say "fuck" to each other when the lights went out and get into and out of trouble before they got back home; and boys like Noah hadn't yet got their face hair, the way their older brothers had, and so had to get back at their brothers in some way—such as finding a skunk to pee on in the shrubbery.

If there was ever a time to look at the facts from a sociologist's and not a psychologist's point of view, it was when you were looking at teen-age boys.

But I didn't go into all that; Sammy was in no mood for theory. We got two cans of tomato juice, giant cans, and a can opener and a roll of paper towels, while Sammy, back in his leather jacketed, public self, tried to "figro" out what else we'd need. As we started back, just past the butcher's he went into a donut shop and bought a dozen, glazed. I thought of all the food I had waiting, and my spirits sank. But Sammy was doing it for Joe and probably knew better than I did what Joe needed.

And sure enough the donuts were gone in half a minute, everyone grabbing for the sugar in his shock, so Sammy had done the right thing.

I doused a freezing Noah with the tomato juice, which must have felt slimy as well as cold, but the smell faded to something we could stand, and I doused him again; but a certain residue was not going to go away, so we started back. Joe was naming all the accidents Noah had had already this year: the time he'd spilled the skillet of hot grease on his shin, trying to fry bacon; the time he'd cut his foot half off on a jagged, broken Coke bottle; the time he'd got ten stitches over his eye from a fall off his ten-speed. It was clear that this misadventure, the skunk, was soon to take its place in the long litany that everyone could recite.

Fritz looked furious, his reddish face tight with rage. (And at that moment my sympathies were with him, I have to admit.) "You *creep*," he said a couple of times to his brother. "You stupid creep." And then, after a few more hurried steps, he began to ask Noah in the most explicit details where on his anatomy the skunk had got him, and would it fall off, and what was Noah trying to get off with the skunk when it happened. All that kind of stuff.

Joe hunched down into himself, and I could see that he was miserable; I looked over at Sammy for guidance, but he was wadding up the donut sack, gone away again.

Noah got into some old jeans of mine because he was so skinny in the legs and hips (or whatever you call the rear end of boys). They came down only to the tops of his calves, of course, and Fritz got to laugh about that a lot. I soaked his pants in the rest of the tomato juice in a big dishpan on the outside porch, wondering what Le Rouge and Le Noir would make of the smell when they came for their snack, if they'd think I'd taken in a tomcat ten times their size.

By the time I had the food heated and ready only Sammy and I really ate anything.

Fritz asked, "What is this junk?"

I said, "Mexican food."

"I don't eat ethnic stuff."

I was pretty discouraged at that point and snapped at him, "So what does your mother cook?"

That got a frantic look from Joe. Was I not supposed to know they had a mother?

"She doesn't cook, stupid; she's in law school. We get our stuff from Gristede's. Nobody cooks, stupid."

Actually he was putting on, as I should have known. I caught him later in the kitchen, eating all the green enchiladas left on his brother's and father's plates. That was so he could hand me back his own in the living room, completely untouched.

"What do you do around here? When my dad's not here, that is." He made a leering smirk in the direction of his father. And as he did, I realized that he'd been looking over at the daybed every other minute since he got here.

I knew the details of my daily life were beyond the comprehension of Fritz Donaldson, sixteen: bake my chicken; soak in the luxurious scum-free tub; work on class notes. "Well, if I'm lucky," I told him, trying to keep it light, "the couple next door has a fight."

Noah laughed at that. Maybe it reminded him in some way of his generally voyeuristic stage of life. Or maybe he thought I'd shut Fritz up. He was huddled with his back against the wall, a sweater of mine around his shoulders and those short, faded, sissy jeans on, and still smelled faintly of skunk despite a fifteen-minute shower. Twelve years old was not going to be his favorite year.

Just then the couple on the other side of the wall really did tune up and have a quarrel (my initial impulse was to take them over the uneaten chocolate cake in appreciation).

"What is this?" Fritz asked. "A fucking ghetto?"

The couple was shouting at each other, the way they always did, where you could not make out the actual words because of the wall, but you could get a tone of voice and the rise and fall of their argument.

Sammy went into the kitchen and came back with my four small juice glasses. "Such are the assets of disadvantage," he said, showing us how to put the glass to the wall, rim flush against the Sheetrock, bottom to the ear. The other three did likewise, somewhat shamefaced, feeling intrusive, down-scale, or silly, depending on their age.

"A *lamp?*" Noah reacted first. "They're fighting about where to put a *lamp?*"

"That's stupid," Fritz declared, disgusted. "I mean, *stupid.*"

"This is where I part company with family therapists," Sammy informed his partner, still listening studiously.

"Why?"

"Because, say, these folks come in for counseling because they fight about the lamp all the time, and the family therapist, he assumes that *lamp* is only a totem for their real fight, which goes deeper and farther back, so their parents are called in, and their children and siblings, if they can be rounded up, and everybody says, 'Now come on, Pete and Shirley, say what you're really thinking, get in touch with your feelings.' And they oblige. And the old parents go over all their sins in raising them, and the kids go over all the ways they've been manipulating them"—here he stole a glance at Fritz and Noah "—and so Pete and Shirley feel good about themselves, and they thank their parents, and they farm their kids out and go home and have this God-awful fight about the lamp. Because the lamp is the whole point. Everything is class, and she thinks she gives better lamp than he does, and he thinks her lamp is déclassé. So sooner or later they're going to split when one of them decides someone with better lamp has come along."

"You always say that: Everything is class." Joe takes up the argument, amiably, his ear still pressed to the wall.

"So?"

"So if family therapy is to save a family, and child therapy is to save a child, then why aren't you in class therapy?"

Fritz looked at his father, nauseated. "Mom's right; you're full of rocks."

"Class therapy, you're right." Sammy continued. "That's my new field."

"Specialty? Lower? Upper?"

"Across the board." Sammy waved his hand for quiet. "I definitely think she's in the right; setting the lamp in the window is tasteless."

Joe put down his glass and got out his pen.

"The train ride was better than this," Fritz griped.

Joe passed around a piece of paper on which he'd written: "What Is This Couple Fighting About?" "It's mine," he said.

I didn't understand.

"Copyright granted," Sammy said.

"Witnesses." Joe stuck my finger in his coffee and pressed it on the page, and then he did the same with Noah.

"How can you be so stupid?" Fritz groaned. "And my dumb brother is going to stink all the way home. Look at him, a dumb pervert in girl's pants." He kicked my chair and disappeared into the bathroom for twenty minutes.

I was worn-out when they left. I'd thought I'd take a shower and put on my robe and we'd be the way we were the night Joe had me imagine I was a Cord owner, but I couldn't even clean up the plates. There was tons of food left, a new event for me, and I was discouraged about that.

"Here," Joe said, "I brought you something." He'd been sweet, thanking me for having them, but worn-out himself. It was worse for him; they were his. And he didn't know how to handle them or to handle all the guilt he had about moving out on them.

He pulled a cassette player and a tape of Respighi's *The Fountains of Rome* and *The Pines of Rome* out of his canvas bag, music which was supposed to go with my blowup of the Arch of Septimius Severus. He played what he said were the two best selections, *Pines of the Villa Borghese* and *Fountains of the Villa Medici*. I didn't have to hear much to know that I didn't like the music at all. And I asked him not to play the rest, being too tired to be polite. I tried not to hurt his feelings by telling him that it was probably just being married all those years to a classicist, but that I didn't like it when people tried to make what they did mean something just by attaching it to something old and crumbling.

But he did get hurt, and finally, he asked, "Well, what do you like then?"

He wasn't really asking; I could see that. He was really telling me that he'd tried to be sweet, that he'd planned how we'd unwind after the boys left, play some classical music, make love, probably eat a midnight plate of his pasta. And that I'd messed it up.

I could relate to that; I'd had the same hopes for my Mexican dinner, my chocolate cake. I knew how it was to need to work it out ahead of time. But the need to arrange things was only a part of it. The other part was that we couldn't act with each other the way we could with other people now because we were lovers. Sammy could have told Joe, "That music stinks," and he wouldn't have cared. Or Mavis Conroe could have brought me the record, and I could have told her to turn it off, that it reminded me of Dabney, and she would have. And that would have been that.

But Joe and I had to get hurt about it. Which is part of what you do when you have sex with someone: you care about everything. A point the therapists were missing about the couple on the other side of my wall, who were obviously fighting about the lamp because everything matters between you and the one you're having sex with.

"What I really like," I told him, as if he'd meant it, "is songs about cars." And I read him the words off the back jacket of Springsteen's *Nebraska*, which I'd bought and which I was going to get up my nerve to ask him to play sometime when I stayed over:

I had the carburetor cleaned and checked
With her line blown out she's hummin' like a turbojet
Propped her up in the backyard on concrete blocks
For a new clutch plate and a new set of shocks
Took her down to the carwash check the plugs and points
I'm going out tonight I'm gonna rock that joint.

I told him that Springsteen was one of my favorites because you could always count on him to have songs about cars on his albums.

Joe didn't comment, and I could see that my reading the rock words about going down the highway had broken the spell he was wanting to set up. But I asked him if he really wanted me to say I liked *The Fountains* and *The Pines* when I didn't. And of course, he had to say no, even if it wasn't true. As he did, and looked dejected.

Then I brought us some coffee, and a sixth sense made me say, "You brought something else."

"Nothing." He shoved his pack away. "You want to walk up to your diner?" He was abdicating.

"No. And don't get mad at me. I hate it when you're mad at me. Show me what else you brought."

"Nothing." However, he opened his pack. "Nothing you'd be interested in." He held up a paperback copy of a book entitled *How to Stop Living Alone Though Married*. By Joseph R. Donaldson, Ph.D.

I sat by him on the daybed, looking at it, and thought about how much I liked him. And the reason was that he didn't go off and do it by himself. I didn't just mean jerk off; I meant he didn't go off and have a life by himself. He had brought stuff to show and tell me; he wanted to bring stuff to the other person all the time. The fact that he did that and was willing to take the risk—in this case that I'd say something hateful about his book—made me like him a lot. And I told him so.

The book jacket said that Donaldson was married and lived in New Jersey with his wife and two sons; that he had a private practice and also worked in a phobia clinic in New York City; that he had degrees from Ohio State and NYU. Then it had two quotes from reviews, one that had appeared in *The Journal of Marital and Family Therapy* and one from *Psychology Today*. The first said it was important; the second, that it had something for everyone. The date was 1976. It showed a younger Joe, heavier, with much bushier hair, no mustache, a checked shirt and bow tie. The same sad face.

"By the time it was published I was living alone and getting divorced. That's typical, I guess."

"Probably."

"The illiterate title was theirs." He was defensive.

The table of contents, which we read together, said:

How to Stay in Touch Like Family Members
How to Stay in Touch Like Colleagues
How to Stay in Touch Like Friends
How to Stay in Touch Like Lovers

The introduction explained that we all have skills at keeping in close contact with people throughout most of our lives, skills we don't use, however, in our marriages, believing them unnecessary. And that this book was going to show us how to use the skills we already have to stay as close to our mates as we do to our families and friends.

"What does the R. stand for?"

"Richard. Actually it's Joe not Joseph. Joe Richard, for two grandfathers."

"This is wonderful," I said, and saw that on the title page he'd written:

To Lutie from Joe
I hope the night we met turns out to be
the night we met.

I kissed him, and he went on explaining. "I modeled the whole thing, case histories, everything, on what Carole did with her mother. I mean, we could be in bed making love or on a plane or asleep, and she was mentally writing her mother or getting ready to phone or making a note about something to get her mother for her birthday. It was incredible. And I got the idea that if her mother could keep her that attached, well, the same tricks could be applied by the rest of us to keep close to our spouses. The trouble was,

I told Carole that: that I'd based it all on her happy marriage to her mother. My mistake."

"What did she do?"

"Kicked me out."

"That must have been what you wanted?"

"It must have."

He didn't look unhappy about it. "It sold twenty-one thousand in hardback. If you can believe that."

"That's wonderful," I said.

It made me want to cry, to think of how out of control he had been at home and then how he'd turned it into something constructive to share instead of turning it all inside on himself.

After we'd made love and he wasn't mad anymore, he told me about his parents. "My dad," he said, "ran a barbershop. Talk about putting yourself at the mercy of other men's wallets. If things get tight, people wait an extra two weeks. They trim the edges at home. They don't tip. He'd grown stoic about that through the years. Then along came the one single event that he could never in a million years have guessed. Men let their hair grow long. 'Even hobos,' he'd holler, 'used to cut their hair before they came to town to panhandle. Hippies, queers, psychos.' He'd call them names, but that didn't change the facts. Nobody but bankers got their hair cut anymore. Dad nearly starved.

"Mom let rooms. Not that she ever called it that. First it was a cousin who wanted to know if she could board her daughter with my mom, in a nice, safe family home, while she went to Ohio State. Mom could tell people, 'My cousin's daughter is staying for the year.' And that saved face. Then the cousin had a friend, and in a couple of years Mom was renting out the two rooms upstairs that had been mine and my brother's; that was so they could keep the house they owned a mortgage on, particularly a fan-shaped rose trellis in the front yard." He looked sort of embarrassed. "If you can figure that."

"I know a lot about what women will do to keep houses," I told him, feeling very close. We didn't come from such different places after all.

10

L U T I E had found she loved her teaching and returned exuberantly happy from each and every class. It might be that she had never truly believed in what she taught before. But now, teaching students who knew her topic better than she did because they came to it instinctively, the classes of dancers and actors who listened so trustfully and earnestly to what they already knew down to the tips of their toes, she couldn't help but believe it also.

The social sciences building at SUNY looked very much like a high school science wing, with slick gray floors, pale gray walls, rat gray trim, and vacant labs. There was an empty room labeled "Natural History Museum," a door marked "Faculty Lounge," which was always locked, an applied anthropology lab with a few Indian relics, and a dozen classrooms. The sociology department titrated quietly in one wing of the gray building (like its related fields, still available for old times' sake), stirring no excitement whatsoever even with courses provocatively labeled "Alienation," "Deviance," "Poverty & Crime." Making no waves on a campus which already knew itself to be an evolving organism, assigning its members parts as needed. Lutie would arrive early, leave her notes in her office, and then walk a long hall to a chrome bench which abutted a floor-to-ceiling window. The bench was never used, was doubtless placed there to keep students from leaning on the glass or crashing into it. She would sit there and have a cup of coffee from her thermos and look out on the back-yard of the campus. Facing down on grass, great oaks with yellow leaves, small trees like tiny willows, and, beyond the parking lot and a gully of maples, the backs of West-chester mansions. There was seldom more than one student hurrying across the back lot. Yesterday it had been a Chinese girl with an artist's pad, in red plastic sandals, orange socks, a black sweater, and an ankle-length green skirt. She'd watched the student cross an old stone wall that edged the side of the parking lot to the east.

Then she would go to the bathroom, brush her hair and wash her hands, and proceed to the large room where she taught a small class Intro Soc. The room had thirty green and black fixed chairs, a light switch which instructed

TURN OFF

SAVE A WATT

and the last hour's notes on the blackboard, these for a class called Power and Poverty. (Lutie always erased her own notes from the board after every class, so that the one after hers—Dr. Birdsong's Visual Soc, which was primarily concerned with sexism in advertising—would find it clean.) Yesterday the previous hour's professor had written in green chalk:

Identify pressure systems
Find contesting groups
Define nature

Lutie wondered if the class knew what this was all about.

Between her classes, which were both on Tuesdays and Fridays, Lutie went to the student cafeteria. At first she hadn't liked the place at all because she wanted it to be like the Holiday House hamburger stands at home and because you had to pay for what you wanted before you went inside. At first to make a selection before you saw it had seemed impossible. But now she had her own favorite, which consisted of a bagel that was fresh and huge and chewy and cream cheese that almost melted in your mouth it was so fluffy and fresh and homemade, and not at all like Philadelphia brand, and all the butter you could spoon on it, which you could get free from a tub by the potted flowers. And she could get that, and a large coffee, for $1.31, as she did every day she was on campus, ignoring whatever specials were tacked up: Vegetarian Crêpe, $1.40, Fishwich, $1.40, Columbo Yogurt, .80, things like that.

There she would sit and eavesdrop until it was time to get ready for her other class, which was called Society and Personal Identity, but was also an intro, under another name.

Teaching sociology at SUNY was carrying coals to Newcastle. It was as if she twice weekly told a dance ensemble that they were a dance ensemble, a cast in a play that they were a cast in a play—so obvious to them was her discussion of the convention of the individual. Any one of them could have danced a number of roles, and did, and anyone could have played a variety of parts, and did (so that she could not be sure from one class to the next if she had the same students she'd had the class before); her theory was their practice, as they sat benignly flexing their calf muscles, agreeably agreeing with her words before she ever uttered them.

Yesterday a boy with a punk haircut dyed orange and a leather jacket (who, last week, was the boy in the toga with the Jesus hair) told a girl in leotards, leg warmers, and what appeared to be a bedspread (who was last week's Lady Macbeth), "We're using Mirror." And she, half closing her eyes the better to get the idea, had asked, "You mean like Image?"

It had been very different teaching at Texas. There, when she traced the thrust of the idea central to the discipline, what is really meant by what we call "I"—going quickly through such versions as Auguste Comte on the illusion of the separate ego, Herbert Spencer's proposal of society as an organism, George Herbert Mead saying that the "self" was a "role" we play—she'd got instant argument from all her students, most of whom were psych majors having to take something outside their own field, psych majors who thought she was totally nuts and who would argue with her long after the bell had rung, citing explicit sources (if they were girls), saying she didn't fucking know what she was talking about (if they were boys).

There she had been careful not to inundate her beginners with too much theory, careful not to take up too much time presenting the inside fights about structuralism, functionalism, interactionism, emergent evolutionism, all that which was of interest only within the discipline. Instead, she'd concentrated in the intro classes on the basic areas of study in the field: community; authority; status; the sacred; alienation. Then, taking each topic in turn, in class and in the outside readings, she would get them to see each area in sociology's context: that we take the view of others toward us to be ourselves and that we take this projected self as real when we act toward others.

In her women's courses, she'd gone on from there to focus on how the fact of being female changed the way you perceived the concepts and realities of family, status, authority, ritual, and powerlessness. As background against which to set this, and because she enjoyed it, she drew on her dissertation work on Mother Right (*Das Mutterrecht*), using the Iroquois of Lewis Henry Morgan and the Lycians of Bachofen to study the practice of matrilineal descent observed throughout prehistory, extending it as it could still be observed in the American South, and exploring the results of its conclusion that only those who came from a common womb were kin.

But that was at Texas; here it was a different world that reflected back her words.

It would be good to share this adventure with Mavis, a friend in the same field who could understand the shift in perspective that a new place brings.

II

M A V I S stopped by for her on Saturday, getting off the Taconic, which she'd taken down from Vassar, planning to get them right back on it to head for Long Island. "The smallest detour," she said. She looked around, delighted with Lutie's apartment. "You've done marvels. I can't believe it. It looks as if you've been here forever. How on earth, in such a tiny place—it looks like a Manhattan efficiency. Where did you get the Roman ruin?"

"I had it blown up from a picture I got in Rome. The one good thing from that trip. This place reminds me of there, Cranberry Park."

"And that?" Mavis pointed to the light fixture Lutie had hung over her daybed-work area; it was a plastic copy of a sixty-watt bulb, two feet long. Lutie liked it because somehow it looked at home with the wicker and ferns, as if the whole room had gone back to the days of the dangling, exposed bulb.

"I got it," she explained, "at a going-out-of-business sale at a light fixture shop in White Plains. The man said that the landlord had tripled the rent when the lease came up for renewal, and he was terribly upset, so he had to move and was hoping to find a place in a mall somewhere."

Mavis laughed. "You know their life stories, don't you? Have you always been such a closet friendly? I don't remember that from Texas."

Lutie felt reprimanded, much the same way she had after the Vassar interview or with Danya and Fudge's lists the first time in group. She didn't know what she did wrong; all she wanted was to do what was expected. Wasn't it all right to talk to shop people? She was alone quite a lot; perhaps she needed other people too much when she did go out? But that couldn't be it because Mavis lived alone and had as long as Lutie had known her.

She'd bought two pounds of Cheddar from her butcher, the one who had a daughter in college. He was proud that Lutie was a teacher and would always holler out, "Here comes the professor," when she stopped in to get her fresh chickens and pork chops. She had asked him what would be the best kind of cheese to take for a weekend gift, and he'd picked out the Cheddar for her. She had told him that at home that's what you did as a houseguest, took along something to eat that would keep and then expected to buy something there, a specialty of the place; for example, at the beach at Port Aransas it would be two pounds of Gulf shrimp from the day's catch. He had understood that. "Nobody wants to cook anymore," he'd said. "Take this. Where you going?" When she'd said the Hamptons, he'd sniffed and pretended to grab the package back. "Take money," he said, and laughed, and he and the other butchers had talked back and forth.

She'd planned to tell that story to Mavis because it was funny, but now she decided not to. Talking to your butcher, even if he did have a daughter in college, might not be all right.

She thought she'd at least done right about her clothes this time, dressing down, the way Sammy said New Yorkers did when they weren't working: worn her oldest jeans, with her best pink cotton shirt (several years old, but a Pierre Cardin) and an ancient white poplin windbreaker, and her hair pinned back with barrettes. Since Mavis had come in painter's pants with a brown turtleneck sweater and a heavy brown belt with a lion's head buckle (which meant it must be Anne Klein, but it was rolled like a Coach), she felt reassured. And her Adidas fit in, she decided, with Mavis's loafers.

She wanted very much not to do the wrong thing with Mavis, because she admired her and their friendship went way back, before Mavis was on her dissertation committee, when both were around the department at Texas.

Mavis was one of those women with broad shoulders and thick waist, narrow hips, and very thin legs, the kind who wear large jewelry and streak their hair and look the same for years and years. She was maybe ten years older than Lutie, not much more, and you couldn't tell except for the wrinkles in her neck, which didn't show with the turtleneck. Dabney had said she looked like a horse, but he was never complimentary. Still, something about her seemed to keep men at a distance.

Lutie had brought along, besides the Cheddar, a six-pack of diet Dr Pepper, deciding that Mavis would be having alcohol and that you couldn't count on places to have iced tea or coffee that wasn't too strong and bitter to drink.

Driving down in Mavis's Honda (which still had a new car smell and a lightweight feel to it, although it was the larger model), Lutie did most of the listening—trying to take her cues from what Mavis talked about and what she didn't.

Mavis explained that she had applied for a Radcliffe fellowship to do a biography, or rather a scholarly reconstruction, of Mozart's sister and had not got it. "It's impossible to second-guess these days what politics go on in things like this. I mean, maybe they got three hundred applications for biographies, but maybe they didn't. Still, I thought the feminist nature of it—I mean, who even knows that Mozart had a sister, much less that they played piano duets together?—would be right up their alley."

"Did they tell you anything?"

"Off the record, very off the record. Someone I know at Harvard, not connected, dropped the remark that I should have titled it *Mozart's Brother*, meaning, naturally, that I should have called *her* Mozart and not identified her through *him*. It defeated the whole point, I thought. Well, I'll try again. Next year maybe. The hard thing is going through the hassle of getting people to write for you."

At the end of two hours and a half they had driven most of the length of Long Island and were almost to Westhampton. The approach to the shore was a total surprise to Lutie, who had been waiting for the causeway and then for the smell of salt and fish, and the taste of both on your tongue, and the way the sticky air clings to your skin and hair so that you know you are near the beach when you are still twenty miles from it, and the way your glasses get fogged over with gritty film and you have to clean them every two miles.

This was completely different. Only a few miles from the ocean, there were still hardwoods—no salt cedar, no palms—and shrubs and grass, none of the stretches of bare ground and sand she expected, none of the pulverized seashells that at Port Aransas made a crunch under your car tires and tore at your bare feet. Here there was not a sign of water at all. Lutie hoped that this was deceptive, that just out of sight, rocky cliffs rose above a mighty pounding sea, with lighthouses and spray dashing into the air, the way you saw it in pictures.

Mavis laughed. "We'll go look at the beach tomorrow if you're all that set. There's nothing to see, believe me."

At their destination Mavis retrieved a key from a small magnetic box stuck inside her friend's mailbox and let them into an apartment similar to the beach condos at home: bedrooms and bath upstairs, modern kitchen, small dining area, conspicuous bar, a lot of bamboo and glass and plastic plants that required no care.

Mavis gestured toward the refrigerator, decorated with yellow daisy magnets, for Lutie to put her cheese and Dr Peppers, poured herself a glass of gin from a bottle over the toaster, and headed for the living room. On the kitchen floor was a box of Milkbone, a sack of Ken-L ration, and a plastic jar of canine vitamins. Lutie perked up. She could use a big dog. She'd missed Cecelie a lot lately. "What kind of dog?" she called.

"You'd probably know its name and have it licking out of your hand by now. There is one, and I have no idea what kind. He's huge and sheds and stinks and eats shoes, and she sleeps with him; that's all I know. Except that when she's not here, he's gone with her."

Mavis turned on the color TV when Lutie came in, then turned it off, set her drink down on a glass shelf secured with yellow brackets, and said, "Let's go to town before things close. You can get the life story of the checker at Gristede's."

They walked the four blocks to a small-town street, with old buildings which housed contemporary stores. Lutie counted six real estate offices, three houseware shops, three clothing shops, three baby stores, one art gallery, and more eating places than she could believe. There were windows of elegant French cooking vessels and wicker bathroom shelves and leather lounge chairs and towel sets in ivory and rose—a marvel of goods. So many things to buy; it made her think of Aunt Caroline and Savannah, and helped her get her bearings. Westhampton was the South.

They stopped to read a menu board in the yard of an old frame house called Main Street Café: prosciutto and melon, $4.95, linguine with garlic sauce, $10.95, coconut batter-fried shrimp, $13.95. Lutie suggested they have supper there (computing what it would cost, which was always roughly twice what the entrée said), but her friend waved that suggestion away. "Let's see what Gristede's has," she said. "I don't feel like being public. We can put our feet up at home. I look a mess."

They passed a pasta store with strips of still-soft noodles and spaghetti drying in the windows like yard bolts or strips of wool awaiting the loom. They were off white and green—very lovely and made her think of Joe. The next store displayed racks and racks of huge steel trays covered with David's Cookies. Lutie pulled Mavis to a stop. "I'll get some for a midnight snack." She knew that Mavis had a sweet tooth.

"I shouldn't—"

"This is a holiday."

"Get an assortment then. I can never decide." Mavis waited on the sidewalk, having a cigarette.

"Are you David?" Lutie asked the man behind the counter.

"This is a franchise. What'll you have?"

"Who is David?" She didn't mind asking, even if it was out of line to be curious, because Mavis was outside and so couldn't hear her.

"Some guy who used to make them, who didn't get a nickel off them, is what I heard. So what'll you have?"

"I'll take"—she calculated what would seem generous but not foolish—"three dozen, mixed. Do they all have chocolate?"

"These are the best," he said, putting in a layer of something dark and fudgy-looking, like chocolate chips only with the cookie made of chocolate and the chips of batter.

"Make it a dozen of those then." Lutie liked to let people sell her what they wanted to; otherwise, if you were a clerk, you would have no control over what you did all day.

"Here you go," he said. He was young and attractive and had a lot of black, curly hair.

"What's your nationality?" she asked, to show that she knew what to say.

"What're you, some kinda wiseass?"

"I'm . . . from Texas."

"That gives you license to insult?"

"I—thank you." She paid him and took her bow-tied box of cookies.

Mavis was gazing in the window of an antiques store called Oldies But Goldies. She looked as if she had sagged a little while she waited. "Did you get his mother's name?" she asked, but gently, smiling at Lutie.

In Gristede's they got salami and prosciutto (which looked like strips of raw slab bacon) and some cheeses, and two loaves of a special dark bread, and some tortellini salad in a vinaigrette dressing with olives and mushrooms that was $5.95 a pound, and Lutie wondered if this was what Joe's boys were used to eating every night. If so, it was no wonder their mother, who shopped at one of these stores, was going to law school.

Lutie, standing and watching Mavis make her selections, noticed that her friend never looked anyone in the eye or said anything to anyone but "Give me a pound of . . ."— instructions like that. Lutie noticed that both the man at the deli counter and the one at the checkout counter seemed used to it, but when they saw her looking at them, each made a sort of wink.

On the street everyone wore a hat: There was a smart tanned woman in white tennis shorts and a tennis visor going in the Main Street Café; a man in a Texas cowboy hat and boots; another man in a jacket with epaulets and an admiral's hat. Something about them reminded her at first glance of the students at SUNY, always in costume. But then she saw the difference: These people weren't in costume. They were wearing what they really thought they were. Even Mavis, now that she noticed it, had tied her hair up in a gypsy scarf, to keep it from getting wind-blown. She amended: Westhampton was Deep South.

They sat on the couch of Mavis's friend's house with their shoes off, while Mavis smoked and continued her gin and Lutie had two diet Dr Peppers. And then she made herself a big Cheddar and salami sandwich on dark bread and piled some of the expensive tortellini-olive salad on top of that as a garnish. She was ravenous. Something about the trip had been a lot more of a strain than she had expected.

Mavis looked dejected. "This is something, isn't it? Places like this. You know what I think? I think the reason that rich people like this have dumpy, cutesy places like this is that it makes them think they've come home. It's the same tacky-nice that their parents had, and now that they've climbed up the scale and know that you don't have plastic slipcovers and shag rugs and magnetic daisies and color TV, that you have real linen chairs and original acrylics and Bartók on the stereo, and you don't say 'drapes,' and you don't eat out of paper cartons—well, they can just take it so long.

"Then they go bananas, and so they invent weekend places like this, where they can go down-scale and pretend that they're putting all their old, outgrown stuff here because that's a savings, but the truth is that here it's just like Mom and Dad's, complete with fake geraniums which you have to remember to wash off in warm, soapy water, and they love it. They can relax. They don't have to worry if they are middle-class, because you're not middle-class if you have two houses, so there, and what the hell. So they rush down here every chance they get."

"I've never thought about that," Lutie said, having a sudden vision of River Bend.

"A longing for downward mobility hides in the heart of the best of us." Mavis emptied her glass and stared at the sandwich makings from the deli. Finally, she wrapped a piece of ham around a slice of cheese and picked up her train of thought. "Let me tell you about my father," she said. "He had these short arms. My mother used to buy him shirts for Christmas, and she'd tell the salesclerk, 'I want a seventeen, twenty-nine—that's seventeen-inch neck and twenty-nine-inch sleeves. And the clerks would laugh themselves sick, and they'd tell her, 'Nobody built like that but a gorilla, lady. . . . Nobody built like that but a orangu-tan, lady.' And she'd insist, but most of the time they wouldn't even show her where the seventeens were. And then she got so she'd take up his shirt sleeves herself, and they'd have no plackets because of having to be cut off so short, and he couldn't get his hands into the sleeves." Mavis was laughing and laughing, remembering. "I can still see him, hollering and hobbling around with his arms jammed in this Arrow shirt, his hands not getting out. Finally, he said to her, 'Short sleeves will have to do.' And the rest of his life that's what he wore, short sleeve shirts, summer and winter." She wiped her eyes from laughing. "My problem is, I keep looking for some guy with arms like Dad's."

Lutie wanted to say that her friend was lucky to have a memory like that of her father, that Joe had said it was a help to you with men. But she wasn't sure whether she was supposed to talk to Mavis about herself and Joe at all.

Both because Mavis was an acquaintance of his ex-wife's and because she might think Lutie was doing wrong to be involved with her group leader. Or, deeper than that, she was afraid that somehow it might not be all right to talk to the man you were seeing about things like that.

But Mavis didn't appear to notice that Lutie hadn't responded. She was more or less thinking aloud. "I've been in the dumps all fall," she continued. "It wasn't just not getting that fellowship. I knew that was a long shot, and besides, they don't give you as much money as I'm making, and I'd have had to sublet and get a leave of absence, a whole lot of contingencies. The problem was, I quit believing in *Mozart's Sister* myself, you might say." She sighed and looked at her glass. "This was to be my big book; I can't keep on dribbling out articles forever on the changing view of women's traditional roles, that stuff, taking polls of people who could care less about what women are up to as long as they are eating regularly themselves, trying to prove trends or at least say something new. I've dredged up everything I can get my hands on.

"What started it was, I accidentally picked up this biography of Alice James. That was my mistake. Fantastic job, it does, of showing you that she didn't have a chance in her day of being Henry James or William James—who's ever heard of Alice James?—and how that, the discrimination, sent her into a deep decline that she never came out of. But the more I read of it, the more I decided that the depression was because she couldn't *marry* Henry or William, not that she couldn't *be* them. If you have those boys for brothers, who on earth can you find for a husband that could live up to them? That thought came to me, and it wouldn't go away.

"I find myself wondering what that says about me . . . because I know what the feminists would say, and they're right, if I ever put a word of that to paper. It's like the downward mobility I was talking about, just exactly like these rich people coming out to get happy with a plastic dinette set: me thinking about taking his suits to the cleaners and shortening his sleeves until he can't get his hands through the holes."

Mavis started to cry; her cheeks were blotched, and her eyes puffy. Her make-up was smearing, and her mascara streaking.

Lutie didn't know what to say. It was the kind of confession which, if made in her family, would cause Mother or Aunt Caroline to say, "I'm putting out amaryllis and crocus this year." Lutie didn't want to be like that, changing the subject when something real came up, something embarrassing. But she had no other experience to go on. She heard the words *The coast here doesn't smell the way it does in Texas* rise to her mind, her lips, but then she knew it was a reflex from her own kin and put it aside.

"Let's eat the cookies," she said finally, afraid that she had done what she wanted not to after all, but hoping it would be taken as an offer of comfort.

She set out all three dozen David's Cookies on a yellow pottery plate shaped like a flower, and they ate them one at a time, taking turns, making sure that each of them got exactly eighteen.

At the last Mavis was crying and laughing at the same time. Talking, in a disjointed way, saying whatever came to her. "I'm lonesome, that's all. The last guy was married; that's what got to me. The crumb. My daddy never missed a World Series in his life. Now that's dumb, to remember that; what does that prove?" She finished off a cookie with a gooey chocolate center. "What's the point of getting tenure if I still take two weeks out of every summer and go all the way across the country to spend it with my mother? I ask you. What's the use of getting all this education if you still can't shake the idea that you ought to have some bald man with a potbelly who hasn't read a book in fifteen years parked in your living room, and you think you're missing something if you don't? Mother's doing fine. After Dad died, she looked it up and announced that gorillas have long arms and that the clerks were nuts. And she's been happy ever since. If you count going steady with her only daughter as being happy."

They finally went upstairs, to sleep in the twin youth beds provided in the yellow-papered, green-carpeted guest room: Lutie in a sugar daze; Mavis sniffing, falling asleep with her robe on over her painter's pants.

The next morning, Sunday, Lutie made some coffee in the Mr. Coffee II and ate some eggs she found in the refrigerator. She drank a lot of the coffee, and Mavis had a beer and two pieces of dark bread from the night before.

Then they went to the beach.

It was a long walk, because Mavis wasn't sure of the shortcut to the private beach, and when they got to a fork where Hampton Close and Old Meadow Bend divided, they took the wrong turn and walked past a lot of beautiful houses, and went past some pine trees, and arrived, finally, at the public beach. It didn't make a lot of difference in November anyway; there were four people in sight.

On sand as flat as any Texas shore, Lutie watched as the steep drop-off gradually became a shallow water line, where you could walk in your wet shoes along the lapping, ebbing tide. It was cold, but not as bitter as she expected, and there were shells after all, not starfish and sand dollars, as you would find on a Texas beach, or any of the convoluted spiral shells that she expected from the Atlantic, but a lot of unbroken clams and mussels. More interesting were the wealth of perfect polished stones, smooth as glazed almonds, uncovered by each receding wave of the out-going tide.

Lutie wondered if the point about having a weekend place was that you didn't like your other options, wondered if you would want a place to go to if you liked what you were doing where you lived. She thought about the pharmacist at the drugstore where Denise worked; she had heard him tell another man one day about how he'd been at that same pharmacy since he was a boy of two, that his daddy had worked there all his life and had raised him there, that when people would ask, "Are those nose drops too strong?" he'd say, "Come here, son," and demonstrate on the boy. And how he, the pharmacist, still wasn't tired of working there himself, seven days a week. And about the butcher, whom she could imagine home on the week-end, taking a lot of his thickest, best steaks with him and cooking them outside on his grill, the way nobody liked to do anymore. And even her dressmaker, Mrs. Rodino, who had dyed black hair and a tight hair net like Gran, who hoped to look fifty and must have been seventy, even she probably, when she wasn't sewing for her customers, would decide to run up some curtains for a friend or do a slipcover for a garage sale.

"I never saw anybody so busy when there was nothing to do." Mavis was tired of strolling back and forth.

"Am I bothering you, collecting these pebbles?" Lutie asked, afraid that Mavis, like her mother, would say, "You think too much."

"Don't mind me. I'll walk down that way a bit and then come back to you. Then let's call it a weekend, okay?"

Lutie took a last look at the odorless, unconvincing ocean and put her mind to those people for whom weekend places meant a lot. She would write Aunt Caroline about Hampton Close and Old Meadow Bend, with their English names and echo of the South, and Mother about the racks of drying pasta and the trays of David's Cookies and the coconut-dipped, batter-fried shrimp. And the strangeness of the eastern shore.

12

Journal: What Is This Couple Fighting About?

THE weekend I went to Savannah we had a bad fight. Part of it was that we were going to be off in different directions, but some of it was that we'd been having trouble before that. The boys went around being mad at their father, and Joe, who couldn't get mad at them, would snap at me and Sammy, when he was there. And then I would get mad at him for doing that.

That Saturday I'd brought the second chocolate cake from my frost-free freezer to Joe's, since it was our turn to stay at his place, where Fritz and Noah were supposed to have a lot more to do, with the TV and all, and were not supposed to have a lousy time the way they did at my place. But that wasn't how it was; teen-age boys do not have a good time anywhere, period.

Sammy says I shouldn't make generalizations about that, that it's the same as quoting those surveys that speak of the six hundred geniuses in Gundy County, Iowa; there's no such group.

But he's wrong.

As I was dumping the uneaten cake in the trash, I told Fritz, "I could have not bothered to bring this and just bought two dozen David's Cookies."

"What do *you* know about David's Cookies?"

"I ate eighteen one night."

"That's stupid, you know it?" He sounded disgusted.

Sammy looked up. "That on the trip to the Hamptons?"

"It goes with the territory."

"I wouldn't know. Never been."

"Don't bother. You wouldn't be welcome."

Sammy and I had been cleaning up while the boys paced around, arguing over the video games, asking if they could take a walk, collapsing on the floor whenever it looked as if they might actually get permission to do so, asking about movies, asking could they go get something to eat besides the slop here.

"How so?" Sammy perked up.

"Hats," I told him. "They all wore hats."

Fritz said, "You're crazy, nobody wears hats."

"Westhampton does. Admiral's caps, cowboy hats, tennis hats. Bandannas."

Joe jerked up from his half-reclining position in the easy chair. "Jesus, Lutie—"

Sammy nodded. "Good. Right. You have to watch for hair, too."

"Hair?" I wasn't sure about that.

"Sure. Sideburns. Hair spray. Beehives."

Joe got up. "Is all this necessary?"

"Ignoring something doesn't make it go away," I told him. "I don't forget Sammy is black."

"Dr. David doesn't either," Sammy said.

"But the way you two go on and on about it, for some kind of effect, as if it was fifty years ago—" He kept glancing at his boys, and that made me mad. What was the problem? Were they not supposed to notice that Sammy wasn't white? It must be that it was the same way that there were people up here you weren't supposed to talk to, like the butchers or the men who sold you light bulbs. Because you weren't supposed to be aware of certain things.

I knew that Sammy wore his leather flight jacket on the weekends out to my place in the same way he'd worn his elevator uniform that first night at group: in order not to be noticed. That's because a black in uniform lulls you, especially an outfit that implies you've served in the military in your day and so know your place in the hierarchy and won't make trouble. Joe knew all that, too. But maybe he forgot when his boys were there.

I wanted to say something to really drive him nuts, like "If you had somebody in a wheelchair, you'd check for ramps, wouldn't you?" but I didn't. Instead, I pointed out he seemed to have forgotten everything he'd been telling us in group.

"Welcome to the North," Sammy said.

"What I don't understand"—Joe was pacing about, warming up to his irritation—"is the way you don't miss a trick about where Sammy can and can't go, but you have a blind spot as wide as a barn door concerning any other male, your kin included."

"Don't you be jealous," Sammy said in his put-on voice that drove Joe wild. "White mens is a figment in the South."

"You can say that," Joe snapped, not turning to look in my direction.

Last week he'd gone through my snapshot album, asking who I was going to see in Savannah. I'd showed him the pictures from Bubba's wedding, which were the most recent I had of all of us; there were two each of Nan and

Aunt Caroline, and Mother and me, and several of them, the sisters, together, and a couple of good ones of the four of us, and one of us with Mary Michael, the bride, who really didn't look as if she were comfortable in the middle of the family.

By that time Joe was shouting all over my Roman living room, "Which of you is the groom?" and "These must be the parents of the bride?"—waving a snapshot of Mother and Aunt Caroline.

"I don't see what you're so mad about."

"A wedding where there's no sign of the groom? It could be that's threatening to me. Not unreasonably so, would you say?"

"Bubba?" I couldn't answer. The truth was I didn't even remember having seen him there.

It made me mad for Joe to be mad so much lately. I had been trying to talk in his language, to swallow my view of teen-age boys as a molting herd of jowly alley cats, telling him that Fritz and Noah were singular and troubled boys, whose problems were unique to them. When Fritz decided to refuse to take the PSAT on the ground that it was a culturally biased test, it was Joe who told him that college was a culturally biased test, for God's sake, that *life* was; I who said he must be insecure.

I was letting Joe cook at my place every time he came— boil the water for his pasta, heat the oil, stir in the egg and pepper—make himself at home in my wonderful kitchen.

When he brought me a cassette of Chuck Berry's "Mabelline," I copied the words out and pinned them up. And when he found me twelve identical postcards of a 1938 tan Packard convertible, I taped them all around the bathroom mirror.

I started buying different kinds of beer from a wholesale bottle-drink store in White Plains, getting two new brands each time, letting him try them all, making him have a preference and rank last week's favorite against this week's whenever he came.

And I wrote out for him with my Mont Blanc pen on my blue Crane's paper a funny quote for him to put over his desk that I'd found in a paperback on how to write term papers: "You might also make a list of transitional phrases, such as *moreover, however, meanwhile, nevertheless,* and *on the other hand,* and keep them handy."

He put it by the Reader-Gram he'd got in the mail from a collection agency threatening him with a lawsuit for non-payment of his bill. It seemed that Carole had sent him a year's subscription to *Psychology Today,* which had been coming for months and which infuriated him—that she could know so little about what he did as to send that and that she'd sent him the bill. It turned out she was sorry; she'd absent-mindedly, she said, filled out a discount ad that came across her desk and had since thrown the address of the distributor out.

The printout scolded:

Dear JOE DONALDSON

Quite frankly we're unhappy with what's happening to our relationship. You've been enjoying PSYCHOLOGY TODAY *for weeks now,* JOE DONALDSON, *and you still have not paid the $8.47 you owe us since we declared "clean slate day."*

That's not fair on your part, JOE DONALDSON. *We've offered to wipe your record clean and wait another whole month for payment. You haven't played fair.*

We can't wait any longer. We told PYSCHOLOGY TODAY *to stop your magazine because you didn't pay. That won't do your credit rating any good with us or them.*

"Clean Slate Day" in NEW YORK CITY *is over—the* DONALDSON *record is not wiped clean.*

We had grown tender with one another; serious but cautious. He quoted Bettelheim to me: "Love is not enough," I quoted Christopher Fry to him: "I love you, but the world's not changed."

But then, as soon as the boys were gone—a convoluted business, in which I spent Friday night, and then they arrived after we were up and dressed, and I rode the train home alone on Saturday, *or* they had Friday night and left late Saturday as they had at Cranberry Lake, and we had our night alone, Saturday—it began to get bad. It got so that whenever we were together, the smallest thing became a quarrel, and I began to wonder if it was all already over with us, something that we had done that would slide right out of our minds when we each went back to where we came from. Mrs. Rodino, the dressmaker, was in a depression because they were taking "Texas" off the air; I began to wonder if we, like the soap, were being canceled in December.

By this weekend I had had too much of all that, and I said right up in his face, despite the audience, "What is this couple fighting about?"

He laughed a little at that and seemed to defuse, slightly.

"You're stupid, you know it?" Fritz said to us, but he flung himself down in one of the upholstered chairs and watched us with interest.

Noah, hobbling from a recent bicycle accident, in a soft, shaggy T-shirt that hung almost to the knees of his bony frame, made a quick smile, picked up an empty drink glass, and pressed it against Joe's back, leaning his ear in close as if eavesdropping.

Joe looked at them and got hold of himself. "Smart alecks," he said, but in a pleased way.

(He really was serious about doing a book called *What Is This Couple Fighting About?*, with a picture on the cover of a woman sitting and a man standing and them obviously deep at it. It was to be a sort of Rorschach, a

Donaldson, he said, in which how you interpreted what you perceived told the therapist, or yourself when you bought a paperback copy in the drugstore and took the quiz at the back, where you were in your life.

(He'd made tapes of Pete and Shirley, as he called my other-side-of-the-wall neighbors, where you couldn't distinguish the words at all; you could hear only the tone of voice, the rise and fall of who was shouting, who was accusing whom, the general pattern of who did the grilling, who was on the defensive, who had brought the fight into existence.

(In the actual fights the lamp was still the major topic, but a new coffee table had entered the picture. Joe had a theory about that, too, that ninety-six percent of all fights were *living room,* as he called it. "It's going to revolutionize our concept of strife. Maybe people never did fight about sex and money: maybe that's an old wives' tale. Maybe it's been living room all along."

(He'd got in touch with the editor who'd worked with him on *How to Stop Living Alone Though Married* and explained the idea to her and got a lot of positive response. Enough to get him on the project in earnest. After he finished whatever articles he and Sammy were going to get out of our Image group, he'd get on it seriously. Six years without a book was too long.)

But I hadn't really been kidding. I was tired of our being cross with one another, tired of having to go to bed behind the boys' backs, of having to save everything until we were alone and so ruin what had been our good time. "What," I asked him, "is eating you?"

He sat back down. "I'm going to stay at Carole's over Thanksgiving. I have to. She's got to study for her first round of exams; she needs someone to help out." He looked defensive.

"Big deal." Fritz got up and went to the bathroom.

Noah blew his nose on the end of his baggy shirt.

"She's manipulating you," I said, out of reflex.

"It's only for the long weekend—"

"She's definitely right," Sammy said, disappearing into the kitchen to make coffee. "The lamp looks tacky in the window."

"What the hell," Joe shouted at me, "you'll be down South with Auntie anyway."

Three

13

THE cabdriver talked them in from the airport in a running monologue. "This booger supposed to be the fast lane. If this is the fast lane, we're in bad trouble."

She had brought Aunt Caroline and Mary Michael each a half pound box of Belgian chocolates, from Neiman's, as hostess presents. The bustling, tiny lady in Candies had confided that she didn't want Godiva anymore, that the rumor was Campbell's Soup had bought Godiva, but that the Belgian were delicious. She gave her a hazelnut and dark cream to sample, and they were, and the box, in a deep bronze and faded gold, was lovely in itself, something you could set out in Savannah when company came.

(The lady from Candies had sent her a handwritten note the next day:

Dear Miss Sayre,
It was a pleasure to serve you.
Enclosed are the receipts for the chocolates. I took care not to mix up your cards.
Yours sincerely,)

She had brought to show Aunt Caroline the most recent weekly letter from her mother. Enclosed with it was a clipping from the San Antonio paper about the head of the Newell Recycling Company, or rather its owner—a man who was marketing a giant shredder that he'd invented which could reduce an automobile to bits and pieces in only sixty seconds. It showed a photo of a Volvo going into a crunching, jawlike machine whose fourteen hammers smashed it into pieces and spit them out on a conveyor belt. The machine sold for one million; Mr. Newell, the inventor, distributor, and owner, had sold twenty already this year.

Her mother and other officials had got to meet Mr. Newell. He was a big name now and very rich. At the cocktail party for him in San Antonio he told her and the vice-president anecdotes about his boyhood in an Oklahoma cotton patch: "Practically all problems in America today are self-inflicted. This country would be better off if it had more people like me." Shortly after that he'd been invited to go to Washington to meet the president, and The University was now considering him for its commencement speaker.

. . . I wore my navy suit, the dressy one, with a new gray blouse. We had a grand time. All of San Antonio put on a party for Mr. Newell and for us. The V-P and I and some friends drove straight from UT to the party. I took along an extra pair of scanty hose; the Argyle Club is no place to get a run.

Lutie had had nightmares about the machine that ate cars, but it seemed something that Aunt Caroline would enjoy.

In the cab she could smell the pine trees in the warm air, and at the same instant all of Savannah and the South came back to her. The sweet gum with its prickly balls and empty locust shells clinging to its bark. The acres of young white sacrificial pine being fattened for the mill. The way the wind shifted and the sickening, stinging odor of the mills was in your nostrils, paper pulp, mistakable for no other smell, and then the way it shifted again, disappearing, and you could see the acres of trailer parks where the squatters who worked the mills lived, and the thousands of retired poor who had come to find the sun.

"Trailer spots rent out at fifty dollars a month," the cabby continued. "Man who runs that place there, Nassau Woods, that's his name, must have three hundred spots. That makes him a rich man, don't it? Even with water, garbage, and taxes, you can figure he's clearing nearly any-body's yearly salary every month of the year with those mobile homes."

"That's a lot." Lutie was friendly to the old white driver, who she decided was having trouble with failing vision.

"That paper mill there is the largest in the world. They employ eight thousand; it's a city in itself out here. Ships carry those paper bags all the way to Europe, coming down our river, they do," he said, a private chamber of commerce, weaving in and out of the airport traffic.

His was a singsong voice Lutie had forgotten. So thick with generations of cotton and levees and tugboats and night crawlers; so full of gleaned information concerning where we were, to the dime and to the minute. She felt a sense of familiarity engulf her. They say the South is slow, but it is slow like ten tons of river washing down on you.

"Where you from, honey?"

"Texas."

"Sun Belt is the place these days."

"My aunt lives here. I'm just visiting."

"Lots of folks say that." He grinned in the rear-view mirror.

"And yourself?" She smiled back at him.

Savannah was a city that she and her mother had visited for as long as Aunt Caroline had lived there; just as Aunt

Caroline and Nan had come to River Bend in the summers, so they had gone to Savannah for Christmas, for the candle-lit services at Uncle Elbert's church, and congregational dinners, and eggnog parties at the homes of friends.

Savannah was a city that Aunt Caroline identified with. Founded as the last and poorest of the original thirteen colonies, it had begun as a miserable place with unpaved streets and vagrants, used first as a buffer zone to protect Carolina from the Spaniards in Florida and later as a buffer to protect the South during the Civil War from entrance by the sea. It had had a brief and glorious cotton boom, paved its streets with the ballast stones of British ships, put on airs; but then, when the price of slaves increased from $600 to $1,600 each and the going rate for cotton fell from 40 cents a pound to 11 cents, it had declined once more. Too poor to build the Victorian homes that flourished on the rest of the eastern seaboard, it lay forgotten for generations. Then historical foundations discovered its priceless treasures of untouched Georgian architecture (Georgian from the king, not the state), and it became, late in its life, the belle of the South.

Aunt Caroline's exodus from The Manse was having something of the same effect. Two of the parishioners from Grace Church, the Rutledge sisters, Ladye and Faith, had given Aunt Caroline the bottom half of an historic house in a newly restored part of downtown. Just recently a few of the old houses from the early nineteenth century, once "cottages belonging to free persons of color," had been renovated and made available. These were small two-story places, with what had been the family's part of the house on the second floor and the old service quarters on the ground level. (That was how you could tell the older homes: You entered through a raised stoop, which went back to the days of muddy streets.)

Aunt Caroline apologized for making Lutie take a cab;

she wasn't sure how to get to the airport herself, since she didn't really drive anymore. Elbert had used to do that, and now she counted on Bubba. He and Mickey, she said, had offered to pick Lutie up, but Aunt Caroline had wanted to have Wednesday night with just the two of them, to catch up. Tomorrow they'd be at Mickey's, and Nan and Sister would call; but tonight they would have supper, just the two of them, like old times, at the 17Hundred90 restaurant.

As Lutie freshened up in the ornately papered guest bath, Aunt Caroline put her things on one of the twin beds in her room. "I want to get a real visit before we get caught up with the others. I could have put you in Nan's little bedroom; but really, mine is nicer, and we can talk like schoolgirls."

Outside was cool and had that soft yellow evening light peculiar to southern cities, filtered by trees older even than the reconstructed slave quarters where they strolled for supper. Aunt Caroline now lived in the middle of a newly refurbished area, part of narrow, museum-quality streets, lovely Georgian houses with walled gardens, old sweet gums, white picket fences, and a mantle of history. It was six blocks, up East State Street, across a small park, to the restaurant, and Aunt Caroline was pleased that her new home placed her in such an historic neighborhood. It made it possible, she explained to Lutie, to invite friends for dinner, the Rutledge sisters, say, and then have a leisurely walk back to her cottage for dessert.

The 17Hundred90, built in that year, occupied the ground floor of a large three-story home, now a small hotel. They entered on the street level and were seated in the main dining room, near what was once the cooking fireplace and now had a gas jet.

"Good evening, Mrs. McCall," the owner said at the door.

The walls were the original brick, the floors worn stone,

the tiny windows shuttered in white; each table was set with a pink cloth and centered with a bouquet of garden blooms. Teardrop chandeliers hung from the low, heavy beams of the old dropped ceiling.

Aunt Caroline had worn a peach wool dress with a shawl jacket, fringed and soft as challis, pinned at the shoulder with a brooch that had once belonged to Gran: a narrow gold bar with two blue stones and a small diamond. Her hair was waved and unobtrusively tinted like Mother's (what Nan called their Princess Grace hair). Her blue-white hands were freshly creamed, the nails lightly polished. In all, she was a less handsome, softer version of Mother, yet clearly a sister.

Aunt Caroline told Lutie about her intention of buying one of the teardrop chandeliers for her own place. She'd asked the manager, and he'd told her where to find them and how much they were. "Such perfect copies," she said, "not real prisms, of course, and I wouldn't pretend so, but only two hundred seventy-five dollars and ninety-one cents if you get it wholesale." She admired the one above them. "What do you think? My dining space is so tiny. One day I hope to have sliding wood doors to set it off; I've seen those in the older homes."

"Will you be having wine, Mrs. McCall?" The waiter was at her elbow.

"Shall we, Lutie? I should think we should, after your trip. Yes, please, white wine, house wine will do fine, for each of us then." Aunt Caroline had allowed herself to forget that Lutie did not drink and so in this way ordered herself two glasses, something she could never do straight out.

"How about an appetizer? What would you like, Lutie?"

"Nothing, thank you."

"The mussels? They're delicious this time of year. Steamed?"

"No, really." Lutie, disoriented, found herself slow to respond in the proper way. It was hard, when you'd been away, to recall that most of what was said in the South wasn't said. She should have demurred. Provided a small discussion. Something on the order of "At home it's oysters, and in New York it's clams. I should try the mussels, yet they're all so filling. Still, it would be a shame to pass them up. But perhaps next time . . ." A far more gracious way to decline than she had managed.

"We'll not have appetizers then," Aunt Caroline told the waiter, and they listened as he recited the day's menu.

They would have the terrapin soup, of course, it was a specialty. And the limestone lettuce with house dressing, the buttermilk. Aunt Caroline chose the grouper, the catch of the day, to show that she was local and familiar with the customs. Lutie tried to slow her pace, debating aloud between the red snapper with capers and the chicken tarragon. Both sounded good; perhaps her aunt should decide.

"Snapper, I'd think, dear, wouldn't you? Chicken, well—"

They would have the spoon bread, which came with everything, that fine soft-centered cornmeal equivalent of Yorkshire pudding. And perhaps wait to select a dessert. The raspberry cream sounded grand, but there were the flaming mincemeat tarts. They could be splendid but were very rich. They would see how they felt.

It was a quiet, pleasant place. Aunt Caroline had found it some years before her uprooting; not belonging to the old supper clubs, she had wanted a place both elegant and cozy that was not on every tourist's list.

Now, soothed by the good service, she told Lutie what a fine two years it had been. "It all happened like a miracle. I remember that I was feeling down at the time; I had been passed over for Chatham, Elbert having died the very week invitations went out, and it seemed the last straw, the dreadful timing. I had worked so hard to become a part of our little community, to make the Savannah branch of the Sayres amount to something. You have no idea. Texas isn't the same at all, as Florence could tell you. Here, if you're not *from* here, you're not here. That's the plain and simple of it. I could point out until I was blue in the face that we came over a hundred years—*one hundred years*—before they did, and I might as well be telling that my papa sold piece goods, for all they care.

"But then, after your uncle's death, it turned around. The Rutledge sisters, whom you know, Ladye and Faith, who have always been the largest givers at Grace Church, became very solicitous of my welfare, feeling that it was the church's obligation to look after me, and it wasn't just that I got my darling cottage, as they call it, rent-free, that could be expected—after all Elbert's years there and the three-fourths full retirement he was entitled to. It was all the little intangible things: being asked out to their place on the Isle of Hope, going along on house parties to Tybee, being included in their card parties. It was almost as if they made a pet of me." Aunt Caroline laughed. "I'm their project. That's it, pure and simple.

"I thought that if your father hadn't been in Oglethorpe and you weren't in Madeira, and certainly I have no hopes of the Married Women's Card Club, as even three-generational Savannahians don't make that, then you had to accept that you were a newcomer the rest of your life. But I don't feel that anymore. It sounds foolish, Lutie, but I feel like a debutante at sixty-three."

Lutie congratulated her and complimented the snapper, which was so tender.

"Did you know"—Aunt Caroline lowered her voice and finished the first glass of wine—"that they've put Mickey up for the Junior League?"

Lutie smiled to indicate that was good news. Forgetting

herself, feeling she had missed a cue somewhere, she asked, "Weren't you calling her Mary Michael, Aunt Caroline?"

"Was I?" Her aunt frowned warningly. "I don't recall that. That must have been a nickname of Bubba's. I can't keep it straight; she calls him Junior until I find myself doing it, and if he's not calling her Mickey, then he's calling her Mick." She turned her attention to the flaky grouper and the advantages of ordering the catch of the day.

After the smallest pause Aunt Caroline continued on the new topic. "Frankly I was surprised at first. But it seems her family, the Dennys, have been active in First Presbyterian and a lot of people know them. Mickey is an old family name. I don't know if I told you? Her father's name is Mickey; imagine, it's a tradition, handed down in every generation to the first-born, boy or girl. Originally it was an Irish name, although they've been here too long to be considered Irish, if you know what I mean. That's a peculiar Savannah custom; I know of women named Peter and James and Will. It takes some getting used to, but on the other hand, it has something to say for it. The family doesn't have to wait around for a boy. Mickey and Bubba have promised to let me name their first Sayre, whichever it is, which you know is a sweet gesture to me. Isn't that dear? Besides, her sister already has a Mickey."

The last time they had eaten in the 17Hundred90, just the two of them, was before Uncle Elbert died, when Lutie had come to see her aunt alone, to get a rest and recover from a brief, unpleasant hospital stay.

At that time their conversation had been full of Aunt Caroline's hopes of being invited to join Chatham, the only newly formed supper club in the city which carried the prestige of the older clubs. "The idea is to take couples," she had told the recently divorced Lutie. "I don't mean to step on your toes, dear, but I am only saying how it is with this particular group and their policy, this group of old friends who like to meet for supper. The Chatham Club. Naturally, I'm sure, if a couple were to be invited and the husband died, then the wife would still be included; that would be only right. But the idea is not to get into the confusion of divorce. Now don't take offense."

As usual, Aunt Caroline had not come right out and said that she was lobbying to get into this coveted and possible group; rather she and her niece had had a long amicable conversation about her idea of instigating high tea, as something social and special that she, Caroline Sayre McCall, could do, which no one else was doing and which she might become noted for. To which she could, naturally, invite certain distaff members of certain selected couples.

The actual content of her talk with Lutie had centered on the idea of planting apricot tea roses against the brick wall at The Manse and putting small tables outside, and perhaps asters, pinks, and delphiniums, to have something in bloom all year round.

"I've never quite belonged in Savannah, you know," she had confided to Lutie. "It's not enough to have the genealogy, things such as UDC, the Colonial Dames; they can't be bothered here. It is much more personal. I don't know how to explain it, but everyone is kin not so much to a family line, the way we're used to, but to specific people that an outsider has no idea who they are. 'She's Jenny's daughter,' they will tell me, or, 'Her grandfather married Agnes's grandmother.' And frankly I'm lost.

"The Rutledge sisters have been simply darlings to me about all that. Did I mention them to you and your mother before? The largest donors in Elbert's church? Well, that's not the point. Lovely people, really. The elder, Ladye, had a brief marriage, something of a scandal in her day, and he left her, if you can imagine it. Left her, as the story goes, 'for someone who had nothing to offer but sex and companionship.' Which is a delicate way of putting it, don't you think? At any rate, I thought, as something different from their card parties or sherry evenings, I'd have my high teas. Caroline's teas. Don't you see?"

They had chatted about what she would serve—scones, although Aunt Caroline was not sure exactly what they were, and crumpets, although Faith Rutledge had told her they were simply cold biscuits with raisins, so perhaps a hot bread, and the paper-thin cucumber sandwiches you always read about, and separate pots of piping hot teas, one for heavy cream and one for lemon.

Aunt Caroline had waxed eloquent about her menus and the garden setting for her social coming out and had made a small scale drawing of the backyard at The Manse and then, having tucked that away in her bag and returned her reading glasses to their case, had asked Lutie, as if in passing, "Now you're not still mad at your mother, are you, dear?"

And then Lutie had understood the reason she'd been urged to make the trip and, seeing her mother's fine hand behind the scenes, knew that Aunt Caroline would call her sister this very night to give a progress report.

"No," she said. "It wasn't her fault."

"Well, of course, we both know that. It was a natural enough mistake, in the anxiety of the moment and being afraid for you. Your mother has given her life to raise you, Lutie, don't forget that."

"I don't, Aunt Caroline."

What her aunt referred to was that she had come home from Rome with Dabney, pregnant but not telling, uncertain what to do, as clearly their marriage had ended with the trip. Back at Redoaks, debating, she had begun to spot on the aubergine rug. She should still remember sponging the carpet over and over with cold water, more frantic about the stain on the rug than about what was happening to her. The doctor, when she finally called him, had called her mother instead of an ambulance, and her mother had driven out in the late summer afternoon to see what was going on. And had whisked her daughter, by that time in a faint on the carpet, off to the hospital—where the doctor took the baby.

A nurse had explained it afterward to Lutie. "Honey, what he said was internal bleeding was just your bladder filling up, but they use that as an excuse, so as not to get themselves in trouble, saying it's an emergency, so they can go ahead, when it's not. It's none of my business, but I was thinking that if it was me, well, I'd want to know the story, so next time I'd know that I could carry one."

Lutie had called Dabney from the hospital, still groggy, to let him know. Even though they were past mending, she had wanted him to feel that she wouldn't lose one and not tell him about it. But he had never called her back.

Six months later she found out why: He had been unable to locate her in the hospital. "I tried *Sayre*. God knows I had more sense than to think she'd put you in there under my name, which I know she couldn't call to mind under oath. . . . I even thought of Miller, your grandmother, for some reason. But they had nobody registered by any name I'd ever heard. I give up, you tell me."

Lutie's mother was contrite when Lutie confronted her. She could explain it all. What had happened was this: When Lutie was born, back in the army, on the base, she'd told the nurses to notify her husband, but in those days they doped you up so you hardly knew what you were doing, and so she'd given her name as *Sayre*, not being able, for the moment, to remember her married name of *Pinter*. Which bit of amnesia had made Lutie's father very bitter.

156

So this time, remembering all that, and wanting to do it right, and, naturally, full of concern for her only daughter, she'd got flustered and told the hospital *Pinter*. Pleased this time to have got it straight.

"I was so worried about you, dear, don't you see? Not wanting you to go through what I had, having to raise a child without a father—don't you see, Lutie?"

Lutie had, and let it go. "I hardly think of it anymore," she'd said.

"Well, then," Aunt Caroline concluded, her duty done. "Now let me see. What would you think about having keys to the garden made, for certain special friends, such as the Rutledges, so they could let themselves right in?"

Now, as they finished the present meal and Aunt Caroline asked the waiter to refresh their memories about dessert, Lutie had a vague premonition that perhaps this meal, too, had as its purpose making its way back to her mother, to set her mind at rest on another score.

Aunt Caroline debated, discussed all the options, and then ordered for them: two Camille Glenn's Mincemeat Tartlettes Flambé. "Aren't you going to drink your wine, dear?" she asked, leaning toward her niece.

"You have it, please."

"Well, really, I shouldn't, but it needn't go to waste. And after all, we are walking. . . ."

"What do you hear from Nan?" Lutie asked as the dessert arrived.

Aunt Caroline sampled a bite and pronounced it too heavy on the cloves.

"I hope she's enjoying herself."

Perhaps it was a little too heavy on the molasses, too.

Lutie waited.

Aunt Caroline finished a mouthful. "To be honest, dear,

I haven't even told your mother, so this is in the strictest confidence, but Nannie and I have had the teeniest-ever falling out. She's so career-minded, not the least thing like her mother, I'm afraid."

Lutie considered the words, picking them over for the real message. Since her cousin had been marketing her needlepoint designs for some years, *career-minded* would have another, more definite meaning. It must have to do with Bubba's wife, who was offering Aunt Caroline a contact with the community that Nan hadn't. That must be it. Thinking it over, she realized she'd heard her mother tell University friends about how far out Lutie lived, almost as if she were in another town, practically to Johnson City, and how her real interest was in her country place. ("Why, you can't believe her garden, all that cooking and canning. It's a marvel; you wouldn't know she was my daughter. It's so peaceful out there, with the rockers on the porch.")

She and Nan, growing up, had heard the sisters talk about how Caroline had moved to Savannah too late to establish herself for the League and how Florence, naturally, working full time, had had no time for volunteer placements.

Aunt Caroline sounded noncommittal. "I imagine she's been busy. But you two girls can catch up on the phone when she and Sister call tomorrow."

Lutie sipped her coffee, feeling her way along. "I've missed my cat," she said. "You remember Cecelie?"

There was another small pause. "Nannie isn't keen on animals, you know. Well, still, I'm sure you can ask her. The truth is, we haven't really been in touch. Oh, it's the teeniest rift imaginable. And she gets on with Sister; they have their jobs. So all of us have benefited from our little trade, haven't we?"

Lutie considered. She took another sip, still skirting. "Isn't it grand about Mother's outstanding woman award?"

158

She was reminding her aunt that there were other ways besides the League to make a go of it; there was the Florence Sayre Wing of the hospital after all.

"Really, it is. I'm so proud of Sister. To have done all that single-handed." Aunt Caroline finished off the second glass of wine and patted her mouth with the pink napkin.

Lutie pushed aside her unfinished flambé and guessed, "It's Cecelie, isn't it?"

"Oh, Lutie, your mother made me *promise* not to tell. But when you brought the cat up first thing, I didn't know how I was going to hold the secret another minute. I can't bear your being up there all this time missing her. Honey, Nannie just can't get on with animals, and I don't know why in the world she didn't tell you that, I don't. But she's so career-minded these days—"

So that was what that had meant. "What happened?" she asked.

"I promised now," Aunt Caroline said, "so you have to *swear* that you won't breathe a word when they call tomorrow. Well, the thing is, it ran away. Nannie says she never even saw it." Aunt Caroline signaled their nice waiter for the check. "At least that's what Sister says. As I told you, Nannie and I haven't been too close, and so I didn't hear it directly from her."

"But it's been three months—"

"I promised Sister."

"I understand."

"You mustn't let on. But when you seemed to miss it so, honey . . ."

Lutie made an effort to adjust her thoughts. She tried to picture the tabby in the underbrush, stalking the wild turkeys, chasing them as if they were mockingbirds. She imagined her showing up on someone's doorstep, a stray, and being taken in. People wouldn't chase her off. It wasn't so bad to be a runaway. Lutie folded her napkin. "That was delicious," she said, "Just what I needed."

"Wasn't it?" Aunt Caroline asked, relieved.

At bedtime they each had a glass of skim milk and a Belgian chocolate. Aunt Caroline turned back the beds, folded up the quilted chintz spreads so they wouldn't get wrinkled in the night, and took the pillows out of their chintz shams. Then she settled herself, and her niece, beneath old down comforters from the linen closet.

"Tell me everything, now, no secrets," Aunt Caroline whispered from one fruitwood twin bed to the other.

Lutie tried to think. What was there to whisper about in this snug house with its interior wall of brick and its wainscoting and tasteful Federal trim?

She had taken a small tour before lights out, admiring such touches as the hand-rubbed shelf in the company bath, the collection of antique thimbles. Throughout the early-nineteenth-century quarters Aunt Caroline had put very personal groupings of her mementos on all her best reproductions: a copy of a George IV satinwood card table, a copy of a late George II mahogany tripod table. At one end of her bow-fronted dressing table, on a starched white runner, sat a gallery of her family: small assorted gold-framed pictures of Gran as a young, slightly blurred Marjorie Sayre Miller; Caroline and Florence as little girls in white afternoon frocks; a later studio portrait of Nannie and Lutie in similar Florence Eiseman dresses. The four of them on the banks of the Guadalupe at River Bend; the four of them, older, in shades of rose, at Mickey's wedding. One of Aunt Caroline as a bride. At the other end of the dresser was her heirloom silver-backed brush and mirror set, with a scrolled S for Sayre.

(There was no picture anywhere of Uncle Elbert. As Lutie lay in the soft bed on the ironed sheets, she wondered

if she would have noticed that on her own or if she was
seeing the cottage now through Joe's eyes.)

"No secrets now," Aunt Caroline admonished, drowsy
from the half glass of sherry which was ritual at bedtime.

"In New York," Lutie began, much as one tells a long
bedtime story to a child, "there is a place where people go
in the summer, called the Hamptons. It's really several
places, and some are more expensive than others, and each
one has a special flavor, and the people who vacation at
each like theirs best, and some have other names like Water
Mill and Montauk. Where we went, my friend Mavis and
I, was to Westhampton. First you have to imagine an island
so long that it runs from Savannah up the coast past
Charleston. . . ."

By the time she got to David's Cookies, Aunt Caroline
was fast asleep, snoring softly.

14

———————◆———————

"'HELLO, Mickey. I'm Lutie."

"I know that; you were at my wedding." The pretty girl laughed.

"I guess I was introducing myself because it had been awhile."

"I know, and we missed you and Florence at Christmas last year; but now you're here, and we're pleased to have you, Lutie."

In the kitchen hung with copper pots and floored with a vinyl that looked like brick, Lutie was served a cup of hot cider and given a tissue-paper-wrapped cake. "Mother sent you her brown sugar pound cake," Mickey explained, "as they couldn't be here—my grandmother is very ill. It's an old recipe, and we thought you and Mother Caroline could heat a slice for breakfast or save it for tea. I know she likes something homemade for her teas."

Mickey was a good hostess. Her house was in Ardsley Park, which was Savannah's nicest suburb and had been for years the best place to live, before downtown was suitable. Mickey had carpeted the whole house in dusty rose and cocoa and had matching two-seat sofas covered in brown and rose colonial print in the living room, and, on the marble mantel, cream china vases filled with fresh pink carnations and baby's-breath.

Mickey wore a cocoa brown wool skirt and a bow-tied rose blouse, matching, unselfconsciously, her décor. She took Lutie on a tour, pointing out what she and Bubba (whom she called Junior) had been given, what they'd bought, what refinished, what pieces they still longed to find: the tiny cherry end tables, a walnut drop-leaf, a sea-scape of Factors' Walk with its ballast stones. She identified the portrait gallery grouped on the breakfast nook wall: These were her parents; this, their place on the island; this, her sister and herself at Agnes Scott; this, a group of class-mates; this, her grandmother as a girl. . . .

Lutie found her cousin Bubba drinking cider in a wicker chair (like the ones she had brought to Cranberry Park) on the veranda. He was waiting for his brother, they were to have a game of croquet before the Thanksgiving repast. She pulled up another chair to sit and visit. "This is a lovely house," she said.

"It's an investment. We had to take a fifteen percent mortgage, but even so, I'd do it over again, with the rates dropping by the week. In ten years it'll be worth double." He made an expansive sweep with his hands. "How's your mother doing with that place of hers?"

Lutie chatted, only half paying attention, trying to see something previously unnoted in this cousin who had al-ways been the pudgy one. Some quality she'd missed she could relate to Joe, as promised.

"I've told Mom, you know how the old girls are about houses, that one of these days she'll have herself a place on the island. Now where is that brother of mine?"

Bubba, soon to be bald, looking middle-aged, although

he couldn't be but thirty-six, had a paunch much larger than she remembered or than he'd had before. Otherwise he was unchanged.

At that moment Langley Graham McCall arrived, parked his new Cutlass in the drive, and ambled down the steep, sloping lawn toward his brother. He was also losing his hair, puffy in the face, expanding in the rear, and he was only thirty-four. Narrower in the shoulders than his brother, he was more of a dandy, his huge thighs concealed by a pair of pink and green plaid golfer's trousers.

He was also a lot friendlier.

He gave Lutie a robust hug and cheek kiss. "Lute, my gracious, let me look at you, aren't you lovely now, in that dress? What is this? An underskirt, now isn't that the fashion? I expect up North you wear it with boots. My, let me take a good look."

He beat his brother at croquet; old men they looked, the two of them, standing with their hands clasped behind them on their rumps, the essence of patience as they watched each other shoot. Looking exactly as they had for years at birthday parties, in their Florence Eiseman suits.

(What Joe didn't understand, having the psychologist's bias that everyone is distinct, is that everyone isn't; some people are a group all their lives. Elbert Junior and Langley G. were a group.)

Lutie was pleased that her Ralph Lauren copy had passed inspection; she had remembered to wear her pearls, and had washed her hair at the crack of dawn and set it on giant rollers so it would brush out fuller, and had worn red hose to complete the look.

Mother and Nan called at half past eleven, Savannah time, just as Aunt Caroline had arranged. She and Aunt Caroline and Mickey took turns talking to them, while Bubba and Langley stayed on the porch, talking investments.

164

Mother had been invited to be part of the vice-president's party to go to the Turkey Day game with Texas A&M. "We'll all go over by bus and then come back to his house for dinner. Some of our old Arab friends are *excluded*, so it should be quite a day."

Nan, her voice faint and defensive, said, "Hi, Lute, we're trading—aren't we—like we used to pajamas. Tell them hello, my old, fat bubbas. I don't miss being at Miss Mickey's pink palace, but don't tell her I said that. Aunt Florence says to hush, so I guess I will. See you in three weeks, that's about it, isn't it? Talk to you later."

Lutie, as she had promised, didn't ask about Cecelie. Nor did she ask about Redoaks. Nan was going out with her "own friends," Mother had reported. "We both keep so busy."

The turkey was stuffed with oysters and chestnuts, and the cranberries made into a compote with orange and coconut and served in a fluted orange rind, and the sweet potatoes had been made into a soufflé with pecans, and the fresh green peas had been lettuce-steamed and prepared in the cream sauce which was the specialty of Mickey's mother. The food, like the house, all matched and overdone.

There was no wine—long habit from church days. Lutie imagined that when Aunt Caroline wasn't there, that was not observed, any more than her aunt observed it when her sons were not around.

Langley said grace, a job he had inherited from his father. "Bless this fellowship, O Lord, and we who share in it. . . ." That was added whenever company, in this case Lutie, was present. "Bless this food, O Lord, and we who are about to receive it." Lutie, head bowed, tried to remember her uncle's blessings. There had always been additional lines, between the fellowship and food, for those less fortunate, the sailors at sea, the homeless. . . .

Langley was doing his part for the Savannah branch of the family, as Aunt Caroline had taken to calling them. Lutie had imagined that with Bubba's wife presenting this nice proper house and being put up for the Junior League, Langley would be left out in the cold, the teensiest forgotten, as his sister, Nan, was. But that was not so at all, for he was working for Historic Savannah and had been in on the start of the restorations. He had also put in valuable time on the Telfair Art Museum, which Aunt Caroline had thought might be too new to bother with but had turned out to be both exciting and prestigious, and Langley G. had been among the movers from the start. He was also, it was revealed—as they worked their way slowly to the percolator coffee and pumpkin chiffon pie with whipped cream—doing a chapbook on the siege of Savannah, which was being locally printed, at his expense, with the proceeds of sales going to benefit Telfair.

He explained, neatly timing his remarks to end with his last bite, that often historians came from other locales and therefore missed the nuances and that this gave him a vantage point, having grown up in the city.

15

FRIDAY Aunt Caroline and Lutie took a walking tour of downtown Savannah on their way to have lunch with the Rutledge sisters, Ladye and Faith.

"This has always been a royalist city." Aunt Caroline picked up her running commentary. "It took a week at sea from English Georgia to Georgian England." She liked to show off her knowledge. "Did you know, Lutie, that they planted mulberries to feed silkworms at the beginning? Isn't that hard to imagine now, when we know it as the home of the cotton gin, to think it was first settled to grow silk— if that's what you say? Raise silk? Harvest it? Whatever. No matter, it took ten acres for every one hundred mulberries. So it was hardly profitable anyway."

She explained *tabby*, a sort of cement of oyster shells and lime, which you could see visible in foundation blocks of old houses, and they admired a Regency with portico, the old Isaiah Davenport house, and an American Federal. They stepped in and out of the morning sun slanting through the moss-hung oaks as they passed the shady parks, complete with benches and pigeons and leaves scattering in the balmy wind.

They strolled away from the river all the way to Forsyth

Park, the oldest and, at one time, the finest of the city's twenty-four squares. Retrieved from pigs and mud at the turn of the last century, it had been landscaped in formal style and reinstated for Sunday strolls. Aunt Caroline, recounting its renaissance in Victorian times, saw that it now sported slides and swings and modern wooden free-form acrobatic gyms (treehouses without trees) on which children—all black—were playing. "Well," Aunt Caroline said, "I suppose since they moved them out of the State Street area . . ." She smiled and nodded at two little boys, whom even Lutie recognized as Cuthberts.

Then they turned and made the walk back, edging the squares central to the city, past Grace Church, to Aunt Caroline's street again. Only this time they turned left instead of right, heading for the Rutledges'.

"Do you still go to Grace?" Lutie asked as they walked past the historic church.

"Naturally, they've been so solicitous, all of them, doing everything possible, they truly have. The Session has practically adopted me, and as long as Ladye and Faith are there at least, you know they are Grace's largest donors, I must be counted on to be there, too. Not that I don't sometimes think it would be a relief to go to First, where they don't know me, and simply join up as Mickey's mother-in-law. Start over. One gets so embedded in church life, to tell the truth, all the factions and dissent, even in a church as old as ours. You know President McKinley got married at The Manse, did you know that? Did I say McKinley? Foolish. Wilson, wasn't it? Not that it would be fitting at this point for me to leave."

The Rutledge sisters were dollhouse collectors, Aunt Caroline explained as they turned onto the brick sidewalk of their home. "Not that you say dollhouse. *Miniatures* is the correct term. They can spot a Montmorenci Stair Hall or a Blackwell Parlor or a Cecil Bedroom in the twinkling of an eye when they go calling. And they hunt all the time for the tiniest addition: an oval double gate-leg table no bigger than a demitasse, a Rhode Island pad-foot bed the size of a tea napkin. Can you imagine a genuine Charles II two-handle porriger on rim foot, circa 1670, used as a washbasin, for proper scale? You can't imagine the patience and the research. You must be sure to notice everything. Their pride is on the piano, their newest. I long to get them some piece they don't have and am always searching for a set of tiny Delft tiles or a stamp-size crewel hanging, but my eye is not that experienced. Whenever I see something, the price is already up, and everyone knows about it."

She wore a beige coat suit the color of her hair, a soft lavender blouse, and an oval locket which had been Gran's. She had approved of Lutie's new royal blue trousers and wide-shouldered jacket for going to call. "You look quite sophisticated, dear."

The meal began with a court bouillon, from a Louisiana cousin, which required real red snapper head and bones soaked overnight in white wine, parsley, onion, and peppercorns, all strained through a cheesecloth. "No one takes this kind of trouble in restaurants anymore," explained Ladye, the main cook. This was followed, at a leisurely pace, by suprême du volaille Maryland, potato balls rolled in almonds, and banana fritters. A glass of port was served as a breather before dessert and to let them have a chance to get acquainted properly with Lutie.

They took her on a tour of their home, which included their Georgian dollhouses, replete with treasures, and a look at their portrait gallery and a glimpse of the walled gardens out back.

Dessert was a generous serving of Corrie Hill Hurt's Lane

Cake, an old, old family recipe, closely guarded, from an aunt in Pineapple, South Carolina (simply called Carolina), a rich white cake filled with pecans, whipped cream, raisins.

After the luncheon the ladies had arranged to go to an auction. "Something you shouldn't miss for the world," Aunt Caroline told her. "Such marvels: walnut spool beds for sixty dollars; sunburst quilts for eighty; oak washstands; beveled mirrors; mahogany wardrobes. Not that I have an inch of space myself in my precious cottage, but you can sometimes find something, a blue floral stoneware pitcher, a pillared temple clock, even an oval picture frame, for only a few dollars. And there's always a drawing, some true treasure. Last year there was a rare eighteenth-century American porcelain sweetmeat stand from Sotheby's; it was made at Bonnin and Morris in Philadelphia. One year it was a Simon Willard tall case clock. It's always something enormously valuable, and to tell the truth, Lutie, I sometimes suspect that it may not be a true drawing, that it is set up so that some collector can purchase the item, by prearrangement. Still . . . It makes for excitement. You'll have something special to relate to your mother. Maybe even find her something for Christmas."

She had talked breathlessly, wanting to show off her knowledge of the subject, her appreciation of what was valuable and what was not, darting glances at the Rutledges with every breath.

They, in their turn, scarcely heard her, looked at her with no more interest than they would have accorded a Grand Rapids table. She, Caroline McCall, bored them.

Lutie, however, being new prey, fascinated; their fixed eyes with the heavy turkey lids never left her. They had pawed at her during the house tour as if she were a new doll and they older, cracked dolls grown malicious in their disuse.

"You've a nice seamstress, dear," Ladye had said, picking

at a shoulder seam of Lutie's black jacket. "Or did you do it? Do you sew? No? Callie's niece, you know her, Caroline, Bertha's granddaughter, sews. So clever. Doesn't she, Faith? And nicely."

"Lost your young man, didn't you?" Faith, deaf, shrieked as they stood in the gallery hall. "Isn't that what I hear? Ran off, didn't he? Caroline, didn't we hear that from you? You'll find another—provided you want one."

Faith was in the sort of ruffled children's party dress which has a matching parasol, and high-button patent shoes from another era, and white nurse's hose, and smelled of Lysol.

Ladye was a giant with matted hair, matted Georgette dress, ropes of grimy, oily pearls.

Lutie couldn't stand to be in their house any longer. She felt hurt for, embarrassed for, Aunt Caroline.

(It raised also the question of her mother. If all the years of kindnesses on the part of the V-P had been like this. If he, who was the center, the mainstay, of her mother's life, looked at her as a bad tenure decision. It might be that he found Florence Sayre tedious, that he had to be prodded into including her in every University function. Lutie, standing in the harpies' grand home, tried to remember what the V-P looked like. Surely she had seen him on those weekend feasts at Redoaks; he was their reason, their premier guest. Yet at that moment she could not swear that he had ever been there. It cut at Lutie to think of the sisters, those beautiful, larger-than-life women of her childhood, being treated in such a way—and having to be grateful for it.)

"Lessons," she said lamely, "really, I must. Aunt Caroline, you go on, don't trouble, I can find . . ."

She suffered the prying fingers and shrill voices of the Rutledges' disappointment.

On the porch her aunt, let down, fussed. "I could have

asked Mickey had I known, Lutie. She loves these affairs, her family has an interest in collecting, but I wanted us, dear, to have a trip all our own with the Rutledges. I'll have plenty of time to see Mickey; you're only here such a short time. I do get tired of taking her around so that people can meet her—which you absolutely must not repeat, even to your mother—and I'll be glad when this year is over and she's in the League and that's the end of it. You have no idea the labyrinthine complications of being sure that each member of admissions has met her once and seen her at least twice, which they say is essential, if they don't know you. I'm sure I'll be exhausted by the end of the summer. You won't change your mind and go with us? You quite charmed them, you know."

"Make my apologies again."

"You know where the key to my little cottage is, in the garden?"

16

HER decision to duck into Grace Church was almost chance. She wanted to be off the street and out of sight before the ladies were ready to leave for their outing. Also, she had the idea of seeing a picture of Uncle Elbert, so she could report back to Joe.

Entering the narthex, she read: "This entranceway was refurbished to the Glory of God and in loving Memory of William Vance Rutledge." She stood for a minute to get her bearing, feeling followed, then entered the sanctuary: a very old room with stained glass windows, vast dome, and ornate interior columns. With its carved boxes, flagstone floors, and dark wood pews, it was quite awesome and somehow British. A residue of George's reign, which she had never felt before, never having been inside with no one there.

Idly she read the handout history at the door. Noting that the Elders once sat beneath the pulpit while the minister preached from the high lectern, that the doors to the right and left of the pulpit had been designed as slave entrances leading to narrow winding stairs behind the organ, that the building had escaped the ravages of the War Between the States.

Lutie found the church secretary, a thin woman whose desk plate said "Dorothy Desmoreaux." She looked familiar, but Lutie couldn't be sure.

"Hello," she said, holding out her hand. "I'm Lutie Sayre. Elbert McCall's niece. Mrs. Desmoreaux?"

The woman stood and stared at her. "Yes? May I help you?"

Lutie faltered. Asking for a picture sounded foolish, coming as she was from her aunt's house. On an impulse she said, "I wanted to see, I'd like to see my uncle's books. Check a reference. I'm a college teacher, you see, and here on a visit. . . ."

The woman didn't move but stood there. "Are you at Caroline's then?"

"Yes, ma'am. But none of his things is out; it's a new place she's in, you see. And I thought . . ."

Mrs. Desmoreaux put her hands, palms down, on her desk, someone who refused to lean getting a little support.

"The son has the bulk," she said. "Your cousin Langley. We got only what was here. You're welcome to see what there is: one shelf in the church library. His other effects I put in a file, primarily the notes which were on his desk that day. No one ever came for them."

"I don't want to put you to trouble." It had been a bad idea to stop in. The woman seemed dazed, and the topic of her former pastor obviously was a sore subject with her. It had been two years; Lutie hadn't thought to lead up to her request, not considering bereavement to apply here.

"His sermon." Dorothy Desmoreaux continued purposefully. "He was working again on Isaac and Abraham, which he did when he was under stress. He would go back to it; it was, you might say, his touchstone. It had to do with his being Isaac to the Lord, that was my interpretation. Whenever he would say, 'Dot, I'm going to have a go at the sacrifice of Abraham,' I'd know. It was a tragedy. It was. A tragedy." The thin woman pressed her fingers sharply against the bridge of her nose. She stood as if in a suit of armor, her brass-colored hair nearly gray, her cheeks rough as if from a nipping wind. She wore no make-up or jewelry, but a very good green tweed suit. Calvinist was how she looked and what she clearly was.

"Well," Lutie murmured, not quite sure what her response should be. She couldn't pretend to be still torn up about her uncle's death yet did not want to intrude on the woman's distress. "Yes, ma'am."

"Do sit down," the church secretary said, doing so herself. She rustled around for a moment and then rang a bell that sounded like a tardy bell.

A young man appeared, slender, quite small, very fastidious. Charleston, Lutie thought, in reflex.

"This is Elbert's niece," Dorothy explained to him.

"My dear." He took her hands in his, half leaning toward her cheek in the way one does with strangers who are the kin of friends. "My dear, we have grieved so. Who ministers to the minister?" He wiped at his small, well-bred eyes. "It is a question as old as the cloth."

"She wanted to see his books," Dorothy told him. "I'm sorry"—she turned her weathered face to Lutie—"I didn't get your name."

"Sayre. Lutie Sayre."

"My dear." The minister seemed still on the verge of tears. "Come with me."

Lutie reached out a hand. "Dr.?"

Dorothy apologized again. "I didn't make proper introductions. I'm afraid."

"McCauley. Charles McCauley."

"What a coincidence, isn't it?"

"Yes, I know. Certain members of the congregation have simply gone on saying McCall; it simplifies things. I answer to either." The young man made a gesture with his hands, a slight annoyance, an acceptance. "The Session mentioned it to me in advance. Most of them call me Charles. That makes it easier."

"Shall I?"

"By all means, please do."

As she followed Dr. McCauley into the pastor's study, Lutie wished mightily that she had not stepped into the building at all. The fleeting urge to see her uncle had vanished some time ago. She was already very rattled from the clawing nature of her visit with the Rutledge sisters and felt she had no reserves with which to deal with this wholly unexpected font of welling emotion in these people who ran her uncle's church. She didn't know if that was part of the way believers dealt with death or if it was something they produced for the supposedly bereaved. She looked about—she had never been in the study before—for some object to comment on and a graceful way to make her exit.

Dr. McCauley had settled down in his swivel chair and was continuing in the same tone. "I can't tell you how grieved the entire congregation was at your uncle's decision to take his life. We are not Roman, and there was no sense at all in the Presbytery of mortal sin. Certainly he received a full church burial service, that was not the issue; but among the congregation, as among the clergy at large, it caused, I must tell you, a soul-searching. Self-reflection, if you will. I won't call it guilt, that was not in order, but self-reflection. Raising, as I said, the matter of who is to minister to the minister."

Lutie heard the words, but they didn't connect. She felt blank, wanting to say, "I have to go, thank you." Not able to grasp what the gentle clergyman was disclosing. "Yes," she said, the way one nods at people one can't hear in crowded places.

"Had we known or even guessed—I speak for the rest of them, for I was in Carolina at that time, called to another church, yet even I had heard of it long before the opening was made public here—we would have given him our full support."

"Yes," Lutie said.

Dr. McCauley looked extremely distressed, as if at a primary lapse in manners or decency. "If there is anything I can do. His family here has preferred to heal their own wounds, which I can have nothing but understanding and sympathy for. Actually"—he clasped the fingers of his delicate hands together—"you are the first person in Elbert's family I have spoken to." He made a feeble smile. "I welcome the opportunity."

"I don't understand."

"What, my dear?"

"What you're saying. It was his heart. Aunt Caroline said they found him slumped over his desk."

"She was sparing you perhaps." He coughed politely.

"But how do you know?"

"My dear, there was hardly an attempt on his part to hide the fact."

"What do you mean?"

"He shot himself, in this room."

"I can't believe—"

"It's common knowledge."

Lutie felt herself faint and tried to grab onto the desk, hitting her shoulder as she fell.

It was dreadful. When she came to, swimming up out of nausea, not remembering and then remembering, they both were standing over her.

She got up and sat back down. "Please," she said. "I'm sorry."

"Miss Sayre, believe me, I had no intention. We've suffered over this for two years now, and I had assumed, since it has been much discussed within church walls . . . Do forgive me. Would you like a glass of water?"

*1*77

"Yes."

"Would you prefer to be left alone?"

"Not yet. I'm sorry." She wanted the glass of water. That seemed something specific that would help her wash it down in some literal, inexplicable way.

After she had drunk, she told him she'd like to look at her uncle's papers.

"Dorothy can help you; she has kept his notes as he left them. So far only our ecumenical luncheon group, which meets weekly in his name to share our concerns with one another, has looked at them. You're welcome. Any way that we can help. Let me call Dorothy."

"Is this a bad time? Are you working?" She tried to find her lost manners.

"My sermon can wait; I'd welcome a distraction. Dorothy and I will go over the bulletin." He patted Lutie's shoulders with delicate, comforting hands.

The secretary showed her what there was. "This file cabinet here, this drawer. That contains what was on his desk that day. That's all we have. Caroline disposed of what was in his study at home. The books I've told you about."

"Thank you."

"Perhaps you'd like a Coca-Cola?"

"Thank you."

Mrs. Desmoreaux closed the door gently behind her.

There was so little.

Three folders. One entitled "Bulletins." One, "Annual Reports." One, "Misc."

The annual reports were full of such matters as the deacon attendance record, class attendance records, weekly offerings and pledges, receipts and disbursements of the trustees, membership lists (additions: profession of faith, 0, transfer of letter, 19, reaffirmation of faith, 8; losses:

transfer of letter, o, deceased, 20), securities reinvested ($60,000), feeble churches ($300).

The church bulletins had news of shut-ins, class meetings, special offerings, and the order of the Sunday worship service.

The miscellaneous folder had a half dozen pages, all with notes that Uncle Elbert had made to himself. These were what Dorothy Desmoreaux had gathered together from the top of his desk.

Lutie read them carefully, understanding little.

Saturday's Moderator, ask DD unpack copy of paper: Manipulative causality. We consider red-hot the effect of high temp; actually red-hot may be *cause* of high temp. Fast heart cause of anger? We confuse what we want to achieve (cause) with its result. Deny causality.

When dealt with in sufficient numbers matters of chance become matters of certainty. GBS. Ask DD unpack article, attach.

See Schillebeeckx. See Bultmann. Theodicy.

We change the past by undoing our own mistakes. Ask DD unpack source. Think spring conf.???

To the schoolmen, who lived amid wars, massacres, and pestilences, nothing appeared so delightful as safety and order. In their idealizing dreams, it was safety and order they sought; the universe of Thomas Aquinas or Dante is as small and neat as a Dutch interior. To us, to whom safety has become monotony, to whom the primeval savageries of nature are so remote as to become a mere pleasing condiment to our ordered routine, the world of dreams is very different from what it was amid the wars of Guelf and Ghibelline.— B.R. Ask DD context. Think Union meeting, 4 yrs.??? Use A & I???

Abraham and Isaac. Ask DD unpack all prior A & I. In encountering God, Abraham is charged to let go his own will.

Letting go that object through and in whom he is who he is. Consider this the dynamic of Christendom. To lose the object of his desire; to be obliged to deprive *oneself* of the object of long desire, one's self. To sacrifice Isaac is to sacrifice one's own self, one's hope, one's promise. Isaac appears as one's own self in actualized form.

What is sought after is one's self in the other.
God reminds us: Isaac is your promise to *Me*. Meaning of sacrifice is to wound selfishness at its root.

Reverse causality:
We undo our own mistakes by changing the past.
What is sought after is the other in one's self.
God reminds us: The dilemma of Isaac is My promise to *you*.

She opened the door so that Dorothy might come in, as she put the notes back in their folders.

"He thought a lot of you," she told the church secretary. "Every note has your name."

"That was my job."

"Please tell me what happened."

"The facts are brief enough. If you're sure you want—?"

"Yes."

"A black family moved into a house on East State before the area was under renovation. Your uncle, may I call him Elbert?"

Lutie nodded.

"Elbert saw that as a chance to invite them to membership. The man had come from a poor family in rural

180

Georgia, his father had cut crossties for the railroad, and then the railroad had laid him off. The man became a cabinetmaker here, in Savannah, wanting to work with wood, as a tribute to his father. The woman, the man's wife, was a secretary. They had no children. Elbert pressed the Session to take them, on the rationale that they lived in the neighborhood, were not seeking membership as representative of any group. The Session agreed to go along after a good bit of pressure, but then the biggest donors in the church threatened to cancel their pledge. When Elbert was unmoved, they bought the black couple's house; rather, they saw to it that the rising taxes which followed in the wake of Historic Savannah made it possible for them to buy the house, and another similar to it, near the church, for rental purposes."

"The Rutledges."

"That's right." Dorothy looked uncertain but took a small breath and continued. "The couple was no longer in the neighborhood, so the Session had an out, and the matter was dropped. It blew over, although there remained bitterness in some quarters at Elbert for bringing pressure. He went individually to talk to some of the Elders, to mend his fences.

"I can tell you about the afternoon he took his life." She looked at Lutie, wanting to be sure she should continue.

"Go on, please."

"He came back here, dispirited, and related the following conversation to me: That he had gone to a certain member, highly esteemed, and presented his concern man to man. The gentleman had told him, 'Elbert, back in civil rights days we had a meeting, and we were all riled up to make amends and see some justice done, and a pastor who had a score of years on us, and a lot more sense, told us, "Boys, if you're really concerned with civil rights you'd be down

at your church right now worshiping." ' Then he told Elbert that he would do well to meditate on that little message
himself."

Dorothy pressed her thin fingers neatly at the corners of
her eyes. When she was back in control, she continued. "It
angered him that restoration was forcing the blacks out of
the center of town, forcing them out by raising taxes; he
saw it as losing ground. Then, when it hit his own church,
he gave up. I think when they drove the young couple, the
cabinetmaker and his wife, off State Street, that's when he
gave up."

"They were in what is now Aunt Caroline's house?"

"Precisely."

Lutie shook her head. It was too much to absorb. Too
many events she had known nothing about. Finally, she
asked for what it was she'd come for in the first place, not
knowing why. "May I see a picture of my uncle?"

Dorothy rose and led Lutie into the church office.

From a file at the back of her largest desk drawer she
took a faded brown-tone studio portrait of Elbert McCall
and handed it to his niece.

Lutie stared down into the face of the owl-eyed man as
if at a stranger.

17

S L O W L Y she walked from the church toward the river; then turned on East State Street, passing through a series of sunlit squares filled with moss-hung water oaks, benches, sidewalks, statues of statesmen, sparrows. She read the plaques on homes that had been moved from another location intact; that had been rebuilt entirely from original photographs; that had been reconstructed outward from a bare shell, whose old, decayed parts had been stripped away, its beams dismantled, cleaned, the whole reassembled to specifications from old drawings.

The tabbied lower floors of endangered structures, designed by famous men, left vacant for decades, wearing the scrubbed and imposing faces of salvation, abutted one-story servants' houses (now refaced with perfectly matched old brick).

She let herself in through the picket fence of the tiny walled garden of the "Cottage of William Wilson, Free Person of color, circa 1818." A patch of pink azaleas caught the slanted light, flanked by tea roses, stock, and hedges of box.

Forgetting, she dialed Joe from the bedside Princess phone in Aunt Caroline's bedroom. As it rang, she remembered: He was with Carole. She tried to pinch the tears from her eyes the way the church secretary in her good green tweed had done. Just as she was putting the receiver down, she heard Sammy's voice.

"Oh, Sammy, I'm sorry. I wasn't thinking. I was trying to call Joe, and then I remembered he wasn't there. How on earth did I get you? I don't even know your number, do I?"

"Hold on." He picked up on the panic in her voice. "Hold on. It's me, at Joe's. Small incidents occurred and I'm holding down the place for him. Nothing to worry about. Fritz stole a car."

"Oh, no—"

"Boys will be boys."

Lutie made a strained smile. "That's what *I* tell him."

"You may have to tell him again. He's wearing sandbags of guilt."

"What kind of car?"

"Buick Riviera."

"Then he must be, oh, dear—" No one would steal a car like *that* except to get at a parent.

"What's up in the South?"

"I didn't mean to dump this on you." She told him what there was to tell about Uncle Elbert.

"Are you okay?" he asked.

"It hasn't sunk in yet. I don't really believe it, even though they said, they both said . . . I mean, how could I not know? How could they not have said anything? Mother? Aunt Caroline?"

"Joe Richard will want to hear about this. Let me have your number."

"No, that's foolish. There's nothing he can do. I don't want to dump anything else on him anyway, after all that about Fritz. It's just that we've argued about this. But it'll keep." She pressed a finger to the corner of her eye. "Just tell him that he was right."

184

"Now wait, don't hang up until I've done my job. Address, phone, next of kin, I need to get it all. In emergencies you have to be prepared."

"There's no need—" She laughed. It was his way of doing something concrete, and in truth, she felt some relief as she gave him not only Aunt Caroline's name and street but Mickey and Bubba's, and the Rutledges', and the church, and would have given Langley G.'s if she'd known it. It didn't make sense, but it worked; Sammy David, surrogate mother, was making her feel that she hadn't got misplaced. She was laughing when she got off the phone, grateful. It wasn't until she stretched out on the chintz spread that she realized her glasses were streaked with tears.

Aunt Caroline fixed them a light supper at home, just the two of them. She had a shrimp mousse that was one of her prize recipes, although, she said, more suited to the summer, but something she could make ahead, and, to fill them up, baked acorn squash with brown sugar and home-made clover-leaf rolls.

Tomorrow she had planned a tour of the tidal area, with its salt marshes and interesting birds, and a stop for fresh blue crabs and a visit to the Isle of Hope, all of which you had to see when you came at this time of year. And then the Rutledges, Ladye and Faith, were to come to the cottage for one of her fine high teas.

In preparation for them, after the supper dishes had been cleared, she baked little "scones," better, really, than the English version, which she made by rolling strips of pie-crust into cornucopias, and "sweetmeats," as she called the piecrust squares she stuffed and filled with mincemeat. And, of course, she would serve some of Mickey's mother's pound cake, since Mickey had been invited for tea, to make amends for her exclusion from the auction today.

As they settled in for the night, Aunt Caroline wound

up her narrative about all that Lutie had missed. "Really, you should have seen the bedsteads, going for a song. I could hardly refrain from getting this one spool bed, even though I have no earthly place for it. It was a gem." She finished her bedtime sherry and put out the light. "Now your turn. You must tell me what you thought of our lunch and our grand tour this morning."

Lutie, worn-out, could not think the proper oblique way to lead into her questions. After a short silence she blurted out in the dark, "Does Mother know Uncle Elbert killed himself?"

Aunt Caroline sat up and was heard to slip on her bedroom shoes. "That's a lie." She got a robe from the closet. "An outright lie. Gossip I never thought I'd have to hear from my own kin."

"I went by Grace Church."

"Whatever for? I can hardly show my face there myself, some of them have been so cold to me. I can't say a word, not a word, not after the Rutledges have stood up for me, but it has not been easy. You have no idea what I've been put through." She returned to the bedroom with another small glass of sherry, leaving the hall light on. "Who did you talk to? The prissy Charles McCauley or that Dorothy person? Did they tell you who started the rumor? Did they tell you that, or were they protecting themselves?"

"I talked to both of them."

"There was a Negro family, I'm telling you this against my will, Lutie, because it is over and done with, and I wish I could hear the last of it. . . . There was this family, I think they'd been hired by the NAACP, one of those groups, to make trouble for Elbert. Well, they did. It was too much for him, all the hostility and infighting. They found him slumped over his desk, and that's the plain and simple of it. He died, worn-out from the whole matter."

"He shot himself."

"That's a lie, an outright lie. If anyone should know, it's me; I was, after all, his wife. A matter they chose to forget in circulating the rumors. Spreading their gossip. She did, Desmoreaux, acting as if she had the right to give out information about the pastor, taking it upon herself to make statements. Making a fool of herself, plain and simple, as anyone could deduce she had made an attachment to Elbert. If it hadn't been for Ladye and Faith, I don't know how I could have held my head up. It all fell on me; I can say with some pride that I never put it off on the children. I vowed I would move my membership to First before that happened, but Ladye and Faith persuaded me that it would roll over sooner the less we made of it, the less credence we gave it, and it has. I never think of it, and don't you breathe a word of this to your mother. I'd not upset her for the world with the knowledge that I'd been maligned by people I took to be friends. Florence has had a hard enough time herself, with no one to help raise you. I wouldn't trouble her for the world, do you hear? This is my personal cross."

Aunt Caroline sat on the side of the bed with her feet planted on the floor, peering in the dim light at her niece, to be sure she had made herself clear.

After a long silence she suddenly asked, "Whatever did you go there for? You've never been a church person, have you?"

"I wondered what had happened to Uncle Elbert's books. I was . . . looking for a reference." It was lame; it didn't matter.

"Langley G. has the library, what there was of it that the church didn't appropriate. He's become something of a scholar himself, although not as single-minded as his father, a relief to me. With his article on the siege of Savannah and the victory of the British, he considered that he should have a library of his own. There were some valuable books, by the way, collectors' items, in your uncle's collection, I had no idea, but we got an estimate; but Langley said he'd prefer to keep them in the family, that they would only be worth more later anyway. If you'd like, dear, I'm sure he'd be glad to show you. You should have mentioned the matter yesterday." She had perked up. "His article is making quite a stir; Savannah has always been a royalist city."

Aunt Caroline looked old in the dim light without her make-up, in a long cotton gown. "Let's put this out of our minds, Lutie. You've upset me all over again. I'd got it settled, was doing fine here in my splendid new quarters. Let's put our mind on the tea tomorrow. Pale green watercress sandwiches are always lovely, don't you think?"

When the doorbell rang the next morning, Lutie and her aunt were having breakfast. Lutie, numbed from a sleepless night, sat politely sipping fresh-squeezed orange juice in the tiny peach-papered dining area, soon to get its copy of a teardrop chandelier. She and her aunt had been discussing the Savannah sparrow and how that was not the one you saw in the parks.

Lutie found herself again and again pressing the corners of her eyes. "I'm getting a cold," she told her aunt.

Aunt Caroline excused herself to get the door and came back to say that Lutie had a registered letter. "You have to sign for it yourself, he says. Who on earth could that be? Would your mother be sending us a note? She might, really; it costs no more than a call. How clever, truly." She slipped two slices of the brown suger pound cake from the broiler.

Sammy David stood at the door of the historic William Wilson cottage, garbed in an outrageous messenger uniform.

Lutie's hand flew to her mouth, but he shook his head.

"Just sign here, ma'am," he said in his best cotton voice,

pointing to an imaginary pad in his hand. When she pretended to do so, he handed her a note from himself.

As she stepped out onto the porch to open it, she saw a cab parked at the curb, two houses down.

She read:

L.
Will be at the airport. We can catch a plane out at 12:40.
Tell Aunt C. your department chairman was killed on the
Bronx River Parkway.
Joe Richard meeting plane.
Tell those beggroes you've had enough.
S.

Lutie appeared distraught, hurried, when she returned. She explained to Aunt Caroline that her chair, Dr. Birdsong, had taken ill and that she, Lutie, would have to take over the extra classes on Monday. She packed and changed into the gray skirt she used with her new black jacket for traveling, gathered up her papers and make-up, got into her good shoes.

"We've hardly had a visit at all. I was counting on you, Lutie, the blue crabs this time of year. . . . Whatever will I say to Ladye and Faith?"

She promised to write the Rutledges, make amends, perhaps even ask for the guarded court bouillon recipe. She called Mickey to say good-bye and make her apologies about the afternoon.

"I just don't understand."

"I need to call a cab—"

"That's out of the question. I won't hear of your taking a second cab. If you have to dash off, I can at least give you a proper escort."

Waiting for Lutie at the airport was a black man in a turtleneck sweater, brown polyester Sansabelt trousers, Rolex watch, mustache and sideburns, brown Hush Puppies, dark glasses, carrying a *Newsweek*, which he casually slapped against his thigh as he waited at the ticket counter. He was invisible. No one paid him any mind; he was clearly one of the new breed, passing through, traveling on his way somewhere else and not going to stop off here. Probably a computer programmer.

Aunt Caroline did not see him, not even when he stood in line next to Lutie while she changed her ticket, or walked through the departure gate with her, or turned to join her in waving good-bye.

She, the woman with the Princess Grace hair, was saying, "I'm disappointed, Lutie. Such a short visit. We had so much catching up to do. And don't forget"—she raised her voice slightly, pleadingly—"don't forget to keep our little secrets, now."

18

Journal: Married and Alone in Rome

DID I ever see Dabney? I have to ask myself that. Someone I lived with for five years.

I can picture his clothes, rather one outfit, which was what he wore all the time: a tan sleeveless sweater, white dress shirt with no tie and wrinkled collar, tan pants (or, in the winter, black wool), desert boots. I am straining for his face; but he is lying on the bed, and his arm is flung across it. (His glasses are beside him, on a book. Wire-rimmed, they've left a red line on the bridge of his nose, and I know the line is there, under his arm; that comes back to me.) That his shoulders were too narrow for his frame. That, in the days of short hair, his covered his ears slightly, and in the days of long hair, the same. He was never one for fashion.

At Redoaks we'd been simply roommates. On Sundays Mother would thank Dabney for putting in an appearance, as if he were a guest, introducing him to her friends as "This is Dabney, uh, dear, I should know—Lutie's fiancé, husband, that is, now. Isn't he good to come? He's in graduate school at our University also, two birds of a feather. Isn't that nice?"

Surely he got sick of that, yet he never said so. He had free rent; and someone who understood the content and context of his daily job and work.

We did not have sex very often, even at the start. If I wanted it, Dabney was usually too tired. He'd been up studying too late the night before, or he had something on his mind, and as he would patiently explain to me in the dark, so that I would not be offended or feel undesirable, there was nothing a man could do about that; it wasn't a matter of will; the mechanism wasn't under his control. If he wanted it, it was usually when I was too tired to respond, exhausted from the weekends, the house full of familiar strangers. Most nights would end up with us turning away from each other, pretending to be asleep, fighting in the way that we did, which was to increase the distance and the silence.

I could not bring myself to masturbate when he was there. That seemed perverse when you were married. But without ever bringing what was going on wholly to consciousness, I would do so in the bathroom with the door closed and my back pressed against the wall, my feet together, whenever he was gone. Below the level of addressing it, I think I reasoned that if he wasn't home, then it wasn't the same; it was understandable and did not mean that we could not do it together. So that as soon as his car drove out of the gravel drive—for he would sometimes go in before me, an early riser, to get to the library or, later, to teach an early class—I would hurry in, close the door, lean against the wall, and then, after I had calmed down, begin the cleaning, the cooking, a section of my dissertation, as if I had never done it.

I know, now, that I expected that to change in lovely

Rome: sunlit, pine-scented, lavish, crumbling Rome. I think that he must have, too; hoped that when he got to the end of his pilgrimage, his wife would not be so tiresomely the same.

Dabney and I were given the two-week trip as a commencement present by his mother and mine. We got our checks the same day we received our final degrees, he in classics, I in sociology, wearing identical caps and gowns in the same ceremony.

We stayed at a small hotel across from the Forum of Augustus, the start of our self-guided tour, embarrassed to be put in a "matrimonial bed." After all, we'd been married five years; we were scholars. That first morning, sitting high on the outside terrace of the hotel, the Palatine rising over one shoulder, the Capitoline over the other—watching the early light filter down through the pines to the old ruins, priests trudging on foot, Fiats trotting by in formation—I thought I was in heaven.

I was instantly, unexpectedly in love with Rome, suffused, for one thing, with a sense of familiarity because of the language, which was so like the Spanish which falls at daybreak on every Texan's ears, and, for another, with the joy of being, for the first time in my life, constantly, tenderly waited upon. The waiters (of whom we had three at every meal) and I got a common vocabulary worked out: how to say "pot of coffee," and then, because it was too strong even to taste, how to say "pot of hot water" (*acqua calda*) and "pot of milk," and how to ask for more butter. And then, as we got the hang of it, we worked out a lavish ceremony of *tè freddo* (iced tea) served as four courses: the pot of tea, the hot water, a pitcher of ice cubes, that great luxury, and a chilled glass with a slice of lemon beside it. They thought this grand and would serve it to me when other people had wine, and thought perhaps it was the American equivalent of mineral water and would say to all Americans thereafter, "*Tè freddo*, okay?"

Dabney was infuriated. "You can't keep your distance from anyone, can you? You'll domesticate Hell itself when you get there." He shut his eyes in irritation. "For God's sake, Lutie, we're in *Rome*."

So, it turned out, was everyone else.

From the first day Dabney suffered from the weight of a truth he had not before anticipated: He was not alone in Rome.

He could not bear it.

He'd brought with him his own careful journal on the excavations we were to see, had in his room years of typed-up classroom notes and extracts from sources on the Roman Forum. For the last two years he had applied to the American Academy in Rome, for a Rockefeller grant to study in Rome, for a National Endowment for the Humanities fellowship, for a teaching Fulbright. And been turned down by them all.

When he wiped his glasses and blew his nose, I think it was to keep from crying in vexation. He went about looking pinched and petulant and fidgety, like a boy in a museum with his mother who needs to go to the bathroom.

It got worse instead of better. "Look at them," he would say, "what a polyglot crew. Anyone at all can come, and here they all are." Every few feet on the streets or in the Forum, in the Colosseum or at the sidewalk cafés, he was surrounded by them: the once-colonized (blacks, Indians), the once-defeated (Germans with backpacks and wide jaws; and Italians, our hosts, as brown-shirted police lounging on the street corner, having a sweet drink, brandishing guns), the underclasses (those with leftover long hair, shirts with the armholes cut out, reefers)—all with the money to come.

All with more money than he, who had waited his turn, done his decade of study, earned his right to be there.

Two families at the hotel tried his patience most of all. One was a mother and middle-aged daughter from Milwaukee, Wisconsin, who went about in matching tan raincoats, telling us the guidebooks said it could pour unexpectedly this time of year, and that they knew it was true, because this was their fifth trip abroad. They had just returned from Firenze, and the highpoint, they related, had been glimpsing Galileo's middle finger, the actual mummified finger, *dito medio della mano destra de Galileo*, pointing to heaven, under a glass bell jar. Before that, they'd been in Pompeii, but the mother had been suffering with a head cold, so they had missed a tour.

The other group was a threesome, also American: a mother, in Evan-Picone slacks, white linen jacket, white sun hat on well-cut blond hair, with her two wretched sons. She spoke to the waiters in French, but to the rest of us in English, and constantly. While she read aloud from her source books—"dates from the time of Caesar Augustus, which was the beginning of Jesus' life"—the boys would tell the most outrageous jokes. (The smaller of the two, fat and belligerent, would shout at the other, "Hi, Dick Hertz?" and the older, whiny one would reply, "Not mine, how about yours?" and they would whoop with laughter.)

Dabney would crumble a roll and grind his teeth, and the waiter and I would practice how to say "pot of hot water" in Italian, and the sun would rise over the pines, and the gates to the ruins would swing open for all of us.

We went to the Sistine Chapel and took Tour C. So did about three hundred others, including: thirty-six members of Carefree David, forty nuns with medals on their habits, a class of French schoolboys in short pants and alpine hats, the mother and daughter from Milwaukee, the Christian mother and her bratty boys, plus multilingual guides explaining how Michelangelo happened to paint the ceiling, as if talking of home repairs.

The raincoated ladies found us and reported that they were glad to get here this time, that last time they'd missed the Sistine because they'd had to check with American Express that morning. There was nowhere to escape in the jam-packed room of tourists with upward-craning necks.

In the Raphael room, Dabney became ecstatic over a painting of the Church triumphant. Above us was depicted a cheap, gilt Jesus, the merest icon, set on a stone pedestal which had once held a winged marble Apollo, now knocked to the ground, broken into pieces. It was the loving care with which the destroyed Greek figure had been portrayed that cheered Dabney, that and the tawdry appearance of the supplanting Christ. "The church might think it commissioned him to put the classicists in their place, but he's made a fool of the lot of them." Spotting Mrs. Hertz, as we called the white-hatted mother, he screamed out, "Do you see? This is overlay. *Overlay.* It's knocking the balls off the Greek statues."

"Oh, hello," she said, not able to hear him above the babble of translations. "Isn't this worth the entire trip?"

"I can't stand it," he said.

At the Pantheon he found the remains of Raphael: wedged into a niche surrounded by entombed popes, statues of saints, bronze kissing doves. "*Ille hic Est Raphael, Timvit Quo Sospite.*" Gregorius XVI on one side; Jesus with a gold-leaf groin cover on the other.

"I can't stand it," he repeated.

The oldest Greek-style building in Rome, the Temple of Vesta, its columns dating back to 200 B.C., was in disrepair. No one charged admission; there were no tours. It was a home for vagrants; Dabney raged as he found a filthy mattress, a cat's bowl, two stale rolls, a wad of soiled paper. "No one cares." He fumed, kicking at a pile of cigarette butts. "No one gives a damn."

I grew tired of his dissatisfaction. Let there be something that pleases you, I thought, here in the home of all your aspirations. One striated ciprollino column, one wild acanthus, one green smear of melted copper, one damp subterranean passage, one fresco's pale, thin colors. *Like something.*

But no part of it could be right if the whole was wrong, and the whole made him sick. He got a cold. He shut his eyes to what was there; standing beneath the Arch of Titus, he refused to look up.

So I went about my pleasures alone, as I had always done. Finding out if the peas were fresh tonight, if there were nice chicken pieces basting or only backs and wings, whether the lamb was in season, whether the beef was good today, that I could count on the *vitello arrosto* to be delicious anywhere, the noodles in cream with ham, the fresh peach in its wine cup. It all triggered my oldest memories of the South: conversing at every meal about what there was to eat today and what would go well with it.

How lovely it all was, and how happy I was to be there.

Central to it, of course, was being freed from tending Redoaks. The pleasure I took in riding the elevator up three floors to the rooftop table and sitting down to be served food that I had not fixed, so beautifully arranged, so carefully presented. I kept a count in my head: eight more days, seven, six. I could have kept coming to that flat expanse of tile, past the clay pots of flowers and latticed bougainvillea, so Mexican and so familiar, for the rest of my life, sitting at my leisure, looking out at the sight of the incredible hills, so foreign and so much home. . . .

Our last afternoon ended in the pouring rain.

Dabney had made two dozen trips to the Forum, blocking it out, studying each corner, making small scale drawings of what was there, comparing notes from various sources as to dates of construction, restoration, destruction, reconstruction.

At four o'clock we climbed to the Farnese Gardens to stand where Gibbon stood contemplating the decline and fall of the Roman Empire. The Palace of Augustus was behind us, the House of Domitian on our right, a grove of orange trees and sweet acacia on our left.

Dabney was in a slump as he stared down at the Temple of Antoninus and Faustina directly below us—usurped by a Roman church, and at the Temple of Venus and Rome—dominated by another.

An Arab with a wife in a hot pink blouse wandered past our line of vision, he making plans to build himself a spread identical to this.

Tourists passed back and forth.

"Who was that nymph that turned into a tree? I forgot."

"We do want to do a little shopping while we're here."

"Daphne, wasn't it? Or Diana?"

I turned and studied the gardens. A black cat slept on a dirt path beside an ancient cypress and a mass of oleander. Three small kittens slept in a pile beneath a bench beside a row of roses. Beyond the orange trees were boxwood, palms, and stately eucalyptus.

The white-hatted woman arrived with her two feuding sons. Pointing to the statues of the Vestals far below, she instructed: "They were just like nuns; they were the nuns of their day."

Dabney clutched at his notebook and stomped off as the sky opened and it began to pour.

The Arab dragged his wife down a set of stairs behind us into the catacombs of Nero. The woman and her sons followed, and we did also. Inside the long arched tunnel we all huddled, joined by a dozen more, as the sky grew dark and the rain fell in sheets. It washed over our feet, making a shallow river through the passageways. We looked like a herd of wet sheep. Only the women from Milwaukee, in their tan raincoats, were not drenched to the skin.

"This was our afternoon to do the House of Livia, wouldn't you know?" the daughter said.

"Still, this is better than Spain. Spain is one great big ormolu clock," the mother countered.

"Nero," the Christian woman in Evan-Picone instructed her sons, "was a wicked emperor who lived at the time of . . ."

Dabney pulled us out into the drenching rain, up the stairs, through the gardens, his shirt draped over his head to shelter his notebook, his chest icy white and rough with chilblains. We sat below the Farnese Gardens, past potted purple hydrangeas, on a stone stairs by a dripping fern-filled grotto, soaked and chilled, until it was dusk and the deluge had subsided.

Watching a great pine drip onto the sloping ground, I though about the pregnancy going on inside me and about all my hopes for a new beginning here among the palaces of Rome. Surely, I had thought, when he is where he wants to be we can come together.

"It doesn't make sense anymore," he said, of Rome and us.

Coming down into the Forum, we saw a mother cat leave a kitten and run up a crumbling wall by the Temple of

Antoninus and Faustina. The mother cat lay at the top, in the weeds and vines, nursing another black and white kitten; while the one at the bottom of the overgrown wall mewed and ran back and forth, whimpering, trying to climb, falling back down. A German family, watching also, was all for sending one of their children to help it up, but I gestured to wait a bit, that this was how it learned to climb. And sure enough, as the trees dripped into the ruins, the little white-faced kitten got a foothold and dragged itself up, hanging once by a claw, until it, too, lay flopping at the top.

"You could be in your own backyard, for all you see of what's here. I don't know why I brought you along or why I came myself." Dabney put his wet shirt back on and slicked his stringing hair.

We went back to the room, and, as every afternoon, he lay down to take a nap, and I went in to take a shower.

Closing the door, I saw there was a fullness to my waist that had not been there before. Leaving the shower running so it would be hot, I went out to get the robe, which, in my anxiety, I had forgotten.

Dabney lay stretched out on the bed, his arm flung over his eyes, his trousers pulled down to his thighs, jerking himself: patiently, methodically, routinely.

I turned the water off, and he saw that I was there.

He shrugged. "It's simpler," he said. "Forget it. Take your shower." He pulled the spread across himself.

I could see, then, that this was long habit. Something he scarcely knew he did, triggered by the sound of my shower. Recalling the time later, he would remember it as when he'd had a nap.

We had never been lovers, not really. Tending ourselves covertly, not making reference to it: like roommates. And now we were out of school, and, as he said, it didn't make sense anymore.

"Take your shower, will you? And quit staring?"

On the plane back Dabney was enraged by the gross manner in which we were being force-fed in every orifice like geese: "Alcohol, earphones, movies. I can't stand it."

I was thinking how Mother would have enjoyed the long flight, being served snacks on trays, having Stravinsky in her ear as she wrote out postcards telling about the trip. She had never been abroad, had always wanted to go, and would have squeezed out every drop of ceremony from the adventure: making menu choices (the chicken? the veal?); hearing all the soothing messages delivered over the PA system in English, Italian, French, and German; accepting after-dinner candies, a complimentary glass of wine, a blanket for her legs, a pillow; paying for the late movie. Such attention would have lasted her a lifetime.

I told Dabney I would like to have given her, not the trip to Rome or the ruins or the art or the pasta, but simply the plane trip over and back.

"You should have married your mother," he said, turning his face away and feigning sleep.

As we got ready to disembark and go our separate ways, the white-hatted woman thanked the stewardesses one at a time, and when the captain himself came down the stairs from the cockpit, she thanked him as well. "God bless you, sir, for the safe flight."

"Eat snot," whispered the younger, fatter of her sons.

Four

———————◆———————

19

THEY had their last group meeting, and Lutie was sorry to see it end—as is the way it should be. She and Danya and Fudge had hugs all around and told each other they were great people and projected that a mile away. Not true, the projection, but still the heart of it was well meant. They did all convey better who they were than when they'd started out, and that was progress.

For the last meeting they were supposed to wear whatever they wanted. It was interesting that more than half the group chose uniforms again, each at home, Lutie surmised, pretending to her/himself that it would be a joke. But actually it kept you from having to admit to the group, who knew you pretty well by this time, that this was the way you were going to be from now on. Which was sticking your neck out a lot.

Danya wore a rigged-up police uniform, and Fudge wore a Miss America dress with an armful of artificial roses and her running shoes. Lutie did not wear the waitress outfit but, instead, the bright wool petticoat, a sweater top which didn't go with it at all, her fuzzy bedroom slippers, and some woolly mittens (not gloves, but the mittens that only have a gob of space for fingers and opposable thumbs). It was as brave as she knew how to appear: mismatched and disorganized. The group didn't quite understand, but she told them that her cat had run away and her uncle had killed himself and that all the Savannah cousins who weren't up for the League played croquet, and they took her word for it, not knowing what all that meant but seeing that Lutie was Acting Out and being glad of it.

Sammy had just received a grant from the National Institute of Mental Health for a correlation between phobics and enuresis. He planned to go back home to Ohio, he said, where all the little boys were scared of dogs and elevators and wet the bed. He'd told Joe and Lutie that he'd put *black* under "Nationality," "Hobbies," "Religion," "Sexual Preference," and "Marital Status." He was elated and making jokes because he'd got the funds, not for the clinic, but for himself, T. Samuel Davidson.

("What's the T. for?" Lutie had asked.

"Terrence."

"Terrence Samuel is a name your aunt Nannie would be proud of."

"She was. It belonged to her favorite husband.")

The truth was, Lutie thought, that he was going back to Ohio not only to set up a controlled study for his new project but to touch base. And he admitted it was true; that ever since he'd rescued her in Savannah, he'd been thinking that he'd been hiding out in New York too long and ought to put on his shades and Rolex and Sansabelts and slip into his old home community again. To see if it was still as phobic at the sight of coloreds.

Lutie had quit trying to thank him every day for having saved her life and had decided that she'd pay somebody else back along the line; that was about all you could do with true favors.

Sammy, who was celebrating, had helped everyone into the elevator at group in his green uniform and left it on.

And was rewarded when two different people, at different times, looked around and asked, "Where's Dr. David tonight?"

Her afternoon walk was now on the SUNY campus the days that she was there, as darkness had come creeping into the day, taking most of it. With daylight saving in October, it had begun to get dark before six; now, in December, it was dark well before five. Day was a dim strip in the middle. She had calculated an hour's walk to be four times around the central square of brown-brick buildings that formed the courtyard. Someone had mounted a row of fake windows on the outside of the bookstore building: apple green wood shutters, checked oil-cloth curtains, plastered-on views of paper oceans (she didn't understand why institutional buildings got such a negative response for looking like what they were, institutional), and she used these as her markers, lapping them four times as night fell in the afternoon.

She had Mrs. Rodino make her a blue silk blouse to wear for her mother's awards ceremony—an excuse to have something new and pretty when she went into the city to see Joe. The weather was in the thirties, which was cold but was not ugly enough to provide the winter tales she'd heard about. It seemed she should be leaving when there were puddles at every curb, slush that slopped you to your ankles, stalled cabs, a white Central Park, needles of sleet, and a chill factor that made it in the minuses. Instead, there was only a whipping wind which was less than the usual Texas norther that cut through the dry cedar brakes, deadened batteries, and rattled the single-paned windows.

Mrs. Rodino was in a slump. They watched the next to last episode of "Texas," in which a raging fire almost killed the adoptive father and the natural father had to brave the flames to save him (or the other way around). Even though Lutie told her that Texas was full of fires like that, that all of it was authentic, Mrs. Rodino fussed. "Would you believe a game show? They're replacing it with a *game show*." She was broken-hearted. "I hope they let us see who gets the boy. That T.J. really loves him. . . ."

At that time Lutie still thought she'd be gone for good in less than a week, and she and Joe were feuding, so she was surprised, but pleased, when he called and asked her if she would fix dinner at his house for his oldest and best friend, Hurlbert Endress, who'd been in his fraternity at college, and in his wedding, and all the rest.

She was not anticipating loading up the wicker chairs and saying good-bye to the tomcats and the brick carriage road or the performing artists—or Joe. So the dinner seemed a reprieve. And amazing, besides, because Joe was always the one to cook, the one who needed to do the ritual of boiling water, stirring the pasta.

"Hurlbert and I go way back," he'd said. "He's my oldest friend. Knew my daddy before long hair, and my mother before the first cousin came aboard. I told him that you were a great cook." He sounded embarrassed.

As well he might have been, his only real meal at her place having been flavored with the smell of skunk.

They hadn't been doing too well because he was sunk in guilt over Fritz's stealing the car. And she'd made the mistake, the last time he was at her place, of looking up from her journal work and telling him what she thought. That when a tomcat gets ready to go out and tear up the neighborhood, you know that he'll get a bucket of water thrown on him by one neighbor, and hit on the head with a broom by another who is sick of his caterwauling in the middle of the night, and get a hunk taken out of his tail and that his jaw will swell and fester and he'll drag around for weeks—but you don't think it's your fault, or the neighbors' fault, or the other cat's fault. You just think: Here we go. Joe had got really mad.

"Cook?" she had said, amazed.

"I'll do the shopping," he said. "Tell me what to get."

Had he wanted her to be cooking all along? Had he gotten tired of fixing his same-dish suppers? Was Hurlbert the kind who got nervous at the sight of a man in the kitchen? She had no idea.

"I won't know until I see what's at the store. But anyway, Joe, I can't bring enough food for all of us on the train. Why don't you bring him out here?"

"Take your car."

She panicked. "I can't do that. It gets dark in the middle of the day. I don't know the way—"

"Cord owners do it all the time; Chevy owners, too."

"Do they?" She had laughed.

"Get out your map, and follow it with me." So she had traced with him over the phone how to get on the Cross Westchester to the Saw Mill to the Henry Hudson Parkway. He would be at the Ninety-sixth Street exit, waiting at the corner. All she had to do was get that far.

She had a good time in the store, realizing that she'd missed doing what she'd done for most of her life. She decided on a yam and banana soufflé, fig and sausage empanadas but then changed her mind because it was a sweet sausage, and she didn't know if that meant Italian spices, and there were no figs. Instead, she would have a pork roast, stuffed with chestnuts and apples.

She'd set out for the store in the near dark, which it was now at four, already deeply shadowed, the air opaque under the bare-limbed trees on the ridge across her street in Cranberry Park.

209

Loaded with food from Finast, she got on the Cross West-chester (headed the wrong way and had to turn around) and followed the signs toward the Tappan Zee, as Joe had instructed, looking for a turnoff that said "Saw Mill." Suddenly she saw a fork to the left which said "New York South, 87," and had about two seconds to decide what to do, in all the early-evening traffic, but she took it, since otherwise she could see herself ending up across the Hudson, and it turned out all right.

From there on it was clear sailing, and then she was on the Henry Hudson and at the right exit, and there was Joe, in a raincoat, straining to see in the pitch-dark with the glare of oncoming headlights, looking for the Chevy, and then leaping into the street and waving his arms frantically.

"That wasn't so bad, was it?" He'd kissed her and seemed worried, more worried than on the phone, as to whether she would really make it. "You don't have trouble unless there's ice."

She was defensive. What did he know about driving in ice? "I know about ice," she said. "West of town sleets over four or five times a year; you plane all over the shoulders. It was the traffic; you have to know where you're going before you get there."

She had got a pork roast, a bag of cranberries to make hot cranberry bread, walnuts, two sweet potatoes and a banana (plus she'd brought a little mace in a baggie, because she wasn't sure Joe would have any, and two pinches of rosemary for the roast), and a sack of spinach for a salad, and a can of baby prunes and a pint of whipping cream for prune whip, an old country dessert. The walnuts were for it, and she'd use a touch of brandy that Joe had. In her mind she could see the whole plate: the juicy meat, the golden soufflé, the hot berry bread, the fresh dark greens.

Joe was ecstatic as he helped her unload. "Great. This stuff is great. I never heard of any of this before. What do you need? A beater? There must be one somewhere."

Sammy arrived before the guest, ready for his odyssey back home. He'd grown a beard, or was growing one, very neat, and he wore a heavy black wool suit and a Black Watch Shetland tie. He looked somehow slightly like Freud and had even taken to doing something with one eye (she'd have to check the Viennese's photograph)—elevating one brow? lidding one eye?—that made the resemblance amazing. He was too big to be Freud, but most patients wouldn't know what a small man Freud had been. It would, on some level, act as a reassurance; it was his ultimate uniform. Lutie attributed it to getting the grant and told him her theory.

He fantasized about his trip back to Columbus, which would consist of counting the blacks in three-piece suits driving BMWs; and noting that the whites looked more and more like inbred Appalachians escaped across the border from West Virginia, living on white bread and Karo, bruising their children on Saturday nights, spending their days at K-Mart.

Then Hurlbert Endress arrived, a bushy bear of a man in a vast tweed greatcoat and a corduroy touring cap.

A cap. Lutie and Sammy looked at each other.

"So you work with Joe Richard, do you? Well, welcome. I mean it," the old friend said to Sammy.

"So this is her, is it?" he said to Lutie. "How do."

"We'll put supper on and come visit," she told him, giving Sammy the look that Savannahians give their Cuthberts.

"A hat," she said, leaning against the kitchen counter.

"Nobody's perfect," he said.

"He's Joe's best friend."

"Boys will be boys." Sammy made a grin. "It'll be fine. I'll pass out cigars. That always does the trick. What does the help do?"

"I forgot about baking the sweet potatoes for the soufflé. I didn't have time anyway. I wonder if we can boil them. Let's find out; they take a lifetime in the oven. You mash the banana in this bowl with a fork, and chop up the sweet potatoes without the skins and put them in this pan. No salt. Let me see." Lutie washed the spinach and tore the stems off and wrapped the leaves loosely in a dishtowel and put them in the refrigerator. Then she made a dressing, which she set near the stove to steep, from some of Joe's good olive oil and lemon juice and garlic. She dumped the fresh cranberries in a bowl and floured them and added the eggs and butter and flour, all of which Joe had. "Look on the shelf for anything that looks like pie spices. Cinnamon? Cloves?"

Sammy found a very ancient tin labeled "Pumpkin Pie Spices."

"Fine." Lutie dumped in two teaspoons and just a pinch of the mace which was being saved for the sweet potatoes.

"You forgot sugar." Sammy was watching.

"Did I? Is there any brown?"

"No, and not much white."

They got the bread in a greased pan, and the roast stuffed and in the oven, and propped themselves against the kitchen table.

"Let's go in," Sammy said.

"I guess."

"Not long before you'll be home," he said.

"That's *you*."

"All the help is leaving."

"Joe hasn't looked upon me as much help." Lutie bit her lip.

"You going to let him spend Christmas with his ex?"

212

"What can I do?"

"Don't they teach white girls that?"

"What?"

"How to keep a man?"

"That isn't even on the agenda."

"If you were sticking around, I'd suggest remedial work."

"If I was . . . Let's go," Lutie said.

She was in her new blue silk blouse and pearls; Sammy was in his black vest and white shirt. How they dressed up for Joe.

As they went into the living room, he was saying, "She's really a good cook."

They laughed; this was a Joe Richard new to them.

Hurlbert Endress, it became clear, meant no harm. He adored Joe, and that counted for a lot. He was head of a company called Leuchtenkunst, which he said meant art lamp. He looked like Paul Bunyan.

"God, makenspeaken, I'd forgotten." Joe looked buoyed by old times. "This joker would makenspeaken words to our German teacher; we even did it in Germany on our student tour and everybody, I mean everybody, believed it. Eatenlunchen, makenpissen, takengirlen."

They were back in the good old days.

"I'm still doing it, Joe: makenbucken. Traveling all over there, getting designs. Old Art Deco and Bauhaus copies, making the chrome parts out of nickel, getting pulls from jewelry wholesalers, calling hanging lamps Pendelleuchtes, table lamps Tischleuchtes, floor lamps Stehleuchtes, so I can charge six hundred bucks apiece. So only the status-mad can buy them."

"So what were you doing in Poland?" Joe asked. Hurlbert had stopped over, taking a cab in from the airport, before going back home.

"Hardware conference. Mostly what I did there was cry

for my lost youth. Remember I was there in the summer of sixty-one, on the Experiment for International Living, enjoying an idyll of sweet red berry soups, hickory-fed pork" —Lutie and Sammy looked at each other, pleased— "potatoes at every meal. Ice cream vendors. Rolling fields like Kansas, the Masurian Lakes, little boats. Contentenmaken for sure. Not these days. Gray streets, gray apartments. Gray guys missing arms and legs. The entire country is gray. Robotwalken. Not a scrap of meat in all of Warsaw, not even in the restaurants. By the time you get there they've sold out." He accepted another Grolsch beer from Joe. "Of course, this time I was selling, not loafing."

"Which calls to mind the Donaldson motto: Sell services, not goods."

"That was bull. From a guy whose dad sold haircuts to hippies. It was doctor talk, a mistake of your youth."

"I'm stuck with it."

"Not me. Watching my dad tune pianos put a great desire in my heart to be the guy who sold them."

"Your dad was a genius."

"Pathetic, that's what he was."

"And your mother's dead?"

"You're looking at the last of an undistinguished line. I read on the plane that the reason dinosaurs died out was that female eggs were the only ones that developed in warm temperatures, male eggs dying out above a certain heat. We're in the same shape today; just when it's finally time for the world to be ours, no more world. I've been running all my life to get somewhere better than my old man, and I'm a dinosaur. I've worked my life out trying to shed a little Licht on the subject, and then everybody on the street gets federal money, and I'm still coming in last."

"Right on the mark," Sammy said.

214

"That so?" Hurlbert looked as if nothing surprised him anymore. "What for, if you don't mind my asking?"

"Phobics. Guys who're scared."

"That so?"

Dinner was ready, and the plates looked as good as Lutie had hoped. They had seconds of the stuffed pork, had never tasted anything like the combination of banana and yam. "This is swell," Joe said, "really swell." He wore a look of enormous relief and delight, as if he hadn't been sure at all whether Lutie knew how to warm a TV dinner, but that he'd needed to show that he had a domestic woman. Hurlbert had an aunt in the country, who used to make prune whip, but without the walnuts. It took him back, and he had seconds of that with his coffee.

"Delicious," he said.

And in the living room, afterward: "You've improved yourself, Joe. Carole's specialty, as I recall, was the deli sandwich."

"Speaking of which—"

"Tell Hurlbert."

Joe recounted the car theft and Noah's subsequent broken ankle. "She says it's the absent father. My thinking at this point is that my moving back will only give the older son a further chance to get at both of us; you give them a wedge like that."

"It's your field."

"Try telling that to a lawyer."

"I can't advise you, not having had kids. I've got wives scattered here and there, as you know. No regrets about that. I think I decided having kids would turn me into a piano tuner."

Joe looked despondent. "I told her I'd stay over Christmas, try to work out the current situation."

"Let me warn you, once you get back in the sack with an ex, you're hooked."

Joe flushed and looked in Lutie's direction. "That's part of the problem," he said.

She felt her face get hot. It had never occurred to her that Joe would go to bed with Carole. They were *divorced*.

"It isn't the absent father, tell her," Hurlbert went on, oblivious. "Studies have shown what causes the problem in broken homes is the absence of the father's paycheck. That's what she's after."

Lutie went into the kitchen.

Joe came in after her.

"How could you not talk to me about that?"

He pulled the door shut so they couldn't be heard. "What did you think?" he asked. "What did you think it was all about?"

"You said, to look after the boys."

"How many bedrooms do you imagine a law student in New Jersey has?"

"Did you sleep with her?"

"I *slept* on the couch." He looked dejected. "So as not to give the boys any more leverage than they already have."

"How could you not tell me?"

"You didn't care. It was more important to you to go visit your aunt than to stay. I wanted to have this out Thanksgiving, but you had to go tripping off. You're going home to mother Christmas. What am I supposed to say to her?"

"But you're divorced."

"Oh, grow up, will you?"

Lutie looked at the remains of the meal, stacked on the kitchen counter. She didn't understand. She had never understood where men were about sex. They were always having it somewhere in some way that you didn't expect at all and not liking how they had it when it was with you. She began to sob.

"How come it's all right for you to spend the first night you're back—when I'm trying to help you with your uncle's death—covering a notebook with reminiscences about *your* ex and not all right for me to deal with *mine* when there are kids involved?"

"You told me to." She wiped her face. "You told me to find out Whatever Happened to Men. So I was. You told me."

"Well, you might have looked up and wondered what was happening to this one."

"I was going back, that's all. I thought . . ." She buried her face in her hands. "I even intend to find Mr. Pinter when I go home."

He grabbed her wrists in his two hands. "That's it. Say that again: '*When I go home.*' Where does that leave me?"

"It's not my fault you were back with her."

"It is if there's nothing out here that keeps me from it."

"What am I supposed to do?"

"Say, 'When I go home, Joe always has the light on.' Say, 'When I go home, he makes me tea.' Say, 'When I go home, my mind isn't on my aunt Caroline.'" He let her arms go and got himself another beer.

"Oh."

"Do you get the idea?"

"You mean, move in?"

"I mean, move your brain at the very least."

"Live up here?"

"People have run away from home before."

"At thirty-two?"

"Don't ask me."

She turned away. She had to think about it. Was this something people did, used each other to get away? Besides, how did you know it would work? When she'd moved in with Dabney, it hadn't changed anything at all.

"But I promised Mother," she said out loud.

"Fuck your mother," he said, and went back to his old best friend in the living room, who had left wives all over the place.

She came around the corner after him in time for them to see Sammy do his cigar show.

"Like a cigar, Bert?"

"Sure."

Sammy walked up to him and held out three long cigars in the palm of his hand.

"What's your line? You work with Joe, right?"

"Phobias. Castration phobias." Carefully Sammy cut the ends of the cigars with his sterling silver clipper and proffered one to the lamp salesman.

"That so?" Hurlbert said, looking down.

"That's right, brothro."

They sat up late, the four of them, with Joe and his friend taking their stories back to college, and Sammy and Lutie having their own thoughts, all dressed up, each of them trying to pass for what Joe wanted, but not knowing how.

Finally, Hurlbert, outlasted, got up and gave Joe a big bear hug, and put on his greatcoat and his cap.

Lutie felt bad; Bert hadn't wanted the rest of them to be there, and she hadn't wanted him to stay. It was hard to share.

"It was a pleasure, I mean it," he said to Sammy.

"Good-bye, little lady. Joe Richard is a lucky man," he said to her.

They sat for a few minutes, the three of them, then cleared away bottles and cups.

"This is where I came in," Sammy said. "Has she figured out by now I don't live here?"

"I don't think so," Joe said.
"See you around." Sammy waved from the door.
They told him good-bye:
"Give my regards to Ohio."
"Tell your aunt Nannie hello."

20

J o e took her to LaGuardia; it was Thursday, the sixteenth.
Mother's ceremony was on Saturday; that was as close as
she could call it. She knew that his paying for the ticket was
his way of trying to keep some control over their situation,
so she had let him. They stood around exchanging transitional phrases: moreover, however, meanwhile, nevertheless, on the other hand.

It had snowed last night, the first snow, a beautiful still
white covering that she had waked to, entranced, too dry
and gossamer for even a snowball. She'd taken her brick
road walk in it, very early, to see the reservoir ringed in
white, the plaza a snowfield. Coming back, she'd sighted a
small, very persistent bird outside on the stair rail, which
the Peterson's guide identified—from its silhouette and its
che-bek—as a least flycatcher. Whose visits she now associated with snowfall.

The plane was strange, too fast a leap across the country.
(She missed what she liked most about travel: the feel of
the wheel, and the sound of country music. "My tears have
washed 'I love you' from the blackboard of my heart";
"She got the gold mine, I got the shaft.")

As they landed, she watched the purple patches turn into plowed fields; the matchboxes become houses; the flies, cars; the long dark streaks, rivers; the green stamps, parks. Mother had said on the phone, "Come by the office as soon as you get in, so we can have a hug. The V-P will want to see you, I know; he's not in good *wealth* these days, but we're not supposed to know. I'm taking off Thursday, so I can have Friday off to get my hair done and let you help me decide what to wear for Saturday. Staff gets university holidays, so we'll have nearly a month of catching up to do before I have to go back. You *will* stay at my place over the weekend, won't you? So we can talk. Besides, Nan is clearing her things out; she promises to be gone—not that I've meant to rush her at all, of course. We've hardly spoken since Thanksgiving, when we called you and Sister. We're both so busy. But we'll talk about all that when I see you. Oh, Lutie, it's been an age."

Had she told her mother she was flying in? She wasn't sure. She should have told Nan not to hurry, to plan to stay over Christmas if she wanted. She hadn't been thinking about them down here when she'd changed her plans, only of Joe.

She walked down the ramp of the plane into the glare, feeling it close around her. Everything looked strange: men in Stetsons, which she had forgotten they really wore at home, women in tight pants and high heels. All good-looking, like movie extras, carrying initialed luggage, wearing initialed belts and bags and jeans, making a big trip to Dallas or Houston, for a deal or dinner and to shop. She'd forgotten, too, how casual everyone was about going and coming and buying and selling. How much time and space and good looks there were to spare in Texas.

She remembered how overdressed she'd been for the first night of group, coming from this world. Now, used to her new appearance, she felt dowdy even in the airport, like a mousy schoolteacher. She should have put on mascara, carried her good Coach bag, worn her pearls. She smiled at the reentry.

She rented a car, going straight for Hertz, which she knew was cheapest in the long run, not having add-ons, and got a weekend rate, even though it was Thursday.

"Let me just give you a few little directions now," the blonde said, "Just follow your street out here, and you'll . . ."

She was given a Ford and, getting the feel of it, recalled why she didn't like Fords: They had the get up and go of a three-speed bike and steering fine-tuned as microsurgery. Guiding the red-interior, white-exterior four-door, she decided they were for conservatives, who liked to move slowly but be able to get out of tight spots in a hurry.

It was balmy, so everyone had on a suede jacket or a sweater at the most. No one carried an overcoat to be on the safe side, even though the radio said a norther was predicted for evening. They would take their chances; that was how it was here. She liked it when a great blue norther came in: you could be standing at the filling station, putting gas in, wearing shirt sleeves, and you would see the cold front move down the street, as palpable as a hurricane, a wall of cold air, and see the people, block by block, run for wraps, dash for the inside, shiver and hug themselves. Cows, too; you could see cows munching along, stunned by the cold, cram together for warmth beneath the nearest tree—having no sense of memory, thinking the long shadows in the sunny pasture would be forever.

Disregarding Mother's instructions to come by the office, she turned away from the direction of The University and headed out 290 West.

Driving into her old subdivision, she could hardly recognize it, so many new houses had been added or begun: copies of one-story German houses with dog runs; copies of two-story farmhouses like theirs; red-fronted "barns" with lofts. The interest rates might be high, the building industry depressed, but that never bore any relation to what Texas was about, which was growing right and left, as usual.

Redoaks looked vacant when she drove up, neglected; the flat cement porch, with its flagstone walkway, was muddy and littered; there were rainsoaked scraps of paper blown against the side of the house. But a car was there, a waxed two-year-old Olds, metallic brown. So Nan must be home.

She rang the bell, but there was no answer. Finally, she opened the front door, hollering out as she did, "Nan, Nan, Nannie—are you here?" So as not to scare her cousin if she was asleep. Something about the house inside reminded her of the days when Gran lived there and Mother was in town all the time, and she would come home from school and find the old lady locked in, the house smelling stuffy and abandoned. Or worse.

"Who's there?" A thin voice came from upstairs. "Who is it? Aunt Florence?" And then, in a whisper: "Oh, God, Aunt Florence."

"Nan, it's Lutie."

"Oh, thank God," the frantic voice said. And then her cousin came timidly down the steps into the tiny entry where Lutie waited.

Her face was puffy and miserable, her housecoat streaked and wrinkled. Herself, ballooned almost beyond recognition.

"Lutie, Jesus, I thought you were your mother."

"Didn't she tell you I was coming?"

"Saturday. Or maybe she said tomorrow. Except she's so vague. I can't ever get the straight of it. She wants me out of here, but she won't come right out and say that, so she tells me to be sure to tell Caroline when I see her that she wants her to write, things like that. Finally, I asked her, "When do I have to go?" And then she waffled, the way she does. I thought maybe it was you not wanting me here, and if you don't, say so, and I can get packed in a couple of days. I've told Mom that I'm not coming back until after the first of the year, I'm not up to Christmas in the pink palace and being the family outcast. You saw them, didn't you?

"Here—sit down. Do you want a drink? I mean, it's your house, what am I doing telling you what to do? Oh, Judas, come on, sit down or something. Where's your stuff? Is that your car out there?"

Lutie sat gingerly in the living room of the familiar house. The fireplace, always filled with greens in warm weather, or a fire, in cold, was stuffed with smoked, blackened, twisted newspapers. The aubergine rug was sooty and stained. The cushions were off the love seat, laid in a pallet on the floor. One of the wing-backed chintz chairs was missing, the one that usually sat against the front windows, with potted schefflera fanned about it like a palm. The plants were gone also.

"It's upstairs," Nan said quickly, "that chair. When I'm here, I stay up there. You know the big bedroom is the only one with a lock, and it just has that big bed, which you can't really prop up in. You know what I mean: The bed slides."

"Yes." Lutie nodded, still trying to get her bearings.

She knew she was staring at the fat girl before her, trying to locate her cousin Nan inside all that. After all, this must be Nan, the nearest thing to a sister she had. Why had no one told her? How long since she'd seen her? They, she and Mother, had made the trip to Savannah twice in a row, once for Uncle Elbert's funeral (she winced), once for Bubba's wedding. So they had missed a Christmas. It would be almost two years. Was it possible to gain that much in that length of time? Two years? She looked at the immense, dimpled arms bulging out of the housecoat.

"I'm a mess, aren't I?"

"Well—it's a surprise." Lutie patted a place by her on the couch, accepting a cup of sloshy, tepid instant tea that Nan had fixed, in reflex at old manners.

"It's Mickey. If I have to blame it on someone. She was the last straw, if you want to know. Not that things were good before that. Mom being moved out of that house, that was a blow, you know, when Daddy died. Well, with the boys gone, I thought she'd really need me, and I was doing great things with my needlepoint designs, having exhibits at all the Christmas benefits, getting an outlet at a couple of shops, all that stuff, and then she got a chance to get in that restored place that the witches got for her, they must have wanted her all to themselves, and there wasn't any room for me, suddenly, not really. She fixed up what she called a guest room, she kept calling it that, the guest room, this dinky closet space—well, you must have seen it. And I bet she didn't put you in there, on that piece of straw she calls a bed, did she? And she'd say, 'While you're here, Nannie, honey, you stay in the guest room, I want you to.' 'While you're here.' 'As long as you're here.'

"And then she'd go out to lunch with Mickey and leave me there, not ask me along, like I was not someone you could go out with to lady things, not being married. She saw me all of a sudden as this albatross old maid, and she wasn't having any of it." Nan looked across at Lutie as if she hoped to convey by how earnestly she was staring what she couldn't put into words.

"I used to get my weight down every year before you and Aunt Florence came or when we came to Gran's because we had to pose for those awful foursome pictures, every time, and as long as I wasn't too heavy for the pictures and Mom could send them out to everyone, use them for Christmas cards and all that, then she didn't mind too much if I got heavy in between times. But when you and Florence didn't come, that year, last year, and she knew you weren't, she went and posed herself with the three of us, me and the bubbas and her, and then, just with Mickey, the new daughter. And those, of the two of them, were what went out. And I know when Mickey gets in the JL, then Mom won't even remember my name, because I never will, and then Mickey will have baby Sayre —you heard all about that, I'm sure—and then I might as well be dead, as far as Mom is concerned.

"She tells everyone that I'm down here with Aunt Florence, with Sister, as she says, and that they've traded daughters, and isn't that clever, and how marvelous you look, and she sent pictures of your visit Thanksgiving, you and her and Mickey. . . . But I'm not mad at you, don't think that. It isn't your fault, Lutie. It's her way of getting at me because she knows how awful I look."

"You told me you were ready to try your wings. You said, when I asked you . . ."

Nan began to cry, tears filling her eyes and splashing down on big cheeks. "Aunt Florence didn't even invite me Saturday, can you believe that?"

"To the awards brunch?" Lutie couldn't. Her mother had been talking of the ceremony since the moment she'd been told, confidentially, at the end of the summer. This was her day, her moment, her reward.

"That's true. I saw it in the *paper*. A big Sunday spread of all the honorees, she'll show you. Open to the public, it said; anyone can come. And she never said a word."

Lutie knew that special invitations had gone out a month ago.

"You know when Mom got that Wilson house? Well, they had a little ceremony because it had been all fixed up and because, you know, the old bats had a lot of pull in the

226

town, and they posed Mom on the front porch and gave the history in, naturally, a big double spread in the Sunday section of the paper—which didn't mention that coloreds had once lived there—and anyway, Mom didn't tell me anything about it. I was talking with a buyer from Atlanta down at the old hotel, and I happened to see someone who was going, someone from Daddy's church, and she asked me wasn't I going to my mom's ceremony, and when I walked up, Mom almost didn't speak to me; there was Mickey, who was still being called Mary Michael at that point because my mom hadn't got the message about Mickey being old settler then and was going through her whitewash, and there was Mary Michael wearing a size six and handing my mom the house key for the photographer. Later Mom said she'd had her in the picture in case it would help her with the JL, to have herself in the paper at such a historic event. But I knew that wasn't the real reason; she can't stand to look at me."

Lutie asked for a refill of the dusty tea. She knew that what Nan said was so, that Aunt Caroline would not have claimed kin to her, looking the way she did. Anything else but fat was all right, anything. She didn't know what to say. It was obvious now why her mother had wanted Lutie to stay in town until after the brunch. Nan had become a conspiracy of the sisters, closet kin.

"She's having a party out here Sunday, Aunt Florence. I don't know if she told you—here." She handed the cup, acidly strong this time. "I'm not supposed to know. She told me you'd be having some of your friends over. But I knew because people have been calling here to say they couldn't come, forgetting you're not here, and they've lost her number or they never had it, something. They're used to calling out here, I can tell; you must do this stuff for her all the time. I got calls all fall, and I'd have to explain that I wasn't you, and half the time they wouldn't believe me.

And then I'd get so I wouldn't answer the phone for so long that they'd have to track her down in town. She had things at her place, suppers. I know that. And she never asked me. She took me to lunch one time, *one time*, when I first got here, so she could write Mom, and Mom wasn't about to ask Aunt Florence later on, so they could both pretend that I was too busy at the needlepoint shop.

"I never see anybody there either. I'm in the back room, designing for customers, making the shop a mint, doing my stuff and leaving it for them. They don't want me out front either, although they're nicer. I did meet one girl, Peg, who comes out and stays with me, or did at the start, when we could still make things work out here; she says she knows you. But then I stayed in town with her—I don't have the foggiest idea how you stand it with everything falling apart all the time—because this place had got too much for me, and we could go out to eat if we were in town. We got tired of the barbeque places out here, there's no place to go without a date and no place to find one. In town sometimes we'd run into somebody. Though I haven't had a real date since I got to this desert way station. I don't know what I'm going to do. Lutie, what am I going to do?"

Lutie felt it all descend back on her: the house; Nan's distress, so like Gran's; the weekend.

"There's no reason for you to leave," she said. "Not for a while anyway, Nannie."

"Don't call me *Nannie*. I can't stand it. That's all I need, that dumb name."

Lutie apologized. "Sorry, my mind was on Gran."

"What's she got to do with it?"

"The way Mother and Aunt Caroline were with her when she had River Bend, and then the way they were with her here, when she didn't."

"I guess I never grasped that last part. What Mom

didn't want to see she didn't, so I guess the reason we stopped coming was that Gran didn't have the place anymore, but I didn't figure that out. I thought we got busy being kids, me and the bubbas. And Daddy was being depressed all the time, and Mom got busy pretending he wasn't."

Lutie sat her undrinkable tea down on the hearth. "I went by your daddy's church while I was there—"

"I can't stand to do that; everybody stares at me, like we were their welfare family or something. I know Mom wants to move to First, and maybe she will; she'll get it in her head that she should go to Mickey's church, they'll have a baby christened there or something. I told her we could just move if she wanted, but the old bats are holding her there."

"Do you know what your daddy died of?"

Nan blinked and looked away. "Being step-and-fetch-it for three hundred people, is what I think. I think you can just wear out doing all the time for greedy people who don't have the time of day for you when the weather changes."

Lutie was silent. Wondering if Nan was talking of Uncle Elbert or of herself maybe. If she knew or if she didn't want to know.

She got up to go to the bathroom, dreading what she would find, which she did: a build-up of lime on the sides of the tub two inches thick. No shower curtain. A commode that gurgled and stalled weakly in its effort to flush water.

Surely Mother couldn't be planning to have people out *this weekend?*

"What I do remember about Gran's," Nan was saying, "was that Jimmie person who was suddenly the apple of their eye, that kid who could get away with anything. Speaking of when the weather changes."

"Are you sure about a party on Sunday?" Lutie asked, anxiously.

But Nan had leaped up and gone upstairs. "Stay there," she called. "I'll be right back. We can go to the Big Wheel, get a beer. I look such a mess, why didn't you tell me? I was terrified you were Aunt Florence, and then I got afraid you were the geek around the circle. Did you ever run into this developer out here? He is all the time showing up and wanting to have a few drinks. Though it's my fault, because I stayed over there one night. I think he's a nut."

Lutie wondered how on earth he had found Nan. "I do, too," she said.

"It was somebody to talk to. He said you'd had dinner with him once, so I figured what the hell."

"I did, but I wished I hadn't."

"I hadn't had a real date since I got here, and it's amazing how good anything looks after four months. You know that country song, 'The girls all look prettier at closing time!' "

She had come back down, in clean Gloria Vanderbilt jeans stretched across her backside, a loose pretty yellow shirt, and a lot of make-up on. Something was holding her in, and she'd twisted her hair over to one side and held it with a clip. Her lashes were half an inch thick, and she looked a lot better. "How's this?"

"Great," Lutie said. "You look like the old Nan."

"This is the way I look when I go out. I don't show up anywhere the mess you saw me in; but it's getting to me, and I'm drinking too much, beer anyway—"

"The Big Wheel sounds good." Lutie needed a glass of real tea.

"I was having this affair at home," Nan continued as they got in Lutie's rental Ford. "He was married, or halfway, and he was a sort of low-class type, even though he was a lawyer and had a nice house in Ardsley Park. But I was at the end of my rope, and anyway, we got involved and met all kinds of times, things like that, and I was on a nothing-by-mouth diet and looked decent, really decent, so that was fine. But it wasn't supposed to be serious, and I got serious, really serious, in over my head. So coming here seemed good from that aspect. That's about the time you called."

"Did Aunt Caroline know?"

"Are you kidding? Anyway, he was still writing to me, and that's when the worst of it happened, about your mom. I always put my garbage in those thirty-pound Heftys out on the county road, in the Dumpsters, because if you put it here, the dogs, there's a whole pack of dogs—but why am I telling you? This is your place—running loose, and they get into it and get it all over the road, and then you have to crawl out and pick up eggshells and coffee grounds at dawn. I'm used to a disposal, and this about drove me crazy anyway. So. Where was I? Oh, anyway, I had put a big load of stuff out on the county road in the bin, and what happens is, it's against the law. It's only for picknickers, so the county sends a letter to all the names it finds in your trash.

"Can you believe that? That some guy sorts through all the leftovers and rotten mess to get to the envelopes? Well, he does. And so your mother got a letter from the county telling her to stop dumping her stuff out here, that was because I'd had one note from her, apologizing because she was going to be too busy to see me for the next ten years; but also, and this is the worst, the married guy got a note, too, and he got really grossed out. Imagining the whole scene being made public. Actually I got one, too, first, but I just thought at the time that they had radar dogs out there spying on whoever drove out and deposited her sacks in the middle of the night. Anyway, end of that affair. So it's a double zip when I go home."

Was that what happened, Lutie wondered, if you didn't

get married when they expected you to? Had she not married Dabney, would she have been where Nan was? It seemed a contradiction: They wanted you to be married but never to leave home.

"Surely," she asked, "Mother isn't having people out Sunday?"

"I'm telling you what I know; they've been replying all week."

They settled in a front booth at the truck stop in Oak Hill, next to Marcie's Beauty Shop. It was one of Lutie's favorite places because of the homemade biscuits and deer sausage.

The jukebox was playing Waylon Jennings, and the front lot was half-full of semis. Most of the truckers sat at the counter when they came in, drinking coffee and talking.

Nan was telling about what she hated most about dealing with Lutie's mother. "She's letting me stay there rent-free, so she can keep it for you, and I understand that, her wanting you back, but she never lets me forget how I'm not paying rent and that she could sublet it any minute of the day for five hundred a month. She manages to send me that message all the time." She opened a Coors.

"It would have cost her that much to rent it out for one semester—"

"You know how they are, our mothers; they don't cognize anything they don't want to."

Lutie couldn't get her mind off the place. "Could you put a can of Drāno in the commode and use a cup of All in the tub and kitchen sink? I'll get them for you on the way back out there."

"Don't bother, I'll do it. Sure. The place just got too much for me. I'll move the chair back down. I was going to get on it this afternoon, but you caught me—"

"I'm glad I came out."

"I am, too. I felt a crumb for not writing." She made

a weak laugh. "But then you might have got a letter from the county."

"I'd forgotten about the dogs and trash."

"Listen, I'm going to come to Aunt Florence's function Saturday anyway. It said the public was welcome. I don't care if it makes her furious."

"Of course, come. She'll believe she asked you. You watch, the minute you show up she'll tell me how nice it is to have both her girls at her side."

"I hate them both, our mothers."

She had another Coors, and Lutie finished her giant tea. It was tempting to sit there the rest of the day.

When they got up to go, Nan said, "You didn't ask about the cat." She looked guilty.

"Aunt Caroline said it ran away."

"I'm sorry, honestly. I was so scared out here at first, in the middle of nowhere, and there was this cat outside, howling all the time, and I thought I'd go crazy, with that and the dogs barking and running in packs whenever you set foot outside the door. I know you told me you had one, but I don't know, I forgot. Your mom was being such a turd."

21

"'I *am* embarrassed by your cousin, I don't mind admitting it."

Lutie, after supper at Mother's place, was getting the other side of the story.

"It isn't that she's let herself go; plumpness runs in the family, you can take that in hand. It was her coming to town and setting out to embarrass me."

Lutie's mother was in a beige wool dress, gold earrings, still in her hose, but out of her shoes. She was a crisper version of Aunt Caroline, trim except for a slight fold of skin on the inside of the arms, a slight wattle below the chin when she forgot and looked down, as she did now, in her anger at having this unpleasant conversation with her only daughter, who had been gone all fall and who now, on the eve of her public recognition as one of the town's most outstanding women, was taking her to task for failing to be more kindly to her disagreeable niece.

"She may think I don't know what is going on, but a dozen people have reported to me seeing her out at night— I won't pursue it. I had got to the point with it where I was going to tell my sister Caroline; since clearly nothing more was to be gained by keeping my mouth shut, but I do hate dissension. But then that threatening letter came from County Health about the trash, and as I never open the mail it made the rounds of the office. That was the last straw.

"And then any number of my friends, my University friends, who have called Redoaks, thinking you were still there, have been insulted or hung up on. I don't mind telling you it has been difficult. And I will not be made to feel it is my fault. Having your cousin here has been nothing but distress for me, and I can hardly wait to hear that she has headed home. I don't know what arrangement she has with Caroline. Savannah is a sophisticated city; but in another way it's the smallest of towns, and I feel sorry for her. On the other hand, I feel put upon that Sister didn't see fit to prepare me in some way. Nannie is no child; she's old enough to look after herself. When I was her age, I was supporting myself and a child, and protecting my reputation to boot. Hers has been given her—and she's all but thrown it away."

Mother took a deep breath and looked Lutie in the eye. "And I'll be glad to say that to her face if it will make you feel any better."

Her apartment was lovely, done in grays and white, with one nice Oriental, a lot of plants, dim lights. At the other end of the large room from the sofa was an oval dining table with reproduction Queen Anne chairs. There was one bath, two tiny bedrooms. Lutie, half listening, was counting the houseplants. Two aspidistra, two dieffenbachia. She was camouflaging the damage to Redoaks in her mind.

"I didn't think you would have such objections to fixing a simple meal for your mother, after four months away, but it seems I've misjudged this whole situation, in my excitement about the ceremony." Mother looked wounded and rubbed her temples with polished nails. "I've thought all along that you would come home and want to have a little party for me. When you didn't offer to do anything yourself, I took the liberty of sending out a few invitations, hardly a crowd. The V-P and his wife, the mistress of ceremonies, who is also a close friend, the other honorees, and their husbands, although actually only one isn't widowed, sad. As I say, hardly a crowd, but it seemed fitting for me to do something. The weather has been grand, and Sunday is supposed to be nippy enough for a fire."

"The place is a mess."

"You're so good at fixing it, though. And Nan promised to leave it in shape; you weren't to peek out there today. I'm sure that she's got a certain amount of disorder, packing."

"I'll need to use your plants." Lutie gestured.

"Whatever for?"

"What were there are gone. It needs something."

"Take whatever will help, dear, whatever will help. Without your fine hand out there, I'm sure it has suffered a loss of face."

Mother had an imperceptible net on her hair, had put a night cream on, but refreshed her lipstick.

Lutie was still in the jacket and skirt she'd flown down in. The rented Ford was parked on the street. She felt exhausted. They had finished their supper of chicken and broccoli three hours ago; their fifth cup of hot tea had grown stone cold in front of them. "Mother—"

"What is it, Lutie?" Her tone was still annoyed.

"The oven's broken—"

"Have someone out. Doesn't W. O. Harper fix those things? Or are they only plumbing now? No, it's plumbing and electric. You know how to deal with those tradespeople; call them up."

It was walking in molasses to talk to her mother. She was weary of getting nowhere, of being chewed out for mentioning Nan. Still, her anger kept egging her on, an anger that her mother was totally unaware of what was involved in pulling yet another rabbit from the old tattered hat that was their place in the country.

"Why did you never tell me that Uncle Elbert killed himself?"

"I'm doubly sorry you had to see your cousin if that is the sort of misinformation, slander, that she's putting out. Designed, clearly enough, surely you can see, to hurt her mother, Caroline. That was never established, do you hear, *never*."

"He shot himself. Nan didn't tell me; the church did."

"That office secretary more than likely. She had a crush on your uncle from the moment she started to work for him, and it was almost more than Caroline could bear. It was a disgrace, and the church chose not to see it. Although I've no doubt that's why her friends—the Rutledge sisters, isn't that right?—have been protective of her. Trying to make up to her for what she suffered at the hands of that girl."

"Mother, Dorothy Desmoreaux must be at least fifty-five—"

"It seems to me, Lutie, that you've come home with a chip on your shoulder a yard wide and a mile long. It must have something to do with living up there; maybe that's the posture of the people you've been associating with. That Mavis person who got you up there in the first place, one of that sort, not that what they do in private isn't their own business, if they keep it to themselves, but when it affects other people, my daughter—"

"Mother, Mavis Conroe is not a lesbian."

"You don't have to get explicit. We do not need to get into all that. I only meant they have no right to presume as if they had a hold on you." She bent forward and touched her daughter on the knee. "Lutie, honey, what has happened to you? I'd have thought on the eve of my public recognition, the honor of having the Florence Sayre Wing, that you'd have wanted to do what you could. You used to be such a pleasure. Let's not get your homecoming off to an ungracious start. I can't help blaming your cousin, you didn't sound this way before, but I promise, cross my heart, not to say another word about it."

"Mother—"

"What is it?"

"I'd like to take a bath. It's been a long day."

"Well, of course. Let me just go over the names with you of those you'll meet Saturday, and who I've asked for Sunday. Do you know I'm as excited as a girl at her first dance? I've waited a long time for this, you know. The best part of twenty years."

Lutie worked from lunchtime to after midnight Friday, getting Redoaks ready.

She put an Idaho potato in the oven while she cleaned, to see if it worked at all, and how evenly, before she let herself think about the menu. "Just fix something from your garden," Mother had said, refusing to deal with the fact, even tangentially, that the "garden" was now a bone-dry patch of rotted sticks that no rabbit would mess with even without a fence.

She worked the aubergine rug in tiny squares with tepid water, a stiff brush, a towel, to restore it. The wing-backed chintz chair, returned from upstairs, was stained on the seat, and there were cigarette burns on one arm. She worked on that, too. She banked the borrowed dieffenbachia by the front windows and stood the aspidistra to one side of the love seat, having hauled both out in the open trunk of her rented car. She laid a fire in the fireplace, taking out the charred papers and layers of ashes, and hoped for a good strong norther.

The living room alone took three hours.

She scrubbed the kitchen floor by hand, using three tubs of water to scour the muddy gray film from the deep brown vinyl tiles and an entire bottle of Hard Gloss Glo-Coat to bring back the shiny deep color that was essential to the country look that was Redoaks' best face. She needed flowers for the low kitchen windowsills, where she'd always kept geraniums; she'd have to take whatever was up 290 at HEB, probably yellow mums, which weren't the best but would help.

It took two hours to clean the rest of the kitchen, starting with the stove burners, of which two worked—one on high only. The potato had burned to a carbon black mass in one hour, so that eliminated the oven. The dishwasher, as she'd guessed, was full of soured water, filmy and cold. She'd bailed it out and sealed it shut with masking tape, just in case anyone got the helpful idea of loading it. She'd left the sink, which now responded reluctantly, sitting full of hot water and dishwasher powder, the best trick for eating away the layers of chalky build-up.

The bathroom was the worst, and she did its brown floor first, salvaging a few drops of wax from the can she'd thrown in the trash. Next she sponged the wallpaper, brown sprigged with tiny cream flowers, dull and streaked. She would look at HEB for a new shower curtain; the present one was gone, and without it you could see the calcified tub, which she also filled with hot water and dishwasher powder but had slim hopes for cleaning.

The norther hit at 11:00 P.M., when she was hosing off the front porch and flagstones in the dark, using a broom and mop and pans of scalding water heated on the high burner. Deciding that a little decoration would help, she brought out the old star-patterned quilt that Gran had used and tried it out across the porch swing, to make a welcoming touch of color.

Inside, she collapsed with a diet Dr Pepper on the kitchen

floor, the only clean place that she couldn't mess up, and tried to work out a menu that could be fixed on one and a half burners for an uncertain number: five honorees, probably but not necessarily an extra friend for each, the MC, the V-P, his wife, Lutie, her mother. Possibly Nan and her friend Peg, if they decided to get even. Seventeen at the top; maybe four at the least.

She'd grown rusty. Such former staples as the pumpkin bread were out of the question; as were her buttermilk pies. She got out the old cookbooks—the *Vicksburg Settlement Club*, the *Neiman-Marcus Taste of Texas*, the *Houston Junior League*, the *Savannah Heritage*—but left them unopened. There was no point in making herself sick reading about what couldn't be done. She wondered if it was possible to make a pineapple upside-down cake in the big black skillet on top of the stove. Why not? She could try: buy two boxes of mix; add a stick of butter and four eggs; serve it with whipped cream. That might work. Corn pudding was out. No, maybe it could be done, as corn soup, on top of the stove. Served from a hollowed-out pumpkin, if there was still one left at HEB. Certainly that would add a garden touch. Chicken breasts it would have to be, maybe with apples, pears, and chutney. And a boiled vegetable platter: zucchini, yellow squash, potatoes, beets, whatever was in the store, with a hot horseradish sauce, as garnish. Some kind of bread; you had to have bread. Without an oven, it would have to be whatever black bread was on the shelf. She would make an herb butter for it. And that would have to be that.

Wine. You couldn't buy wine or beer in Texas after midnight on Saturday. She would have to remind Mother, or herself, to pick some up tomorrow afternoon. Perhaps Mother had some put away for company.

There would need to be something for the center of the table, a bowl of onions maybe or red cabbages? No, eggplant, to match the aubergine of the living room, and greens. That would be festive.

She put the best sheets on the little guest bed, where company would lay their wraps, and put a fresh pot of waxy holly on the end table by the bed. The brown checked curtains were dirty, but there was nothing she could do about that, so she tied them back and pulled the decorative inside shutters closed.

That would have to do it. Upstairs she simply would not deal with. She could see where water from the bathroom above had leaked onto the boards of the ceiling (there was a slight warp), but she would let it go. She would make it off limits to herself as well as guests. She had her hands full as it was.

She roused herself at last, realizing that the Culligan water system, long out of salts, would have to be reactivated, recharged, checked out, if they were to have decent drinking water by Sunday.

Finally, as she crawled on top of the guest bed to sleep, missing Cecelie dreadfully, she began to have hazy dreams of River Bend. Wondering if it had been like this for Gran every time her daughters in their sun hats came to visit; wondering if Gran had run out of the energy needed to produce those inviting rooms with their freshly ironed sheets one more time.

22

"'Y o u must be someone's daughter, dear."

"Yes, I am. Florence Sayre's."

"Isn't that nice?"

"I'm very proud of her."

"Isn't that nice?"

The Outstanding Austin Women Recognition Awards brunch was held at Live Oaks, Austin's finest December meeting place. A vast old Victorian house, each of whose rooms had been turned into a dining room, it was, at Christmas, a turn-of-the-century delight. Each room boasted heavy ruby velvet draperies, a live fir tree with red satin balls, a blazing grate fire, and, on the tables, emerald green cloths, red napkins, and lit tapers. The dessert, traditionally, was cherry-chocolate cake, each piece served with a lighted candle.

The recognition ceremony started out as all Mother had hoped. And she, in a deep green double-collared wool dress, pinned with a cameo of Gran's, sat beaming, third from the left at the head table, ready to receive her due.

Lutie studied the audience. All about the ruby room black ladies, friends of one honoree, sat easily with white ladies, friends of the other honorees, mingling easily as if they had been, as most of them had, inhabiting the same homes for three generations. Dressed alike, their pins and brooches from the same era, they asked fondly after one another's grannies. Widows, all of them, of one kind or another. The lone husband, of the Mexican doctor, sat by himself, placed by the door.

(It raised the question, especially after the visit with Aunt Caroline in Savannah, if status among women was always bought at the cost of lives without men.)

Looking up, she caught her mother's eye and blushed, almost hearing the "Oh, Lutie" of her voice.

A very poised MC, in a tan gabardine suit, big round tortoiseshell glasses, short red hair, and an orange ruffled blouse, gave a snappy presentation, the gist of which was that each of the awards could really be claimed by all of the women in the audience. "I'll be bolder and say that each of you has devoted her life to these areas being honored today—finance, the arts, preservation, welfare, health—just as have the outstanding women before you. I propose that everywhere we go we conceal these depths in the surface of our lives. Let's have a round of standing applause for you as well as for them."

Then, after a rousing response, the recipients went forward, one at a time, to thank their colleagues, committees, and compatriots for placing them where they were today. "I could not have done it without you," they said, to a woman.

In order, those receiving commendation were:

Madge Greeley, investment banker, for her contribution to finance, being one of the first women in banking to see how depository institutions took advantage of a "day of float" and to apply that for her depositors' benefit;

Amy Barton, for her achievement in the arts, for pulling the Barton Museum from the red to the black by increasing security measures and thus allowing the old restored home on Barton Creek, which served as a gallery, to receive traveling exhibits formerly considered unsafe;

Croswaite Brown, for historical preservation, for masterminding the restoration of a block of Clarkstown, formerly a Negro residential area, and leasing the houses to lawyers, insurance companies, and teacher retirement, with long-range plans for further restoration to include a strolling sidewalk and a historical square;

Dr. Consuelo Vargas Breedlove, welfare, who had started at Planned Parenthood as a volunteer doing intake records for Spanish-speaking patients and who was now back there, fifteen years later, as head obstetrician, for donating her services to the area of town she grew up in;

Florence Sayre, for her work in public health, for securing three floors of new beds in the city-county hospital, to provide much needed expansion of services in what would be known as the *McAllister* Wing which would have a brass plaque mounted in the elevator in recognition of Mrs. Sayre's tireless volunteer hours.

The five gathered together, arms about each other's waists, for a final group picture and another round of applause.

"You must be somebody's daughter."

Lutie looked closely to see if it was the same woman who'd said that before—it might be they all asked that—and it was, short and bull-shouldered, with a large mole on her forehead.

"Are you someone's mother?" she asked this time.

"My daughter's the banker."

"That's nice."

"She told me she was going over Daddy's accounts to help me out."

"I see."

"She said it was for me."

"That's nice—"

"She's put on airs, Madge has."

"I'm sorry."

"You're somebody's daughter, aren't you?"

Lutie fled toward the speakers' table.

"Aren't you proud of me?" her mother asked as everyone accepted sherry and congratulations: the honorees with orchids on their shoulders and plaques in hand.

"I am," she said.

Florence Sayre's eyes glittered with tears and excitement. "I do wish Sister could have come; I know she has a family to look after; still, this is my big moment."

They waved across the room to Nan, who, with her woman friend Peg, had appeared after all but had stayed far enough away that Mother didn't have to introduce her as her niece.

"That's thoughtful of Nannie," Mother said brightly. "To come and represent her mother, like that, on her way out of town."

She sipped her sherry, looking all about, calling out, waving, eager to expand ever moment to its fullest.

"Did you know," Lutie asked, "that it would be the McAllister Wing?"

"What? Oh, the mayor has to take credit for everything. She has to get reelected, after all." She made a small frown. "Did you see the way she hogged the limelight? I think I wrote you, she even tried to upstage Dolly Parton. It's a shame." She looked around, animated. "Well, there you are. At least it will be our name *in* the building, won't it?"

A young woman rushed up and kissed each of them on the mouth. "You're Lutie, aren't you?" She touched the nipped waist of the gray dress. "You look exactly the way you do in pictures. I'm Jean, Dab's wife. I expect Flo has told you all about me. Don't you think we look a little bit alike, or the way you used to? I felt so close to you even before we met. You have such a marvelous aura and I'm into that; the moment I saw you I knew it had to be you. Dab talks about you all the time, and you know, I think you always belong to someone you've loved, don't you? He and I try to share all the people we're close to."

Dab? Lutie looked at her mother. Flo? This had the ring of the past to it.

Mother patted both girls fondly. "Jean works with me at The University. Not in the office, but in the same building. Isn't that a coincidence? And I don't think there's any conflict of interest; there's no reason for hard feelings. I'm sure I've written you, dear. We pieced it all together one day when she heard me talking about you and your job at Vassar. It seems Dabney hasn't a job yet but is applying all over the country, the way you academics have to. But here, let's talk about something else."

"You made a wonderful speech, Flo, really you did."

Lutie watched the way the tall, affectionate girl touched her mother, smoothed her collar, stroked her hair. She was a real Jimmie Wallace. Dabney had got himself the semblance of intimacy this time, it seemed. She could see the two of them, Dabney and his Jean, at Redoaks, he settled back into a place he was used to, she not being flustered by it, as Nan had been, or buckling under to it, as Lutie did. But, say, tearing out the appliances and instigating a new program of cooking everything on a pot outdoors, organic vegetables, hydroponic tomatoes, or, maybe, buying a microwave oven and, therefore, never having to have the V-P and his pacemaker out for Sunday brunch again.

Lutie smiled broadly to herself at that image, and Mother, misunderstanding, shot her a look of relief, thinking Lutie back to her old self again.

"I've enjoyed having Jean about," Mother said when they were alone. "For company."

"Nan looked good, didn't she?"

"That other person is as fat as she. Wouldn't you think they'd have better sense than to go about together?"

"Peg."

"Whoever." She put an end to that and looked about eagerly. "Now I want you to be sure to say hello to the vice-president, dear. He was asking about you." She searched the crowded holiday room. "There they are; do let's go say hello."

The V-P and his wife saw them coming and hurried over—a bustling, chubby white-haired couple, holding hands.

"How do you do, Miss Lutie?" he said. "It's been too long." He gave her a grandfatherly kiss. "You know my wife, don't you?"

"We were so proud of Florence we could pop, just pop," Mrs. V-P said. "Where are you now, honey?" She peered at Lutie.

"She's teaching in the East, I told you," the V-P reminded.

"So you did, but she doesn't look as if she'd mind telling me again herself."

Lutie smiled. "I am, and I like it a lot."

"It's our loss," the V-P opined, "that we can't hire you here as more than an adjunct. Harvard hires its own; I don't see why we can't. We lose some good material that way."

Her mother brought the conversation back to the main event. "Wasn't it lovely, the whole thing? The cake and candles?"

"Well deserved, wouldn't you say?"

"I like to think so." She was modest, flustered in the presence of her boss.

"You know we think the world of Florence, the world," the dumpling of a wife said to Lutie.

"That's true, we do indeed." The V-P pumped first

Mother's hand and then hers. "Quite a day. We wouldn't have missed it."

And they were gone—in their matching gray suits, he with a white starched shirt, she with a white crepe blouse.

Lutie and her mother were standing by themselves, near a large tree flocked in red, decorated with green velvet bows and strings of real popcorn.

"The V-P is going to try to get out to our little party tomorrow, he promises."

"Have I met his wife before?"

"But you must have, of course, a dozen times, heavens, Lutie, all our gatherings, with all your special meals cooked fresh from the garden."

Mother stopped a waiter and took another sherry. "Now help me celebrate, won't you? Have a little sherry, can't you? Relent a little, please, and let me have my day."

"I'm sorry about the wing."

Mother stared at her plaque. "I worked so hard, didn't I? For all those years? To have to turn my silks."

Lutie nodded as her mother plucked at a passing gabardine sleeve.

". . . know my daughter? I don't think you've ever met, have you? Lutie, I'm so *meager* for you to know the mistress of ceremonies. Such a good, dear friend of mine."

23

Journal: I Was the First to Call You Father

M O N D A Y early I left Mother the aspidistra, the dieffenbachia, a box of real maple sugar Santas for her stocking,
and the keys to Redoaks.

I wondered if Gran had had the same feeling of relief
when she sold River Bend and, with it, her responsibility
for everyone's good times.

Assured that my rental car could be turned in at the
Dallas–Fort Worth airport, I headed up the road: to find
Mr. Pinter.

Waco is where I'd last heard from him, back when he
used to send payments, small ones, every month to Mother.
These would come from the Pinter Publishing Company—
and I saved the envelopes for years, for his handwriting.

Until I was ten, maybe, or later, when we moved to
Redoaks, he also sent me birthday cards, the commercial
kind that said "TO MY DAUGHTER," every year in March,
and I'd look forward to that, though he never said anything but "Love, Your Daddy," at the bottom. And then

they stopped coming, although the checks didn't. Pinter Publishing was in Waco, Texas, 123 Broad Street. I knew that from memory.

"It was a youthful marriage, a wartime marriage," Mother used to say. "He had a wartime commission; we didn't see past our noses in those days. Caroline had already married her preacher. I don't know. It was a youthful mistake, for which I've paid dearly."

I'd called information in Waco; there was no listing for Pinter Publishing, but they did have a residence for Alfred Pinter. Did I want that number? I said yes, but I wasn't going to use it. I couldn't call; I'd have to just show up.

On the stretch of IH 35 between Round Rock and Georgetown, still an hour from Waco, I got a speeding ticket, for going seventy-five in a fifty-five-mile zone. I almost cried, sure that the cop would send me back, the way they do truant children.

I paid the fine in cash (three twenties; they can get what they want on the highway like that), and after all it had taken to fix up Redoaks and do that meal, I was down almost to my last traveler's check.

In Waco, that super-Christian town, I pulled off at exit 17 at the Denny's whose sign is twenty feet in the air, for people like me who need to regroup and go to the bathroom and figure out where they're going. I did all of that and had a Super Bird besides. And remembered how nice it was to be served the Texas kind of iced tea, half a quart filled with crushed ice to the rim and stuffed with wedges of fresh lemon, and a sandwich with fat white unprocessed turkey breast, thick tomato slices, bacon that was crisp. It's the careless abundance that you forget. I ordered another to go, deciding I could use it on the two-hour drive to the Dallas–Fort Worth airport, that it would have to last me until I got back to Joe.

The norther was still fraying the tree limbs outside, and everyone was walking around hunched over in a jacket, amazed that such weather had hit again, as stunned as a bunch of cows in the pasture with no memories, sure that it would be back to normal tomorrow.

I got a city map at a Shell station and located Broad Street, which was, to my relief, a commercial street. Standing talking while they put in gas, in the old jacket and skirt I'd worn down on the plane, I was as cold as the rest of them. Expecting, the same as they, that any minute the crazy cold would be blown away by warm winds from the Gulf, and we'd have decent weather back again.

I drove through a rather empty downtown, past a Big State pawnshop, a jeweler, a barbershop, a couple of banks, a county courthouse building with a Woodman of the World memorial in the front, and then, turning east on Fifth, a one-way street, and south on Washington, I located Broad and the address. It was between Jerry's Diamonds, and Joe Buzzie's Music. And, to my relief, was a printing shop after all.

I was relieved, but at the same time afraid, because the window had WAYTEX COPY COMPANY stenciled on it. Maybe someone else had taken over? Or maybe he had just changed the name, the way Standard had become Esso and then Exxon. WAYTEX might be a more current, computer-age name. I brushed my hair in the reflection of the window of an office supply store (handy) next door and pink-glossed my mouth, for about the sixth time since Super Bird. I took my glasses off and cleaned them on my white shirt, wishing they weren't loose at the left temple and trying to screw the little bolt in with a fingernail. And then took a deep breath.

Should I introduce myself as Sayre or Pinter? I didn't want him to think I'd been using his name, as I hadn't, and surely if he'd lived with Mother at all, he hadn't forgotten

Sayre, which it even, to remember that painful story, said on my birth certificate.

I opened the glass-fronted door and went in. "Hello," I said to the receptionist, a knocked-out blonde who was in the middle of a conversation about Miracle Whip. "May I speak to Mr. Pinter?" I didn't want to say "daughter," in case they had no idea, so I left it at that.

"Who?" She was chewing gum, and half her attention was focused on the friend who was standing by her desk, a gorgeous brunette of the same type.

"Mr. Pinter. Alfred Pinter? I believe this is—" I hesitated. What if he had sold out years ago and that was the reason for the new name? This showpiece receptionist might have been hired yesterday.

The brunette with the mass of curls looked at her fingernails, considered aloud. "Pinter. Never heard of him. Have we ever heard of a . . . Pinter? Oh, you mean *Peewee?*"

"Peewee." The dolly behind the desk laughed. "You can go back; he's in the shop. Just go on back. Straight back."

"We'll have to rag Peewee about this," the brunette teased. "What's the wife's name? Ida? We'll have to let the cat out of the bag on this one."

The story resumed. ". . . Well, they said bring salad dressing, so I thought they meant Miracle Whip, but they meant that bottled business."

It was a long hall. At the back, past offices whirring with copiers, was a large machine-shop room, with a typesetter in the center. A real printing press. Manning it was an old man in too large pleated pants, a dingy tan shirt, suspenders, and runover shoes, the left one held together with a safety pin.

"I'm looking for Mr. Pinter—" Then I saw his face, and my knees went weak. I hadn't forgotten at all. I'd remembered him as taller, but then I was only three. He was average, and he wasn't old, only bent over.

"Yes'm, what can I do you for?" He smiled but kept on with his work. "You from the church, aren't you? We're nearly finished with your job."

"I'm Lutie Sayre."

He cleaned his glasses and peered at me. "No joke, you are?" He came over and shook hands; his hands and face and eyes and teeth were the color of his shirt. "Imagine that, little Lutie." He kissed me on the cheek, and I could smell plug tobacco. "What you got on your mind, honey? It's been a long time. How's your mom? Married again, I always figured, someone more her level. She didn't have much to say for an unemployed ex-sergeant, not that I blame her. After the war we were all scrambling. Well, how about that? Little Lutie."

He cleaned his glasses again, blinking his squinting eyes and staring at me, shifting from one foot to the other.

"I was driving through," I told him. "I live in New York now and thought I'd stop by."

"How in the world did you find me here? Don't reckon your mother knew that, did she?"

"You used to send me birthday cards from this address."

"So I did. Had myself some stationery printed up in those days, didn't I? Job hunting, I imagine. Then I settled down here, with Ida, the new wife. We do fine. She's at the library, and we have three boys, play Little League they do. The oldest is about to grow out of that now, Kevin. Fine kids. I got myself some luck in later years, made myself a place here, through my boys. I thought you might be one of the ladies at the church."

I leaned against the edge of a wooden table that held stacks of paper. I could remember him clearly, the way he'd been. Promising all sorts of things, the circus, pony rides, the zoo. Mother getting angry, and a long summer visit at Gran's with Aunt Caroline, and then we didn't go back, and Daddy was gone. Mother was taking a job, and

253

then, gradually, I lost his face. Sometime in there I couldn't picture it anymore.

Now here he was again, after nearly thirty years, the same big, toothy smile and the way his eyebrows shot up.

"I was just passing through," I said.

"You married? Got kids yourself? I reckon you're up there by now."

"I was married; no children. I teach, in college."

"A professor. How about that? My daughter a professor. I bet your mother's mighty glad about that, though maybe she'd rather have grandkids."

"I don't know."

"You're still a pretty one."

"How old are your boys?"

"Well, now, I just happen to have some pictures here." He got out an old brown wallet.

I could not believe how it stung, to see him produce snapshots of other, later children. "I was the one who made you a daddy, wasn't I?" I asked, unable not to. "I was the first."

"Sure enough, you were. And I was mighty proud of you in those days. I had a walletful of snapshots, same as I do of these kids. A boy has to do sports, these days, and I'm lucky that mine took to it like ducks to water. Here's Kevin; he's the oldest—"

I was looking down at some round face, but I didn't really see it because I was looking at Mr. Pinter's suspenders and the pinned shoe.

Just then a man came in the door, young, in a sleazy tan three-piece suit and slicked-down hair. "What have we here, Peewee? Looks like some fine visitor. If I'm not *interrupting*, on this last order, you see here, the date is left off, and I don't have to tell you that Kiwanis is not—"

"This is my brother's wife," Mr. Pinter said. "Lutie Pinter. The brother who lives in Dallas?" He shifted back to his place at the printing machine. "I'll tend to that, Mr. Tarver, right on it. Give you my word." He studied the announcement. "Sure as the world, we left the date off, we sure did."

"How'd you do?" The man turned to me. "Sister-in-law, is it?" He looked me up and down. "Kissing kin, is it?"

"I'll get right on it," Mr. Pinter repeated, nervous, looking at his boss and then at me, to see if there was going to be trouble.

"Nice business you have here," I said to the slimy man. "My husband and I, we're thinking of opening one like it."

"Are you now? Well, stop by my office, why don't you?"

"I'll visit with my—kin a minute more, first, if you've no objections."

"Glad to have you on the premises."

We were silent a moment after Mr. Tarver left, not sure if he was still in hearing range. Mr. Pinter started up the machine in the corner, a fancy copier, for the noise. "Hope that didn't bother you, honey. I've dropped a few years here and there, you know how it is in the working world, was no way I could explain having a daughter your size around here. They don't know different; my boys are young. Matter of fact, I got a brother in Dallas, like I said. I've mentioned him to Tarver on occasion, as they are both Kiwanis. And for all he knows, you could be the wife. For all I know, too; I haven't seen him in about as long as I haven't seen you."

It was the way he was afraid of the sleaze that I couldn't stand. I wrote out my address in Cranberry Park for him. "Why don't you start up those birthday cards again? I'd like that. I missed them when they stopped."

"Didn't know if they were getting through. Your mom had strict provisions about my keeping out of your life, she said that right at the start, and I didn't want to make

trouble, sending them. Get you in trouble, or myself for
that matter. She was a strong woman, at least in those days."

"Does Ida know you have a daughter?"

"Sure. We don't have secrets. She's glad to have me,
was an old maid of sorts, that's the way they think of it in
a little town, at the library and all that; as a matter of fact,
she wasn't more than your age when I met her. And we
started keeping company. She's glad of our life and admires
that we're known around town, and happy with her boys.
Thinking, as she did, that she might not have any."

"I'm glad for you."

"It was a shock, I'll say, when you first came in. Being
so grown. I must have looked taken back."

"Send me a picture of your family; I'd like to have it.
My boyfriend would like to see it. He's always after me
to bring him pictures—"

"You got a boyfriend? Well, that's nice. I didn't know,
your mother—"

"Yes, I have. We live together."

"That right? Well, things are different nowadays, aren't
they? And New York is a different place, I imagine. That
still won't go down around here; I had to practically
propose before I could take Ida to the movies, but that's
Waco, I imagine. We're a churchy town."

"Joe, my boyfriend, has two boys."

"That right? They old enough for sports?"

"They're teen-age. The older one is very interested in
cars." I coughed. "The younger . . . does a lot of stunts."

"Sounds like you got a ready-made family for yourself."

"Will it be all right if I send you and Ida a Christmas
card?"

"Well, I don't know as I'd want to stir up waters, but
you can send it here. To the printing shop. I'd be glad to
hear from you. And tell your mom I send my regards when
you see her."

"This is between us, this visit."

Mr. Pinter looked enormously relieved and loosened up. "Send it to the house, honey. That's okay. I didn't mean to shut you out like that. I could see the way your face fell I'd said the wrong thing. Don't take offense. I was spooked that this might be something Florence had cooked up. I don't have much desire to reenter your mom into my life these days."

He wrote out his home address, so I'd see that he meant it, on a calling card that said "WAYTEX PRESS." I could see he was getting more and more nervous with my staying; he had a mistake to change, the church ladies to please. Plus the slime.

"You keep me in touch now," he said as he walked me to the door. "You going to stop by and see Tarver?"

"No."

"That's what I figured. You're a fast thinker, Lutie."

I turned and kissed his cheek. "It was good to see you," I told him.

Five

24

Dear Mother,

This week ninety thousand commuters became sociologists. That's because of the train strike. You have no idea when you're not used to such numbers the panic it can make when part of the city grinds to a halt.

I've been going in often, but now they say the bus takes over an hour, even off peak, and that if you don't get in the front of the line, then you have to wait for another and sometimes another. No one likes to be told, "There's only room for five more," because nobody likes to be one of a number.

My teaching is going well. Although it's still in the forties most days, the students have started to come to class in outrageous costumes; they look like a cast of Midsummer Night's Dream.

Some birds are beginning to come back, and I've seen what Peterson's says is a European starling (really a meadowlark). I saw these black birds, with a sort of purple-green gloss, that I knew weren't crows, because they were shaped like orioles.

That sounds like a good idea for you to take your vacation at Aunt Caroline's, for a change, and see the islands off

Savannah, especially as you missed Christmas there two years in a row. I don't know, yet, about my joining you all and Mickey for the summer. But when you call Sunday, we can talk about it.

Love,
L.

P.S. Tell Jean that if you don't keep the level up on the salt in the Culligan system, you have to recharge it and that Pedernales Electric Co-op expects you to send in your own meter readings.

She had told her mother that there was an opening for the spring term at SUNY Purchase and that she felt it would help her future job chances if she took it. So that she could now talk about her teaching when she wrote. Her hopes were that by summer Mother would have got used to her being gone, or at least learned to make do with her new tenants at Redoaks, and that Lutie could stay here, returning less and less, weaning them both.

When she told her landlady that she wanted to sign up for another six months after her lease was up in January, Mrs. Vaccaro had been enormously relieved at not having to find someone else, but she'd said that if Lutie had ideas about staying on, she'd have to understand that there would definitely be an increase in rent. "I may be a widow," she said, "but I'm no easy mark." Her feelings were hurt because her own daughter, who always had her down to Florida for the holidays, had not asked her this year. " 'We're having houseguests,' she tells me. Houseguests! Did you ever? I wouldn't have treated my mother's dog in that fashion." So Lutie agreed to another twenty-five a month and baked Mrs. Vaccaro a buttermilk pie.

When she'd come back from Savannah, she'd told Cleveland Birdsong that she'd used her as an excuse to return early, and Dr. B. had said that on the q.t., she was going to be the permanent chair and that if Lutie wanted to stay, they'd be interviewing in the spring, but that until then she could keep her two intros. "I'll see that those on the inside have an inside track," she'd said. "Not that I can promise."

She and Joe were doing fine; they spent two nights a week at his place and two at hers and had the boys on weekends. And he had promised that if she stayed up here, he wouldn't spend the night in New Jersey anymore. And he'd seemed as relieved about that as she was.

Fritz and Noah weren't doing any better, but Lutie worried a lot less about that than Joe did because she didn't expect them to. Their mother had started cooking Chinese, and so the boys had to gripe about all of Lutie and Joe's efforts at meals and to ask why wasn't there any bok choy and tree ears and lotus roots. Fritz was more or less always in trouble, and Noah was more or less always in traction, and that was how it was going to be. She'd used her spare time to look around the county for video games in the malls and fast-food eating strips and things like that; you had to treat Teen-age more or less the way you did the flu: lay in a supply of Vicks and Sucrets and 7-Up, and wait it out.

All that had been under control; mothers and landladies and department heads and sons you could cope with, because they came in ones and twos, and you didn't have to handle them all at once. But the train strike was a wholly different matter, of a wholly different magnitude.

Ninety thousand extra commuters trying to cross the bridges into the city was too staggering to grasp. It was like those statistics that tell you the debt is in the billions, or the viruses are in the trillions, or the stars in the quadrillions —you turn the newspaper page and want to read about the one dog that ran in front of a particular car.

That was how each commuter felt: wanting to be that

one dog on page one; his or her inconvenience, panic, threat to job, to sanity, to health, to marriage of headline importance. Instead, they had to line up like kindergarteners for blocks, waiting for a Liberty Line bus, a car pool, or a chartered service. Some of them, to save money, rode buses into the Bronx and then caught subways downtown; others, to save time, hired limos and then sat, stalled, while the buses crawled past.

Lutie went into the city on the second Thursday in March, to have a day with Joe. They'd agreed that she would not spend the night, because now there was no 7:15 A.M. express to guarantee her getting to class on time, but that they could have most of the day together at his place. The strike was still new, and they were playing it by ear until they had a better idea of what was going on.

The Liberty Lines, she found out, ran every fifteen minutes from the transportation building across from the County Center in White Plains. There she lined up at nine o'clock with the rest of them: men in chesterfields, clutching *Wall Street Journals*, the daily *Times*, and attaché cases; women in gray flannel suits, digital watches, and good gold chains; other women in bandannas and mufflers; little clots of college students.

"Where do we catch the bus back?" a dazed businessman with scrubbed pink neck and barbered hair asked the bus driver, who was monotonously demanding, "ExACT AMount, EXact aMOUNT, three dollars only, three bills please." He stopped at the question, blinked, went into his other speech: "Madison at Thirty-seventh, Fortieth, Forty-seventh, Fifty-fourth—where you work? I don't advise after Forty-seventh, to be frank; I'm passing them by every day."

It took an hour and a half, with the bus bearing down on the bumper-to-bumper cars, bludgeoning ahead, before they got to Fifth Avenue, where they sat for twenty minutes more, snarled in a traffic jam caused by four yellow school buses, four Liberty Lines buses, and fourteen cars turned sideways, their drivers waving bills and cursing, trying to buy or bulldoze their way into a parking garage that displayed three street signs claiming "FULL."

A woman in front of Lutie pointed out the window to a blonde in skinny black pants carrying a miniature poodle, waiting for a doorman to get her a cab as if nothing were going on in the middle of the street.

"Did I tell you I saw Jackie Kennedy this close?"

"You could recognize her?"

"She looks the same—"

Her friend continued a house renovation story which had been going on since she got on in Scarsdale. "It was a walk-in closet, and they took the doors off, so it was an alcove-type thing. Real pretty. Do you see?"

Behind them a loud woman told, for the second time, about her visit to the hospital. "I come in once a week to get my blood pressure checked. Now it's twice. I'm in the hospital day before yesterday, and I say, 'How do you get something to eat around here?' and one of *them* is behind the counter and tells me, 'You push.' Now what's that supposed to mean? Whoever heard of having to push to get a slice of bread? That's what she says. 'Push what?' I ask her. 'Push what?' Did you ever hear two hundred fifty over one hundred fifty? Well, you're sitting next to it. And no wonder."

As four men, late to work, went up to harangue the driver for not opening the door in the middle of the street and letting them out, the man next to Lutie continued through the financial section of the *Times*, folding each page in half lengthwise in a careful ceremony, and the man across the aisle began to doze, part of a headline visible on his bulging lap: IN SEX DEN.

Lutie sat thinking about Sammy's story of the two fat

men on the stairs, naked except for their shoes, who died wedged on the same step, unable to move up or down, immobile. Maybe that was the way to understand the city in the throes of a strike: It was not thousands or millions of anything; it was two (exponential) fat boys who couldn't go up and couldn't go down and so stayed stuck there until they died from the strain.

She had been unable to park at the County Center, or at a nearby municipal lot, or at any of the adjacent malls, or in any of the train lots, and, so, finally, after thirty minutes of driving around, she had gone back home, parked the Chevy in the drive, and walked to the bus. That took another forty minutes. She could see now that it had been three hours since she left home, and she wasn't there yet. She calculated that if she walked to Joe's from the bottom of Central Park (a half hour) and then from his place to Forty-seventh, where she stood at least a chance of getting a bus home (an hour) and it was two hours home, then she might as well not have come.

The plan fact was, there wasn't time to go to Joe's. She asked herself what a Cord owner would do in this situation —and the answer was that she would put her engine up on blocks and wait for another day.

When the bus finally started up again, crawled down the street, and disgorged a handful of its frantic passengers, Lutie got out, too.

She walked south, and called Joe from the Waldorf lobby to tell him that she'd wait in Oscar's until he came. That way they could at least have an hour or two together.

She closed the public bathroom door behind her and locked it, delighted to have a space to wash her face and hands, put on lip gloss, brush her hair, wipe off her dusty shoes. The Waldorf had small private compartments with marble tops and full-length mirrors and Kleenex and hand lotion, and all that made you feel comforted and was well worth the quarter you put in the saucer in the hall. She had a pocketful of quarters in the new gray skirt she'd had Mrs. Rodino make to go with a puffed-sleeve loose-knit gray sweater that she'd found at Neiman's for only $30. It had a scoop neck and looked nice under her jacket for the city and over her long calico skirt at home.

(The bathroom was a special treat since the last time she'd been in the city, she'd stopped at Grand Central, before the strike, because she couldn't wait to get to Joe's, and there was a black lady ahead of her who tried to grab a stall door before it closed, and missed, so Lutie had handed her a quarter. And then—it was awful—the custodian who walks around the station rest room had followed Lutie into a stall and said, "You mustn't ever give anyone money, don't you know that? Did you give that woman money? Don't you know not to do that?" It had been embarrassing, cooped up in that small space, being shouted at.)

At Oscar's she settled down at the counter with as much relief as if it had been her own living room. It took its toll, being part of ninety thousand reluctant bus riders all shoving and pushing and saying, in ninety thousand ways, "But me . . . but me . . . but me . . ."

Here she and the others were back to coming in ones and twos again, and that felt marvelous. She read the green and white card tucked against her sugar bowl—"ENJOY IRISH WEEK AT THE WALDORF O'STORIA"—and wiggled out of her shoes.

"That's the iced tea, right?" Manuel, the waiter, recognized her. He wore a name tag, is how she knew his name, and he spoke in a heavy accent. He was very dark and middle-aged, and she realized she might have burst into tears if he hadn't been there today, so much was she counting on familiarity. "The bagel today?" he asked.

"Yes, with lots of butter."

An old man, balding, with liver spots, came and sat on the stool to her left. He was in a good thready tweed jacket, green shirt open at the neck, shiny cuffed trousers. Two faint strands of hair were slicked across his forehead, lashed down like ropes.

"Hello, Manny," he said to the waiter. "Let's have the ice cream today, Manny, one dip chocolate, one dip strawberry."

He ate slowly, mixing the two flavors in every bite, savoring the combination, until the ice cream was half-gone. Then, reluctantly, he called out, "I find a piece of glass, Manny," and he held up a small chip of clear glass, which the waiter examined and verified, and they both nodded. "Cross this off the check, Manny, and give me a piece of nice apple pie with cheese." As Manuel obliged, the man in the green shirt returned the piece of glass to his tweed pocket, adding, "A fresh cup of coffee as well, Manny."

On Lutie's other side, at the corner of the U-shaped counter, a wealthy man and his wife talked about food. He, emaciated, was obviously ill.

"You can't taste that at all, can you? Even the bacon?" She ate a club sandwich. "That's too bad."

He nodded. "That's right."

"You weren't able to eat those little chops we had last night, were you? That was too bad; they were very tender."

He took a swallow of water. "That's fine."

They looked, not like Sammy's real parents, of course, but as they might have been cast by Hollywood, with the wasting man distinguished and gray, the woman plump, highly corseted in plum crepe, wearing a fox fur stole. From time to time she would pat his arm, but she never stopped eating.

The five of them who were there, the waiter from Spain, the man who ate part of his ice cream, Jack Sprat and his worried wife, and Lutie, made a congenial group. She, restored and fed, felt a wave of happiness. The Waldorf, she decided, was like River Bend: a lovely place from the past which you could always count on.

Out on the street she was plunged instantly into two hundred thousand commuters, seven million locals, and fifty thousand visitors to the city, and it took her a half hour to get a bus and another two hours to get home.

She decided to wait to soak in the tub, although her body ached all over from the trip. She would take her usual walk first, while it was still light, and that would make her feel back on schedule.

She put a chicken in the oven to bake, set the timer, put a glass of tea in the frost-free refrigerator, and put her journal and her Mont Blanc pen by her plate.

Although she had done a lot of walking already today, it had not been in her Adidas or in a relaxed way, and she enjoyed the blustering cold hike up the bricks, across the carved stone dam, and down. It wasn't until she was descending the narrow steps, leaning into the wind, remembering Noah and the skunk, that she remembered she'd told Joe she'd wait at Oscar's until he got there!

He was sitting on her stoop when she got back.

"I'm sorry," she said. "How did you get here?" She didn't see the Saab, which Carole was using.

"Borrowed a car."

"I forgot," she told him. It was impossible to explain.

"*Forgot?*"

"It was all so frantic, and then, after I had caught my breath—" He wouldn't understand. She unlocked the door and added another plate to the table.

"How did you know I'd be here?" she asked.

"*They* told me."

"They?"

"Your goddamned groupies at Oscar's."

"But how—"

"As soon as I walked through the door, having hiked down forty blocks, you couldn't get a cab today if you were an Arab—"

"I know—"

"As soon as I walked through the door and looked around, some geezer at the counter and the waiter both told me, 'She's gone home.' "

"I'm sorry," It was impossible to explain. She opened him a St. Pauli Girl.

"Do you know why I took up with you?"

"Not really."

"You were Browning's Last Duchess. She who put no more value in his ancestral name than on the hired help or the apple trees or the hounds. She with the heart 'too soon made glad,' she 'too easily impressed,' who 'liked whate'er she looked on, and her looks went everywhere.' " He made quoting signs in the air and with his hands. "Do you know how amazing that seemed? It seemed a miracle. To find a woman who could be made happy by a couple of stray cats, a buckling poster of Rome, and a few cups of tea?"

"And now?" She asked, not wanting to hear any of this, trying to remember what Dabney had said when it was over: "It doesn't make sense anymore." That was how she felt. She'd got herself back together, and he'd come all the way out here to take her apart again.

"I figured out why the duke wrung her neck, and I thought I'd share it with you. It was after the tenth time he'd gone into her boudoir and begun to tell her that he was offering her his heart, and she told him the news about the seamstress's baby, and how the stableman was under the weather, and did he know that the cousin of the former duchess had run off with—"

He ground out a cigarette on the floor, a gesture he knew she hated.

"I'm tired of being Joe of 'Mrs. Spumoni and Mrs. Tortoni and Mrs. Vermicelli and Aunt Linguine and Uncle Sammy and Joe.' " He parked himself in a wicker chair in the living room. "I want to be in a class by myself, can you understand that?"

Lutie took off her Adidas and sat on the daybed. "Yes, I know. Dabney said the same thing to me. Mavis said the same thing. I *know*, but I don't understand. What do all of you want? A person can't go around by herself all the time; you have to realize there's everyone else out there, too. Don't the rest of you get lonesome all wrapped up in yourselves?"

"Even when I drive a borrowed car way the hell out here to tell you I've had enough, I'm just one of the crowd."

She didn't answer. She was not ashamed that she wished she were back safe at Oscar's. It had been so hard to leave them, the man with the chip of glass and the waiter who remembered and the man with cobalt in his system and the woman with the fox fur. She had hardly been able to make her feet move and had gone back twice, once to pick up a WALDORF O'STORIA card and once to leave a whole dollar for a tip.

"In the cowboy movies," Joe explained, "the man in the white hat says to the man in the black hat, 'Would you like to step outside and say that?' and then the two of them go through the swinging doors, leaving their cohorts behind— do you get it? *leaving their cohorts behind*—and have it out, hand to hand."

"I don't want to be the black hat."

"Take your pick."

Lutie had her back up. "You said, *you said*, that nobody changes. That that was the basis on which you did your therapy. Well? Well? I'm the same Lutie I was at the

271

beginning, and you can't fuss at me because you want the fact that we went to bed and fell in love and I moved half a continent away from my mother to make me somebody different."

"When I was twelve, I had a girl friend who had a shoe-box of paper dolls, and whenever I came over, all she wanted to do was get out those paper dolls and play with them."

Lutie brought him another beer and herself a diet Dr Pepper. She pulled the other wicker chair around so that they could sit with their knees touching.

"Maybe," she said, "when the duke came to her boudoir and started talking like that, she was afraid he wanted something she didn't know how to give, and so she brought in the seamstress and the stablehand for reinforcements."

"She could have said so, before he cut her head off."

"Maybe your twelve-year-old girl friend thought the only reason you stayed was that she had those paper dolls."

He pulled her up and put his arms around her. "How can two people ever be a group?"

She knew the answer, but she hadn't the words for it. It had to do with Gran. With seeing how she was when they all had time for her—Mother, Aunt Caroline, Lutie, Nan, Delia, even Jimmie—and then how she was when there was only Marcie at the beauty shop and the sales-woman in Better Dresses. And then how little was left of her when she had no one at all who cared.

It had to do with the fact that even if you let it be true, the way Joe said, that nobody changed, you had to make provisions for the fact that they changed *in relation to you*. If you didn't, you were going to end up like Gran, sitting in the rocker on the porch, watching the sun go by, mad every day that it set behind your back.

That was the danger, and she wished she'd known

how to say that in Rome, or the Hamptons, or even at Redoaks. . . .

Needing Joe to understand, she put her hands behind her and turned in his arms so that he was still holding her, but they were no longer looking *at* each other; they were looking out. "Like this," she said. "Like this."

"I'll show you," she offered, and, filling her pockets with Seanips, led him out onto the stoop in the dark.

"You can't do it without the rest of them," she said. And after a whistle or two the tomcats came, Le Rouge and Le Noir, the red tabby pawing her pocket, the black kitten waiting his turn. The waning hangnail of a moon had not yet risen over the bare limbs of the pear tree; no trains whipped past in the distance. After a while it grew bitter cold, and the smell of snow fell in the dark; but still they sat, wrapped in a blanket, all of them: Lutie and Joe.

The author of eight novels, Shelby Hearon has been awarded a Guggenheim Fellowship for fiction and a National Endowment for the Arts Fellowship for creative writing. Her previous novels, which include *Afternoon of a Faun*, *Painted Dresses*, and *Armadillo in the Grass*, have twice won the Texas Institute of Letters Jesse Jones award for fiction. Her short stories and articles have appeared in *Redbook*, *Texas Monthly*, *McCalls*, and other magazines and anthologies. She has recently won an NEA/PEN short story prize.

A native of Kentucky and long-time resident of Texas, she now lives in Westchester County, New York, with her husband, philosopher Bill Lucas. She has taught at the University of Texas, the University of Houston, and as Distinguished Writer-in-Residence at Wichita State University.